LOS ANGELES GIRL

ELLEN DE STEFANO

PUNISHMENT FOR CLAUDIA

RICHARD STEELE

Safe Sex is essential: your very life may depend on it. Please remember that some of the sexual practices that are featured in these works of fiction (written in an era that pre-dates lethal STDs) are dangerous and they are not recommended or in any way endorsed by the publishers; by the same token, we do not condone any form of non-consensual sex for any reason: it is reprehensible and illegal and should never become a part of a person's real life: rather it should remain firmly in the realm of sexual fantasy.

Past Venus Press
London 2004

Printed and bound in Spain by Bookprint
S.L., Barcelona

THE *Erotic* Print Society
EPS, 17 Harwood Road,
LONDON SW6 4QP

Tel (UK only): 0871 7110 134
Fax: +44 (0)20 7736 6330
Email: eros@eroticprints.org
Web: www.eroticprints.org

ISBN : 1-898998-89-2

Foreword by Michael R. Goss

The history of erotic literature had always been clandestine, and, apart from furtive purchases of under-the-counter hardcore, American readers between the end of the war and the mid-1960s could only openly buy paperbacks with lurid covers that always promised, like first dates, far more than they actually delivered. However, the sale of two trashy paperbacks at a newsstand in New York's Times Square was to change the history of erotic publishing in the United States forever.

Previously there had been several landmark cases involving the publication of books that extended the boundaries of what was legally acceptable. These included James Joyce's *Ulysses*, D.H. Lawrence's *Lady Chatterley's Lover*, Henry Miller's *Tropic of Cancer*, John Cleland's *Memoirs of a Woman of Pleasure* and William Burrough's *Naked Lunch*. All novels which today we celebrate and study as major works of literature.

The pivotal moment came when Robert Redrup, a Times Square newsstand clerk, sold two pulp sex novels, *Lust Pool* and *Shame Agent* to plain-clothes policeman, for which he was tried and convicted in 1965. William Hamling, who published the books under his Nightstand imprint in San Diego, paid Redrup's legal bills to the Supreme Court and the resulting case, *Redrup v. New York* in May 1967, truly opened the floodgates of what was acceptable.

Hamling, and his lawyer Stanley Fleishman, firmly believed that he was not selling, as was said about his books, "commercialised obscenity," nor would he admit to "titillating the prurient interests of people with a weakness for such expression." Hamling felt his books were giving people who would never have the skills to read and enjoy *Ulysses*, *Fanny Hill* or *Naked Lunch* what they wanted.

The judge presiding over the case of Redrup, Justice Potter Stewart, went far beyond his established just-left-of-centre position on obscenity to the most radical of outlooks. Apparently the vote to affirm Ralph Ginzburg's conviction for his magazine *Eros* was his personal wake-up call. In his Ginzburg summary Stewart wrote:

Censorship reflects a society's lack of confidence in itself. It is a hallmark of an authoritarian regime. Long ago those who wrote our First Amendment charted a different course. They believed a society can be truly strong only when it is truly free. In the realm of expression they put their faith, for better or worse, in the enlightened choice of the people, free from the interference of a policeman's intrusive thumb or a judge's heavy hand. So it is that the Constitution protects coarse expression as well as refined, and vulgarity no less than elegance. A book worthless to me may convey something of value to my neighbour. In the free society to which our Constitution has committed us, it is for each to choose for himself.

Stewart's arguments were persuasive enough to convince the court to reverse Redrup's original conviction by 7-2. This decision by the United States Supreme Court affirmed that consenting adults ought to be constitutionally entitled, under the First Amendment, to acquire and read any publication that they wished, including those agreed to be obscene or pornographic, free of interference from the U.S. Government.

Under this guiding principle the Supreme Court adopted a policy of systematically reversing without further opinion ("Redruping") all obscenity convictions which reached it. Scores of obscenity rulings involving paperback sex books, girlie magazines and peep shows were overturned.

Despite an attempt to reverse the tide of pornography by new Chief Justice

Warren E. Burger in the 1970s an explosion in paperback publishing followed. Carpetbagger publishers burst into life across America, including Brandon House, Essex House, Greenleaf, Lancer, Midwood, Pendulum, Pleasure Readers, Star Distributors and many others. Every aspect of human sexuality was covered in a sexual anarchy of threesomes, foursomes and more-somes in every combination of genders and colours, often including the whole family, their pets and assorted farm animals to boot. Every genre was exploited from incest to Nazi sex with everything in-between in a total assault on the values of bourgeois culture. One can imagine publishers and authors sitting in bars coming up with titles in alcohol-and dope-fuelled brainstorming sessions which would then be commissioned out to a stable of jobbing hacks for around $500 a book.

Past Venus Press will reissue the highlights from this post-Redrup period, many of which were originally considered to have had no literary merit whatsoever and to be utterly without redeeming social importance. But that, of course, was part of their charm.

LOS ANGELES GIRL

ELLEN DE STEFANO

Past Venus Press

Prelude

In the darkened photographer's studio, the girl stood naked, legs apart and arms akimbo, her full, firm breasts thrust proudly up and out so that the nipples pointed in slightly different directions.

"Last time, hunh?" she smiled, now lifting one of her breasts a little higher than the other.

He grunted in sympathetic agreement. She was leaving for New York at the weekend.

"Like this, Steve?" she asked.

He squinted through the camera's viewfinder and pressed the cable release a few times, the shutter sounding loud in the calm of the big basement room.

"Yeah, honey that's good... now turn..."

The brunette laughed throatily and turned her bottom towards the camera, and slowly bent low to clutch her buttocks and spread them wide, gradually changing the pose from erotic to downright lewd. Through the camera's viewfinder he could see clearly a hint of wet pink flesh between the hair fringed lips of her vagina as well as the darker punctuation mark of her crinkled brown anus, stretched between the widely parted, fleshy globes of her bottom. Lit by the studio lamps alone, her pale body shone against the black backdrop and, for a moment, took on an almost vulnerable appearance. Steve felt a sudden surge of lust and his penis lurched inside his pants; this one had been such a great lay... and when there had been the three of them together it had been really wild... but just as quickly the professional in him took over and he strove to drive all such thoughts from his mind.

"Come on, hon, you know that's not the pose I want."

She straightened up and shot him a mock-sulky look over her shoulder and resumed a more sedate pose. Steve started to take photographs and smiled to himself.

There was always time to fool around later, he thought...

Chapter 1

A cool, light breeze cut through the hot midmorning overcast of Los Angeles smog and blew gently through the split-bamboo blind shading the half-open window of the shabby beach cottage. The girl sprawled lazily on her stomach over the bedcovers, absently sipping away at a mug of lukewarm coffee and puffing at the short butt of the filtered cigarette, its smoke blue in the shafts of sunlight.

She stared through the bamboo slits with mild disinterest, observing the passing scene of summer people, brightly clad in scant bikinis and straw bonnets, making their way to the sandy beach area, a few blocks down the street. Already the hot sun had warmed the asphalt to such a degree that they delicately quickened their steps against the tickling heat and rapidly made their way down to the soft sand in brisk paces. She reached over to the bed stand and placed the half-empty mug on the scarred wood, not bothering to place a protective covering under it, then turned over on her back and propped her hands beneath her head. Stretching her firm youthful legs to their fullest length, she glanced down at her softly tanned body, now bursting forth from the flimsy silken material of her robe. The creamy spheres of her upraised breasts contrasted in stark whiteness against the tanned flesh surrounding them, accentuating their full voluptuousness with seductive appeal. She ran her long tapered fingers over the curve of her small waist and onto the full expanse of her generously full thighs, pleased with the beauty of her body, and at the same time frustrated that she had not yet been able to acquire a modelling job to prove her talent.

Not wanting the familiar depression to

take hold of her, she got up quickly from the bed and made her way into the small bathroom, turning on the cold water to its fullest pressure and splashing it freely over her hot face and throat. She loaded her toothbrush with a mint-flavoured paste and brushed vigorously at the small, even white teeth behind her well-formed, sensual lips, trying to get rid of the bitter aftertaste the coffee had left in her mouth. Just over the sink, a panelled mirror reflected the tired look in her eyes and the expression of sheer misery on her face. She had never felt so frustrated before in her life. When she had made the final decision to leave home, and the restrictions her parents had placed on her, she had been sure that her youthful beauty would guarantee her swift success in the modelling world of Hollywood. If it had not been for her savings, now almost gone, and her roommate Barbara's generosity, she would have been forced to return home months ago.

Della wrinkled her nose and dabbed her mouth with Kleenex, thinking that she was indeed lucky to have met Barbara when she did and that there was still time to break into the modelling scene if she applied a concentrated effort with the more popular agencies in downtown Hollywood. How right her friends had been when they had cautioned her about beauty being a commodity that Hollywood maintained a cold indifference to, it being there in such abundance that she was able to walk down the street at Hollywood and Vine, scarcely attracting a second glance from the passers-by. She leaned against the sink and, making a determined effort to get dressed, went back to the bedroom and gathered together the ensemble of clothing and portfolio of pictures that she would need for the day of canvassing the local agencies.

Her thoughts travelled back to the time when she had first met Barbara. Funny, she thought, she had met Barbara many times before, reading magazine stories about hippies, in the movies, and in novels. But until a few weeks ago, she had never come face to face with a swinging hipster – a casual, completely free girl who lived only for today. A girl who smoked marijuana, slept with whom she liked, gave herself without guilt, completely sexually free from inhibitions. The refreshing change from her own dull life into Barbara's world had been just the tonic she had been looking for. Everything had been exciting and stimulating, exactly as she had imagined it would be. The intellectual discussions on every subject under the sun – ranging from psychology to sex and art – which went on until dawn with the all-pervading air of freedom, to say or do whatever you wanted to without criticism or admonishments.

All of this was such a contrast to her life back home on the San Francisco peninsula, where everything seemed mild and boring by comparison. And her parents, though she realized they loved her deeply, always maintained strict limitations on her life and could not seem to understand that, for her own happiness, she would have to make her own way without their help.

All through high school, she had dreamed of her day of freedom, never considering going to college for she found textbooks uninteresting and dry. Of course, the football games and proms were a lot of fun, but still the years dragged by in unendurable slowness. After a lot of coaxing, her parents finally allowed her to attend modelling school where she had learned the basic application of makeup and posing, which was so critical for a successful modelling career. When she had completed the course, last fall, she took her savings and went straight to Los Angeles, where the cost of living was a lot lower, the salaries higher, and most important of all, her opportunities for a modelling career, much greater.

Della walked over to the dressing mirror attached to the back of the closet door, and pensively studied her reflection in the full-length mirror. She slowly removed the silk

polka-dotted robe and critically let her eyes travel up and down her figure, running her hands over her luscious curves and studying the picture of herself as searchingly and objectively as she could.

Her long golden hair fell loosely around the nape of her neck and curled softly at the top of her shoulder blades. A summer of sunbathing and swimming had naturally lightened her tresses and had deepened the lightly tanned skin on her face and body. Large hazel eyes, speckled with green, looked out sullenly through a dark thick fringe of lashes and her full mouth slightly puckered in a perpetual pout that gave her the little-girl-lost look that she despised. No matter how expertly she applied her makeup, she could never seem to achieve that certain degree of sophistication that seemed so essential for successful modelling.

Although the graceful animal lustiness of her appearance had so far not been able to land her a job in the modelling field, it had certainly been no hindrance in attracting males, even to the point of having to fight them off. She had met and dated many different boys, but had never let herself get involved enough to give up her virginity… at least not until last summer when she had met Danny Ritter.

The memory of those wonderful days even

now stimulated the blood in her veins and sent it rushing through her body, awakening the hidden urges of her sex drive. Her hands came up to her breasts and, only half aware of what she was doing, the girl began to stroke them methodically, rubbing her fingers gently, persuasively over the firm globes, bringing the delicate pinkish-brown buds to a pulsating point as she let her mind drift back to the delicious memory of her first seduction.

* * *

The hot August sun burned down through the thin material of her organdie dress, as she steered the MG convertible down the winding coastal highway that led from San Francisco and ended in Santa Barbara. She had purposely started out early, wanting to enjoy the scenic, breathtaking view from where the bent cypress trees leaned toward the cool Pacific Ocean over jagged cliffs of rock and sand. Each curve she rounded offered a new panoramic scene of splendour, truly unequalled in beauty, and temporarily subdued her adventurous mood with a new feeling of peace and calm.

Earlier that morning she had packed the bare essentials she would need for her trip to Los Angeles, not forgetting the portfolio of shots the modelling school had furnished her with at graduation. These would be essential if she wanted to be represented by a reliable modelling agency. She kissed both her parents goodbye, and inwardly felt no regret or misgivings about leaving home for the first time, for at last she would be free to live as she choose, with no restrictions or limitations.

She stopped in Monterey for lunch, enjoying a full plate of fresh abalone with a small carafe of dry white wine. Everything seemed even more wonderful than she had imagined it would be, now that she was able to enjoy her newfound solitude at leisure.

After lunch she roamed around the small shops on the dockside, browsing over the small trinkets on display, set out to attract the multitudes of summer tourists that invaded the small town each year.

Reluctantly, she left Monterey and continued down the coastal route until she was midway to Santa Barbara. By then, the wine from lunch combined with the hot sun and concentrated effort of manipulating the small sports car around each curve had tired her out. Her thin summer dress was completely drenched with perspiration, especially where her back touched the hot leather of the car seat, and she longed for a swim in the cool, blue Pacific. When she spotted a small motel by the side of the road, she gratefully pulled over and checked into a room for the night.

As she was unpacking her suitcase, she discovered to her chagrin that she had left her swimsuit back at home, and there was no shop near where she would be able to purchase one. The small motel was managed by a retired couple and was now almost deserted because the summer was nearing an end.

Tiring quickly of the heat in the small room, Della decided to take a long walk down the empty beach and cool off in the ocean breeze. She walked by the surf's edge for a good half hour, letting the small waves curl around her ankles. How wonderful it would be to go for a swim, she thought, the water looked so clear and refreshing!

Suddenly an urge to be completely free and unrestricted overcame her inhibitions and she looked up and down the beach to be sure that no one else was around. The coast was clear, so she quickly shed her thin dress before she could have any second thoughts about it. Her bra and panties came next, and she stood posed on the shore for a moment or two – a stunning and beautifully naked nymph, her young body a golden tan, except where her swimsuit had previously concealed her firm breasts and loins from the sun.

The white portions of her flesh were accentuated by their stark lightness, making a delightful contrast with the rest of her graceful body. The perspiration on her body quickly evaporated in the cool ocean breeze, and she felt a delicious refreshing rush of air sweep between her half-spread legs and caress the silken pubic hair exposed at her loins.

How wonderful it was to be so completely free, she thought, glancing down at her pale-skinned breasts. Why on earth shouldn't we be able to bathe like this all the time, just as Mother Nature had originally intended for us to do, without fear, displaying our nudity.

Without further thought, she plunged into the sea, diving beneath the cool waves and feeling a tremendous release go through her as the salt water lapped and caressed her nude charms, making her nipples tingle and her skin pulse from the sudden stimulation.

She swam gracefully through the water in a slow crawl, fully aware that she was getting an unmistakable sexual thrill from her nakedness and from the feel of the sea on her unclothed body. When she grew tired from the pace, she turned over onto her back and floated gently; smiling as she watched the waves glide over the swells of her upturned breasts, making them quiver and ripple, with the buds of her nipples just breaking the surface and sticking upwards towards the late afternoon sky.

Through the clear salt water, she could see the darkened v-patch of her pubic mound, with the tiny hairs floating out from her body in all directions. She arched her back and thrust her stomach up to make her crotch appear above the water, secretly delighted at watching the soft dark blond pubic hair cling wetly to the fleshy mound between her loins.

Della lazily spread her legs, stretching out her arms at the same time to form a starfish shape. She let her head fall loosely back, and closing her eyes tightly against the glare of the sun, listened to the faint swish of the sea as it lapped onto the sand about 50 yards away.

Suddenly, without warning, she sensed another body in the water not far away from her. Her animal instincts had sensed the faint ripple of water that crossed the natural pattern of the gently flowing waves, and she opened her eyes at once, trying to spot the intruder.

Della swiftly turned over, and treading the water with her long, graceful legs, squinted around her through the glare of the water's reflections to get a full view around her, but no one was there. And yet she was sure she had noticed movement of some kind. She tensed her body as the horrible thought passed through her mind that possibly sharks could be in the area, for she had read about their presence on the coast and how they were capable of attacking a helpless swimmer without warning.

It was at that moment when Danny Ritter broke through the surface of the sea only inches from her nude body, a broad boyish grin on his lips, his white even teeth dazzling in the sun. Della scooted back and cried out in alarm, too astonished by his sudden presence to think of what to do next. Danny, on the other hand, seemed completely relaxed and unembarrassed, treading the water and nodding his head pleasantly at her.

"I'm sorry," he said. "I didn't mean to frighten you!" He peered at her more closely, drinking in the beauty of her glistening hair and skin. "I didn't expect to find anyone out here so late in the day," he continued, "but the water's wonderful isn't it?"

Della stared back at him, still speechless with surprise. The swimmer next to her was handsome and very powerfully built, and his sandy coloured hair still managed to curl slightly, in spite of the wetness. She could see the animal strength of his thick-muscled arms, now glinting water droplets that clung to the thick curling dark hair on his chest. She shivered and tried to avoid his frank stare, for she could already feel her resistance siphoning out of her body and a hot burning coal starting to smoulder in the pit of her womb. They were only a few inches from each other and the thought of his maleness – his complete animal attraction – in such close proximity to her unprotected sex made the blood rush to her head.

"What's your name?" he persisted. "I'm Danny Ritter, I have a small summer cottage just over there," he said, pointing to a small cluster of trees on the horizon.

Della told him, trying unsuccessfully to hide her embarrassment. "Look…" the words were rushing out of her, spilling from her lips with mounting panic. "I don't have anything on… I left my swimsuit at the motel…"

He threw his head back and laughed a slow, wonderful, natural laugh. "Well, it looks like we're both in the same boat," he grinned cheerfully, looking back at her again. "And I was wondering just a few seconds ago how I was going to explain myself to you. Look, don't let it bother you. I'm not embarrassed… why should you be?" He shook the water from his hair, his earth-coloured eyes ripe with good humour, then narrowed them in sudden seriousness and locked his gaze steadily on her face. "You're a very beautiful woman," he said in almost a whisper.

"Thank you," she mumbled, hating herself for not being able to hide the naked look of mutual yearning that she knew was revealed in her eyes. The sun glinted down on the thick, curly hair on his tanned chest, and his arm brushed against her body, sending a burst of electricity running through her that jolted a flame coloured blush of colour to her cheeks. Her hand came up to her mouth; she could feel the warmth of his skin against hers, and could smell his salt-clean body odour.

She was about to make a move to leave, wondering how she was going to get out of the water without treating him to a full view of her nude body, then a particularly violent wave sent her body crashing helplessly against his, with her head going under the sea.

She felt his strong powerful hands reaching under her armpits and lifting her back above the water. She sputtered, the salt water gagging her throat, and he held her loosely next to him until the spasm passed. Her breasts were now brushing against his huge expanse of chest, and the smooth roundness of her belly was moving seductively against the flat of his. All at once Della was lost in the fire of the moment, with every muscle in her body tensed and strained against his with an uncontrolled urgency. Danny's mouth was on hers and she felt his lips pressing tightly, his arms encircling her at the same time and drawing her with undeniable strength against his hardened body.

She could feel her pointed breasts being

slowly crushed into his chest, and with a wild thrill of intensified pleasure... Della realized that his cock was already stiff and hard! It thrust urgently against the hairy mound of her throbbing cunt in pleading back and forth motions, and he reached down and gently ran his hand over the awakening mounds of her tits and down over her belly to the soft fleshy folds of her cunt below.

Tiny goosebumps sprang out over the whiteness of her sensitive flesh, with her body becoming alert now to the caresses of the magic hands that were stroking her flesh into a hot sheet of desire. God how she wanted him, perhaps it was the heat of the day, combined with the freedom of a deserted beach that contributed to her feeling of helplessness and yearning. Though, whatever the reason, she found herself returning his passionate kiss almost immediately, her sea-moistened lips pressing against his and her body no longer resisting its contact with his. She dug her fingernails deep into his back, just above the line of his buttocks, urging him against her with a fierce and intensely demanding persuasion.

Danny felt her body squirming and thrusting against his with a mild surprise. He didn't expect their sudden stormy encounter to arouse such deep, unexpected passions in them both, passions that could not be chilled by the coolness of the seawater still swirling around them. He kissed her, shutting his eyes, and it was as if he had kissed her many times like that before. His lips grazed her hair and the quivering lids of her wide-set eyes, and then he pulled away from her and bent his head, his hand coming back to her cheek. "I know you," he whispered into her ear, "I know you so well... even though we've just met."

She responded to him with another passionate kiss, driving the tip of her tongue firmly between his teeth. She wriggled it all around deep inside his mouth, licking carefully at the back of his teeth and at his palette, firing him with a desire to possess her utterly and completely.

His hands slipped softly down the curve of her back until be felt his fingers moving on the supple cheeks of her small firm buttocks. Danny held them there for a moment, lifting the soft orbs gently, then began to massage them, rubbing his hands firmly over the beautifully rounded globes and marvelling at the soft, sweet sheen of her taut flesh.

They finally pulled away from each other, both breathless from their passionate struggles, and tiring from the constant treading to stay above water. Unhurriedly, the couple swam back to shore, with Danny leading her to a small sandy inlet, protected on either side with a wall of jagged rocks. When Della felt the sand under her toes, she stood and ran toward the shore, and fell on her back on the floor of the cove, temporarily exhausted. He ran from the water after her reaching her quickly and bending low over her completely exposed body.

"God, you're beautiful," he said.

He pulled her gently towards him and looked directly into her open eyes. "Do you want me to please you?" he asked with almost a boyish shyness.

"Yes... Oh God yesssss," she cried out, pushing her body up against his in hot urgency.

After that there was no more need for words, their eyes communed, saying all that it was necessary to say. Both Danny and Della had accepted suddenly without question that their desires were going to be fulfilled...

She felt his hot breath on her cheek, then Danny's lips again pushed against hers with a renewed urgency, this time with his tongue extended between them. It slithered like a warm, wet snake into her mouth, tasting the wet juices of her saliva, working her already hot lust into a furious, raging urge.

He cupped his hands over her up-thrust breasts, first softly milking at the fleshy mounds with tenderness, then working at them wildly with his fingers digging into the firm muscles and squeezing tightly, bringing a small cry of pain from her parted lips. He worked the pointed buds of her nipples between his thumb and forefinger, backwards and forwards until the teats jerked up into sharp little points.

His hands dropped to the under curve of her white breasts, and he leaned down, clamping his mouth hard over her generous parted lips with a suddenly brutal, unrelenting pressure. She cried out loud in pain, though thoroughly enjoying the uncontrolled passion of his hot lust, then began to suck and pull at his tongue until it was drawn its full length in the moist fleshy depths of her mouth.

Their bodies welded together with each muscle and tendon a part of each other, licking and writhing together as a single unit, gradually building up the tempo of their dual lust beyond the thought of inhibitions or shame. A sharp gasp emerged from somewhere deep within his throat as Danny lifted his mouth from hers and buried his teeth in her softly rounded shoulder, biting down painfully into the flesh and leaving a red welt, then moving on to another unmarked area, sucking and nibbling each tender spot as his mouth travelled down to the creamy mounds of her shivering tits.

"Ooooooh, God," she suddenly groaned, digging her body deeper into the soft sand beneath them. She quivered uncontrollably from the sudden unexpected tingling sensations that shot through her body, and dropped her hand between the area of his wide-spread knees, grasping his hard erected cock in her hands. Danny moaned a deep low pleading sound as she pushed against it with her fingers sliding the foreskin back over the round rubbery head.

In return, Danny anchored his hot moist mouth tightly to an erected nipple and began a gentle sucking pressure, swirling his tongue in tortuous tiny circles, around and around the pulsating bud until it came to a sharp peaked point. At the same time his hands coursed lightly over the soft firmness of her belly and thighs, while his mouth continued to play for a long delicious moment teasingly around the throbbing tits.

"Ohhhhhh, darling," she groaned... she had never called anyone darling before.... With ecstatic pleasure and longing, Della fondled his pulsating cock, at the same time coaxing its head towards the centre of her gaping unfulfilled cunt.

But Danny hesitated, sensing the girl's virginity, and wanting to prolong her yearning to a point that would make his entrance as painless as possible for her. His experience in lovemaking had begun in his early youth, but of all his sexual encounters, he could count very few virgins... and none as eager and willing as Della. This moment for him was so spontaneous and refreshing that he wanted with all of his being to give the writhing girl beneath him the same pleasure and fulfilment that she was giving to him, so that it would be locked in her memory long after their satisfactions were consumed.

His mouth slid down over her now quivering belly, his penis sliding from her hands as his body moved reluctantly away from her. He drove his wet tongue for a moment into the tiny indentation of her navel, bringing small mewls and grasps of pleasure from her open mouth, then crouched lower, moving his lips in maddening patterns of indecent sensations, gently nipping at each tongue-kissed area with his sharp teeth.

Della felt her thighs being pressed gently open and she made no move of resistance as he hunched down between them. She groaned, the exquisite feeling of air rushing over the rising bud of her exposed clitoris, and rippling up to her throbbing tits, drowning out any feeling of control or hesitation from her burning body. She was now a complete and willing slave to her newfound lover's manipulations, and she let the straining muscles of her thighs slowly relax while she anxiously waited for his next move.

Danny's tongue flicked forward, the tip of

it teasing moistly against the tiny bud of her clitoris, causing it to throb into erection with burning pain.

Della wrenched forward from the electricity of its contact. "Aaaaaah, mmmmmm," she moaned, "do it more... oooooh, it's so goooood!" She sucked in her breath with another gasp as she felt his fingers spreading the soft hair-covered lips of her vagina wide apart, with the coolness of the ocean breeze touching against her there.

Again he drove his hard, pointed tongue deep within the confines of her wide-open cunt, this time mercilessly spearing it in and out of her with the rapidity of a fast-moving drill. Della responded immediately to the tortuous fucking of his tongue, grabbing at the tangles of his wet hair and pulling his mouth deeper into the crevice of her hot aching loins. His tongue was now circling around maddeningly inside of her, the tip flicking against the wet sensitive walls of her pussy, causing her hips to buck and writhe uncontrollably. She began to murmur words of love to him without thought of their meaning, gently coaxing his manipulations to continue, she never wanted the delicious feeling to end. Her breasts heaved out against her chest, and her legs splayed out wide as she jack-knifed her knees upwards to open her cunt as wide as she could to his probing tongue.

"Oooooh... don't stop... don't ever stop," she chanted through her lust-dazed passions, unaware of her begging, pleading groans, only feeling the multitude of sensations that were making her his slave.

Now that her luscious cunt was poised fully exposed to his view with the afternoon sun glinting down on it and picking up the crystals of moistness that decorated it like a thousand tiny gems, Danny could wait no longer. He lunged his hips forward, sending his cock within the confines of her gaping channel, tight and resisting in her unexplored passage. Her body stiffened, the tightness of her virgin hole reminding her that she was going to suffer while gaining the rewards of her first sexual encounter. But now she didn't care about the pain and discomfort, in a way, her suffering added to the indescribable pleasure of release that was now flooding through the gates of her wide-open loins, paying tribute to the freedom of expression that she had so desperately sought all of her life.

She felt his hardened cock push gently into her, reaching the midpoint of her craving hole, then hesitating as if fearing to proceed to the depths of her womb. Della sensed his indecision and gripped at his shoulders tightly, forcing him to meet her eyes.

"Do it now!" she commanded, staring

desperately up into his eyes. "I'm ready, Danny… Now! Fuck me! Fuck me, darling!"

Upon hearing her provocative words, Danny exhaled a stifled roar of lust and eased his prick slightly out of her cunt, giving him greater access, then thrust it with all his might, all his strength inwards, tearing the thin fleshy curtain of her hymen! He no longer thought of holding back or the tenderness of the moment, and let his rampaging cock take full control of his body, plunging in and out of her tight, moist hole with a driving lust. He fucked into her with a savage, unrelenting power that he had never used before, even with the lowest of whores… and her pain-filled cries continued to drive him on, his pounding and surging body surpassing the roar of the waves around them.

Della's head snapped forward as the rest of her body collapsed under the pressure of his pounding loins, her open mouth devouring and gorging at Danny's shoulders, burying her scream of intense pain by sinking her sharp teeth cruelly into his muscular flesh. A hot, gushing pain streaked from her ragged, lust-torn cunt and up through the rest of her trembling body. Her lover had suddenly turned into a cruel torturer, ramming a white-hot iron between the lips of her wet, viscous opening with unceasing repetition. But then, gradually as her inner muscles expanded and became accustomed to the burrowing rod, it slowly began to please her as the thought passed through her mind that she was actually able to contain so massive a weapon… so huge and solid a prick!

Then, as if by magic, the intense pain gave way completely to a new and stimulating sensation, new and deep inside her… a sensation that she never before had known or could now believe was real. With each new in- thrust of his rock-hard instrument, now lessening in its fury… titillating sparks of fire burst from the passages of her vaginal walls, electrifying her whole being from the depths of her womb to the tips of her erect nipples. For a moment she dreamed that she had surpassed the confines of life and was now floating in the limbo of an unknown heaven… she had never realized that such joy could be felt, and silently prayed that the delicious fucking she was being subjected to would never end. With the slow ebbing away of pain, Della began to adapt herself to Danny's rhythmic fucking of her body, moving her hips and loins in time with his movements and allowing her mind to savour every moment of the intimate act.

Danny looked down, thrilling at the sight of the small, warm trickle of blood running down her thighs, and he knew then for sure that his powerful cock was initiating the girl onto the long path of womanhood that she was about to embark upon. Now he was ready to bring her to the crest of her passions, peaking all emotions and feelings that she might have known before him. With his cock firmly imbedded in her, he fumbled his hands beneath her buttocks and lifted them off the sand. He settled his fingers snugly around the wet cheeks and drove his prick more securely than ever into Della's slightly bleeding vaginal passage. His hips rotated in slow, circular motions as his cock dug into the hot slippery depths, and Della responded by grinding her own hips in imitation, clenching and unclenching her buttocks, feeling his hands pinching roughly into the soft flesh of her bottom, bruising the skin and then probing cautiously around the puckered ring of her anus.

"Oooooh," she moaned and chanted as he felt the full expanse of her insides flowering open to receive his rod deep in her womb. "Yes... Yessss..." she murmured as her body followed him, moving in wild abandoned jerks beneath him.

Suddenly she felt a throb deep inside as the thickness of his cock flexed in frozen rigidity, and he drove his middle finger past the tight muscular ring of her tiny anus.

"Auuuuuggggghhhh!" she groaned, her face contorted in the half-smile of erotic pain.

"Do... do you want me to stop?" he panted, not moving his finger from the tight hole, and slowly rotating it around and around until the firm muscle gradually adjusted to the lewd intrusion.

"Oooooh," she gasped, shaking her head from side to side, not wanting anything at all to stop.

He continued to move his finger around inside, stretching the rubbery softness wider and wider, while at the same time his lengthened shaft began a new firm in and out stroking, driving her into a greater frenzy of lust.

A deep moaning sound from deep within her lungs burst forth, slowly dying into soft whimpers of pain for a moment and then building up into greater moans of pleasure as her anus slowly became more accustomed to the impalement. He slid his other hand slowly up from the soft moons of her ass to where his cock was sliding smoothly in and out of her pussy and could feel the soft hair-lined folds clasped tightly to his plunging cock, pulling and giving with each long, hard thrust into her.

Della's hands reached down under his, feeling the spot where he entered her, the sensation bringing softer moans of abandoned pleasure from her mouth and at the same time spreading her legs to a wide spread-eagle position, attempting in greedy desire to swallow the whole of his cock into her now-gaping channel. She could feel the edge of a foamy wave lapping at the soles of her feet, and realized that the rising tide had slowly crept around them, and was now gradually encircling their bodies, threatening to engulf them both as they wallowed in lewd connection in the sand. But her body was paralyzed under the hypnotic spell of his enflamed lovemaking, and right then she would have rather drowned in the tide than to stop the exquisite feeling overwhelming them both at that moment.

Danny, too, felt the surging tide imprisoning their bodies, and realized the danger of them both being trapped between the rushing waves and the ragged rocks behind them, but he continued to fuck deeply into her, the excitement of their perilous position igniting his body with renewed energy and purpose. He had to fuck her to completion, and quick, before it was too late to escape from the cove!

He lunged forward, his weight smashing her full firm breasts flat against her chest. Thrusting his hips forward at the same time, he let his long, thick cock plunge into her cunt, pushing the soft moist flesh of her vaginal walls in rippling waves before it. The loud smack of his balls beating against her upturned cheeks resounded sharply above the roar of the incoming waves.

"Oh God... Oh God! Hurry – hurry – hurry!" she screamed, grinding her cunt against his rod with a mounting panic.

A large wave burst over their twisting bodies, completely saturating them and temporarily pulling Danny's plunging organ out of her expanded hole, lubricating it with salt water from the angry sea behind them.

"No! noooooo," she protested, "finish it, for God's sake, fuck me!"

He frantically rammed his long shaft again deep into her belly, filling every part of her insides. She had never been so filled in her life and his cock speared into her without mercy or thought of injury in its haste to reach its final completion. She renewed her own rhythm quickly, determined to reach her climax before he could withdraw again, gyrating and twisting her body beneath his urgent pounding, until... half swooning, she felt a great soaring sensation in her loins... a wild, fantastic explosion burst from the hot pit of her twisting loins and spread like a rampaging brush fire through her twitching body, finally reaching the depths of her entire being, and re-bursting into a thousand minuscule explosions each igniting the other like a long string of fiery, exploding roman candles.

"Ooooh... it's soooo good!" she groaned,

as her tensed body flooded with waves of tranquillity and complete release. She could feel her own juices oozing from inside her and gushing around Danny's hard pulsating rod, still plunging in and out of her expanding and contracting channel.

Above her, Danny could hear her cries of fulfilment punctuated by a soft grunt with each powerful lunge he made into her, blended with the tempo of the crashing ocean waves slapping against his back. Her body was now wet and slippery from the sea water, and he reached forward, digging his fingers into her shoulders to gain more leverage as he continued his hurried rhythmic thrustings.

"Oh... Oh... Ughhhhh!" he gasped and groaned, as he felt the hot, thick fluid burst forth from his loaded balls and spew itself deep within her hot, wet, clasping cavern. Della clung to him desperately as she felt the hot sperm shoot through her, mixing with her own fluids, and then gushing out again, overflowing down on the soft flesh of her inner thighs, only to be washed away by the next ocean wave that sprayed down on their trembling bodies.

Still gasping, Danny pulled himself reluctantly away from her, and lifting her with him as he stood, braced his weakened knees to keep them from buckling beneath him. They stood there for a moment, clinging to each other and let the wild surf wash against their legs, trying to recapture the strength they would need to swim back to the open beach on the other side of the cove. No words were spoken, for none were needed at that moment to communicate the intense satisfaction that swelled deep within their bodies, and then hand in hand they waded through the foamy sea water, past the breakers, out to the calm, cool waters that would lead them back to a safe shore.

* * *

After those first wild moments, Della and Danny spent a wonderful two weeks together... swimming during the day and going for long walks in the evening, sometimes talking to each other about their individual views on life, and what future hopes or hidden ambitions drove them to their separate goals. Della discovered that first night when she moved her belongings from the motel to his cabin, that he was a struggling writer of the new left "hip" group and that he was now trying to complete a novel written in a campy commercial style solely because he had run out of money and had no other source of income. She sensed that the uncompleted book was a strong force behind his sudden moody silences that periodically overshadowed their bright moments together, and tried to ignore them, hoping that their newfound happiness would bring him away from those sombre moods. But as the second week drew to an end, his moods increased in frequency, and lingered over him longer than before. Finally, when she could stand his shifts in temperament no longer, she decided to leave, knowing that a day longer with him would forever ruin the memory of their first passionate encounters.

She waited until later that evening when he drove down to the small general store to get some beer and cigarettes. At first, he insisted she come with him, but she feigned a headache, trying not to reveal on her face the tightness that had balled up in her chest for want of him.

He hesitated at the door. "Is something wrong, Della?"

She stood there, her heart pounding, then rushed over to him and put her arms around his waist, burying her head in the wide expanse of his chest. "No... nothing's wrong," she mumbled, fighting back the tears that were swimming under the lids of her eyes. "I'll be all right."

He kissed her lightly on the ear and closed his hand about her waist, stroking the roundness of her hips. "I'll be back soon, baby," he said, and stepped out the door.

The muffled roar of his sports car was still

an echo in her ears, and she brusquely wiped away the hot tears that were blinding her vision as her numbed body went through the motions of packing her clothes, finally taking them out to her car. She paused a moment, and viewed the sunset still breathtaking in its brilliance, then turned on the ignition and slowly drove back to the coastal highway.

Chapter 2

Della stood before the mirror with her eyes half-shut against the reflection of her nude body, as the vivid memory of her brief affair with Danny completely permeated her soul with unfulfilled yearning. To this day, she had remained true to his memory, hoping somehow he would be able to find her in the vast cosmopolitan city that she now felt lost in. A few days after she had driven away from his rented cabin, she had written him a long letter, telling him of her deep feelings and why she had left in such haste, but the letter had been returned unopened... he had left the cabin, with no forwarding address.

She walked back over to the bed and stretched her naked body over the soft mattress, as the memory of Danny and his lovemaking gradually drained her earlier ambitions of job hunting. She reached down and placed her long fingers over the hot pulsating moistness at the opening of her cunt, still feeling the pressure of his body driving into hers during those magical two weeks. Her body flinched in surprise as the touch of her own hands brought forth small shoots of electricity surging through her loins. God she was hot! She drove her fists into the soft mattress at the total frustration that enveloped her ripe body, praying silently that somehow she would be able to find him again.

A soft knocking at her bedroom door interrupted her enraptured thoughts, and she quickly drew the bedspread over her nakedness.

"Who is it?" Della called.

"It's just me," Barbara answered. "Are you decent?" Without waiting for an answer, the girl pushed the door open and came into the room. She stopped short in apparent surprise when she saw Della's naked body outlined under the thin bedspread. "Oh, you're not dressed... and here it is almost noon! Well, never mind, dear, I'm not that prudish, you know."

Della blushed at her last remark, knowing it was directed at her shy habit of either leaving the room or turning her head away whenever she walked into Barbara's room and found the girl in the nude. Which happened very frequently, since Barbara seemed to spend most of her time either naked or in a scantily dressed condition. The girl never missed an opportunity to tease Della about this – and though Della tried to cure herself of her innate shyness when confronted by the nudity of her own sex, she could never seem to get over the silly inhibition.

Barbara was an intelligent girl, and Della envied her self- assuredness and composure that she seemed to maintain under any and all circumstances. However, the novelty of Barbara's way of life was beginning to pall; she knew she didn't really fit into her group because they had an entirely different upbringing from her and, besides, they had never known the security of a home life which Della found she still longed for. Maybe her rebellion against her parents didn't mean that she rejected their philosophy of life entirely... maybe she had been wrong to leave home in such haste.

"What's wrong?" Barbara asked. "You look down in the dumps."

"Oh not much, I guess," Della answered, half-heartedly gazing back at her roommate, and secretly envying her beautiful dark looks.

Barbara Hope was a tall and lissom, dark-haired girl in her late twenties who seemed to maintain a substantial income from the rental of the two small beach bungalows, and working part-time as a model. Many times before, Della had urged her to show the stills of her past modelling, wanting to compare them to her own portfolio, but each time, Barbara had put her off, making the excuse that they were not really good samples of her work. Finally, Della had stopped asking, silently resenting Barbara's reluctance to show them, and passed it off as Barbara's subtle way of fighting competition within the trade.

Now, she stood before Della in full confidence, dressed deliberately in the sloppiest fashion possible. At the moment, she wore a faded polo-necked sweater and a pair of tight, blue jeans. They had shrunk through countless immersions in the washer until they now stretched only as far as the girl's calves, while around her crotch they clung so tightly that the outline of her sex was plainly visible. Her long, dark hair fell loosely over her shoulders in uncombed tangles, almost hiding one side of her face. Barbara wore no makeup, and relied on the sun to softly tan her cheeks to a soft amber tone, though it did little to hide the perpetual circles of dark around her eyes, mementos of a thousand sleepless nights high on Benzedrine or other pep pills. The whole effect served to give her a striking, gaunt appearance that was not totally attractive, in spite of her classical, even bone structure.

Barbara carried herself with the casual, sleek grace of a stalking panther, her hips slim and narrow, jutting up to her amply ballooning breasts, still firm enough to hold their shape without the support of a brassiere. Now, as she ambled over to where Della sat, her buttocks rippled under the tight material, revealing their firmly rounded fleshiness with each step she took.

"Cheer up Sport," she said. "I've got some good news for a change. First and foremost... I'm going to throw a blast tomorrow night. God knows it's about time; this place is getting too dull for words. And to liven up the show, I'm going to treat my guests to a super new supply of hashish." She laughed at the surprised look on Della's face. "Well, don't just sit there like you've got a bad taste in your mouth," she said good-naturedly as she flopped into the over-stuffed easy chair by the window, "you know, I must say you're just about the most unhip roommate I've ever had, and to change all that, this time I'm going to insist that you have a few puffs with the rest of us."

Della smiled, ignoring her last comment. She had never tried hashish before, and wasn't really interested in getting "high," but Barbara always insisted that she was missing a good thing by not trying the drug... perhaps this time she would.

"So what else is new?" Della asked dryly, lighting up another cigarette.

"Just wait till you hear this!" Barbara jumped up from the chair with a new wave of enthusiasm and sat next to Della on the bed. "Two real good friends of mine, Steve and Ginny Albright, are looking for new models. They run a photo studio over in Santa Monica, and they've got a big reputation in the business."

"That sounds great," Della said, "what do they specialize in?"

"Well, er... right now they're looking for cheesecake models, you know, the fresh dewy type, like in the Playboy foldouts." She placed her hand on Della's arm. "Hon, I know you're just the type to fill the bill, I'd go myself, if I were a few years younger."

"I don't know," she hesitated, "I never thought of posing for pin-ups before... besides I'm mainly interested in breaking into fashion... not, something like that."

"Don't be a fool." Barbara took the cigarette from Della and took a deep drag. "You've been pounding the pavement for months with no luck yet. Hollywood is a tough place, kid, and I'm giving you a chance to at least get a start. Steve phoned me this morning, and I set up an appointment for you. If you want to back out, that's up to you, but don't say you never got a chance at it."

"I'm sorry, Barbara, I didn't mean to sound ungrateful... I'm just not sure I want to get into that type of modelling."

"Listen, believe it or not, I do happen to know people who have perfectly respectable businesses!" Barbara chided. "Steve and Ginny, incidentally... they're brother and sister... operate this legal, absolutely proper pin-up concern. Artistic, glamour pictures... some in the nude, some in lingerie. And they pay fifty dollars an hour, even for models like you without experience! If nothing else, at least be practical. How many weeks do you have to go before your savings run out?"

"Only a few," she said slowly starting to accept the idea. The last thing she wanted to do now was to go back home a failure and prove to her parents that they were right from the beginning.

"Well, if you really think it's wrong to pose in your underwear or in the nude... forget it. I know Steve and Ginny want their models to look natural and relaxed when they pose."

Della leaned back on the pillow, unconsciously letting the bedspread slip down the rising buds of her pointed nipples. The thought of posing for Steve and Ginny Albright was gradually taking the shape of an exciting adventure in her mind. After all, hundreds of famous actresses had started their careers by posing for such photos, and had gone on later to greater fame and stardom. During her adolescence, she had secretly nursed her dreams on the glossy issues of Hollywood magazines, which was her one escape from the dull suburban reality that she lived in. These dreams had always inspired her, and were actually the reason why she chose a modelling career in the first place. She could remember all of her girl friends in high school, always talking of marriage and a family, but she had never been attracted to the thought of long years of dull, routine, boring home-life. No, that was definitely not the life for Della Wilkins, and she had known it for years.

During those long peaceful nights in Danny's arms, she had confided these dreams to him while they were resting from the heated exertion of their lovemaking. Those moments had been wonderful and unforgettable, with just the two of them alone together, sharing their individual hopes and aspirations. He had admitted to her that he saw himself as an *avant-garde* novelist, writing stories that depicted the hypocrisy that existed in the social mores of the twentieth century. Most of all, he wanted to play his part in the sexual revolution which was now gaining momentum by helping to destroy the final remnants of Puritanism and neurotic guilt which still prevented complete freedom in the arts.

His visions had inspired Della, and that night he told her of a world where sex and nudity were accepted everywhere without fear and shame. She could recall the passion in his voice when he spoke, and now she wanted to help him in her small way by proving to herself that she could live up to his beliefs. She might be playing only a tiny role in the emancipation of sex by posing for nude photographs, but at least she would be taking part in it.

The thought of this new adventure of free expression sent tiny shivers of excitement up her legs and back, and suddenly she felt very grateful to have such an unselfish friend like Barbara. She looked at Barbara with a new sense of admiration and friendship for the girl.

"You must think I'm awfully stupid," she said, leaning over and squeezing Barbara's hand. "Of course, I'd love to have the job... when do I start?"

Barbara looked back at her with surprise. "Well!" she exclaimed, "I'm glad to see that you're using your head, for a while there I was sure you were going to turn Steve's offer down. But, before I call him back, are you sure you don't want to think it over a little longer?"

"No... no, I'm positive about this, Barbara. I feel sure now that this might be the big break I've been waiting for, it just took me a little while to get over the shock... that's all."

"That's great, kid," she said. "I made your appointment for Monday morning so you'd have a little time to rest after the party, at least you'll have something to celebrate now." She glanced down with admiration at Della's firm, white breasts. "I know Steve and Ginny will be very satisfied with you, so don't get stage fright."

Della blushed and pulled the bedspread up to her shoulders, not realizing before that she had been so exposed to her roommate's eyes.

"Oh, come now," Barbara mockingly drew her own arms in front of her. "You'll have to get rid of some of that prudery before Monday, if I bother you, how do you think you'll react before a camera... with a man behind it!"

Della blushed again and nodded her head. "I know I'm shy, Barbara... but I can change... I know I can." Then a thought struck Della. "Incidentally, how long have you known Steve and Ginny?"

"A few years," she replied. "On and off, that is, you know how it is in the trade. But don't worry, I've done lots of posing for them before, and you have nothing to worry about."

"Did your work with them ever lead to anything else?" Della asked.

"Anything else like what?" Barbara said giving her a strange look.

"Well... like bigger stuff... you know what I mean... magazine work, talent scouts..."

Barbara smiled. "No, I'm afraid it didn't," she said. "For one thing, I don't have your innocent, fresh appeal... besides, I was already too experienced and cynical when I met Steve and Ginny to be a new discovery. You have to understand that what people want in their sort of business is girls who show their bodies off but still retain a quality of innocence... as if they don't really know what sex is all about..."

Barbara had a sad, distant look in her eyes and her lips were set in a firm line as she paused and took another drag off the cigarette. Della felt a sudden rush of sympathy and compassion for her roommate, for she realized that Barbara's maturity had been forced upon her at an earlier age. She had grown up too fast, experiencing everything there was to see and live, and now, sitting there so close to her, Della realized what it was that made Barbara seem incomplete: she had no more dreams to dream, or ambitions to seek.... That's why she lived, for the here and now, and getting "high" was probably her only escape from the self-made prison that enclosed her.

"Whatever that inner spark is that a photographer seeks, I just didn't have it," Barbara continued. "I don't think I ever had it." She made a gesture as if to shrug off the solemn mood that permeated the room, but the bitterness in her voice and words saddened Della, though she knew there was little she or anyone could do to help Barbara.

Barbara leaned back on the end of the bed and put her hands behind her head. "Anyway, let's change the subject, talking about myself is just about the dullest thing I can imagine!"

Della could feel the warmth of Barbara's thighs next to her feet under the thin material of the bedspread. They were slightly trembling and despite the older girl's outward display of cool cynicism, Della could see that her eyes were slightly moist with unshed tears.

"Don't be afraid to show your true feelings around me," Della said with understanding. "You're my best friend, so don't try to act so cool and detached. If there's anything you want to get off your chest, you can tell me… but don't keep it all locked up inside you Barbara, I can't stand to see you suffer like this."

Barbara looked up at her with hopeless misery in her eyes. When she finally spoke, her voice was soft and trembling.

"Oh Hon… I could tell you so many things," she half whispered, wiping the tears from her cheeks with the back of her hand.

"Then tell me Barbara… I'm not trying to pry. I don't care how you've lived before," Della urged her softly. "You'll feel a lot better after you've talked about it. It might make a tremendous difference to confide in someone… someone who's really sympathetic and only wants to help you."

Barbara crawled up to the front of the bed and positioned herself next to Della like a small child seeking comfort from her mother after a bad nightmare. "My story," she began, her eyes staring fixedly across the room, "is as old as time itself… I loved and lost. Only there is one slight difference: the person I loved and who rejected me happened to be another woman."

Della froze! A strange, sinking feeling… like the first downward dip on a roller coaster churned inside her stomach. But there was nothing she could do about her position, after all, it was she who urged Barbara to tell her her problems, and she had to stick it out now, or the older girl would never have faith in anyone… ever again.

She continued to listen breathlessly as Barbara related, in brief, unemotional terms, the facts of her first love affair, a growing curiosity awakening in her as she looked down at the older girl and realized that she had known the intimate caresses of another member of her own sex.

Della herself had never, so far as she was aware, ever met a lesbian before now. Certainly, she had never been approached by another girl or even felt the slightest desire to experiment with bodies identical to her own. But gradually, as Barbara's voice calmly narrated her early experiences, Della could feel a slowly mounting interest in such strange pleasures. It was as if she were a small child again, becoming aware that there existed certain mysterious areas of behaviour that, up to the present, had been completely forbidden to her.

She lowered her eyes and tried to hide the spark of growing excitement within her as Barbara told her of the earlier painful experiences she had endured as a young girl. When Barbara was fifteen, she had fallen helplessly and totally in love with a much older girl, who, in return, had merely used her as an instrument of pleasure. Barbara found out later that she meant nothing more to the lesbian than a soft, exciting body that she could use and instruct in the secret delight of Sapphic love.

When the older girl had finally tired of her and gone on to convert another "fresh" inexperienced novice, Barbara let herself go completely, and even to this day had never been able to shake off the memory of that first, gloriously fulfilling love affair. Over the years that followed, she had gradually integrated herself successfully with the more liberal, arty, types of Manhattan Beach, knowing that these people would not chastise her for the way that she chose to live.

"... But don't think I'm completely homosexual," Barbara finished. "This may sound a bit strange to you, but I like men just as much as girls. You're so young now you might not understand what I'm saying right now, but to me... affairs aren't that enduring. You go to bed, enjoy sex with another person... man or woman, and in the bright light of day that follows, you still know nothing at all about their inner feelings. It's all for the pleasure of flesh, and releasing your physical needs and when your current interest begins to fade, there's always someone else to fill the vacancy." Barbara's voice broke and a stifled sob escaped, softening the bitter tone of her voice.

On sudden impulse, Della moved her hand almost instinctively to Barbara's head and started to stroke her hair gently, not saying anything, just trying to show her that she sympathized and understood. There was no other way to show the older girl how deeply she regretted the bitter disillusions and suffering that she must have gone through in the past years.

Barbara turned and for the first time during the long discussion, looked deeply into Della's eyes. "Can you understand me Sweetie? Can you understand how I got the way I am today?" Her eyes were full of misery as she reached her hand up to the side of Della's face and gently brushed her fingers across the soft, firm flesh in a light caress.

"Y – yes, I do understand… and, it's made me feel very close to you… very close."

She whispered the last words, hearing her voice tremble and murmur them in warm response to Barbara's needs. Her hand was still resting on Barbara's head, her fingers now entwined in the girl's long, dark hair. She felt as if she was on the brink of a staggering discovery about herself, as if Barbara had unwittingly stirred desires deep within her that she had never before recognized.

Her thoughts rushed through the complexity of her mind like a series of electrical impulses, knowing immediately what the final answer would be. Freedom of sexual expression after all, could go as far as the two persons participating would agree upon, and Della truly wanted to give her body to Barbara to prove that sex could be an emotional as well as a physical relationship.

And it would be so much more meaningful than the "one-night-stand" bed partners that her roommate had met before. Besides, she was terribly intrigued by Barbara's frank account of her homosexual activities. The story had aroused her to a point where she now felt an almost uncontrollable urge to find out for herself what the caresses of another girl would be like...

"W – would you like to make love to me, Barbara?" she whispered, scarcely believing her own words.

The older girl narrowed her eyes, ran them wonderingly over Della's blushing, downcast face. "Do you really want me to?" she asked, not being able to hide the trembling excitement in her voice.

"Oh, Yes... Yes I do, more than anything!" Della's heart was thudding crazily beneath the bedspread as though it were going to jump right out of her skin. She was afraid for a while that Barbara might think that she was being too forward in her enthusiasm, but she didn't care now as long as everything was agreeable to the girl lying beside her. After a long silence, Barbara finally raised her arms and gently enclosed them around Della's narrow waist.

Della took a deep, trembling breath and exhaled, feeling all the pent-up tensions finally releasing themselves from her tortured body, for she knew that she had reached the point of no return. She felt strangely passive; as if she had given up her freedom of choice when she made the initial approach to Barbara, and was now unable to do anything but follow down the path the other girl led her.

Chapter 3

Just outside the beach cottage, the sweltering summer day lay over the beach community with a blanket of humid heat that gave no sign of lifting. Noxious black clouds of LA smog had drifted from the inland industries and down to the ocean, now filtering through the slotted bamboo curtain and into the bedroom where the two girls sat almost trance-like, staring at each other with the full conscious knowledge of what they were about to embark upon.

The fluid light of the semi-darkened room played across the white translucent valleys and peaks of Della's young body, now completely uncovered and open to Barbara's admiring gaze.

"It's so hot and sticky outside," Barbara purred, "let's take a bath together so we can be more comfortable."

Della nodded and shyly followed Barbara

out of the bedroom and down the hallway to the large spacious bathroom that was situated on the opposite side of the cottage. The younger girl was unable to pinpoint the precise moment when she had decided to give herself to Barbara, but no matter what her real motivations were – whether they were a simple desire to experiment, an affectionate wish to show Barbara that not everyone regarded sex as purely a self-gratifying pastime, or merely her own repressed perversions coming to the surface – she had to go through with it now…

She let Barbara take her hand and lead her slowly into the cool bathroom; the dull Friday morning had magically been altered, changed by fate into a day of vital psychological meaning for her. The room itself was a welcome break from the stuffy bedroom that they had just left. Barbara had redecorated and modernized it herself earlier that year, and used her practical efficiency to tile the walls in soft blue mosaic squares. A white synthetic fur rug carpeted the floor, wall-to-wall, and streamline glass cabinets and shelves lined the walls, giving ample storage room for toiletries.

Della curled her toes into the deep piled rug as Barbara secured the lock on the door. Barbara stepped up closely behind her and lightly placed her hands on the soft rounded shoulders, beginning to knead Della's skin gently, relaxing the tensed muscles into a satin smoothness. Then, lowering her head, Barbara touched her mouth softly to the nape of Della's neck, planting tiny, wet kisses in a winding trail, stooping lower and lower until she was on her knees. She reached up and planted her wide-spread fingers on the base of the younger girl's spine, kneading there too until the rigidity of her muscles had surrendered to her expert massage.

Della could feel the tension flow from her body in waves of exciting sensations. She swallowed audibly, as she felt the adrenaline pumping through her limbs with sharpening intensity, and she let her body go completely limp, submitting to the lovemaking, which she herself had invited.

Slowly inching her body up to a standing position again, Barbara turned Della around to face her, running her eyes appreciatively over the beautifully tanned body in its complete nudity. Della blushed deeply, still feeling extreme embarrassment under the other girl's frank stare, then turned away suddenly, leaning forward over the bath and inserting the plug as she turned on both faucets full blast.

While she was in this revealing position, her buttocks splayed slightly... opening the cheeks and revealing the divine crease that sheltered her well-hidden back orifice. Then, turning around once more, Della looked back at Barbara who was now slowly removing all of her clothing with the seductive movements of a stripper, all the while never taking her eyes off of the trembling body in front of her. Della felt another flush of fear mounting in her stomach, she was still not sure that her new sex adventure was wise, but it was too late now to stop, she knew that.

She strained further over the bath to adjust the flow of cold water, and as she bent forward again, Barbara could plainly detect the pink and partially opened lips of her vagina that protruded faintly from between Della's fleshy thighs.

She gazed avidly upon the taut-muscled legs as the girl stretched herself. Della was seemingly unaware that she was presenting this intimate area of herself to Barbara's inspection and this added to the lesbian's enjoyment of the situation.

Barbara felt her breath quickening at the thought of the impending seduction and felt the hot burning coal in the deep centre of her loins grow more and more sensitive as she continued to view the vulnerable openness of Della's wide-spread legs. When, at last Della straightened up, she turned slowly to face Barbara, her eyes hot with excitement. Barbara had removed her sweater and bra, revealing a luscious set of tits as large as firm, giant grapefruits.

Barbara moved through the steam that was beginning to fill the room and laid her fingers on Della's waist. Her fingers trembled at the touch... the girl's skin was so incredibly soft, so sleek and smooth! She fondled the flesh around Della's waist for a few moments, and then eased her hands down until they cupped the fleshy hipbones.

"Take off my jeans, for me," Barbara whispered, "I don't want to take my hands off you... not for one second."

Della nodded still speechless at the emotional intensity of the moment, and eagerly, swiftly moved her delicate fingers to her belt... unbuckling it and drawing the zipper slowly downwards.

Keeping her hands where they were, Barbara waited breathlessly until Della had begun to pull her jeans down over her hips, then slipped her feet together and wriggled her legs seductively until the tight-fitting jeans had fallen in a limp bundle around her ankles.

As she stepped daintily out of them, she felt Della's hands go around her waist and press into the base of her spine... just above the tight elastic waistband of her panties. The older girl took a slow, deep breath, expanding her huge white breasts to their full size and sucking in her stomach at the same time to ease the removal of her flimsy panties. Della fitted her fingers into the waistband and drew them sensually down, pausing when the panties were halfway over the black patch of her pubic hair, to view the voluptuous curve of the upright, dark pink-nippled breasts jiggling sexily in front of her parted lips as if urging her to fondle them. As if to speed up her disrobement, Barbara reached down and quickly skimmed out of the silken panties, then stood entirely nude before Della, enjoying the look of total admiration in her eyes.

Della realized at this moment that she didn't feel even the slightest embarrassment at gazing upon another girl's nude body. All at once, without warning, it seemed to be the most natural thing in the world to appreciate the nakedness of feminine beauty! She could feel her own nipples hardening with desire and starting to strain to a pointed peak.

Della glanced down quickly at her breasts. The points were stiff and sensitive... her normally quiet and soft-textured nipples had grown thick, bursting into flower like over-ripened buds!

Barbara, sensing Della's growing lust, began to sway her breasts towards her, bending her legs a bit to bring her nipples into delicious contact with the equally hard buds which belonged to Della. The electrical contact took Della's breath away. She almost gasped aloud as the older girl's free hand massaged her own breasts in tiny teasing circles, tweaking the soft nipples into a firmer, almost tormenting hardness. Without warning, Barbara scissored her legs open with the agility of a limbo dancer, exposing the thin slit of her vagina, nestled teasingly in the soft dark hair between her thighs. Sheer wanton desire burned out at Della from her dilated pupils, now half-hidden beneath her slightly closed eyelids.

Della blushed slightly at the guilt flickering through her conscience... Did she really have the right to have such strong desires for a member of her own sex? She squirmed her own buttocks nervously, feeling the edge of the cool, tiled wall behind her. Barbara brushed against her once more, and she jumped at the unexpected contact and the more unexpected shock it had brought. Her breath quickened as Barbara began to move rhythmically from side to side, letting her full, globular tits brush again and again into Della's... feeling a glorious thrill each time the pointy buds made contact with one another.

The steady splash of the water behind her forcibly reminded Della that the bath must be almost overflowing. She stepped backwards and reached out her hand for the

taps… reluctant to tear her eyes away from Barbara's marvellous breasts. Sitting on the edge of the tub, she ran her fingers through the flowing water, testing the temperature. It seemed just right: not too hot, not too cold.

Della lifted one leg up and lowered her foot over the side of the enamelled tub, deliberately remaining in this open position for several moments so that Barbara could feast her eyes upon the soft, pink, moistened flesh of her cunt. The thin, curved slit had peeled apart and the inner lips were succulently revealed to Barbara's steady gaze. A light trickle of hot moisture began to run down the inner thighs of Barbara's long, tapered legs as the warmth of the younger girl's passion fused with her own lustful feelings. But, she made no attempt to conceal her premature emission, though it was obvious from Della's widening eyes that she had noticed the clear, warm fluid escaping from the inner confines of her womb.

The steam-filled room had grown very hot now and beads of perspiration stood out on Barbara's completely naked body. They ran slowly down from her neck to drop in tiny rivulets between the deep valleys of her breasts. And, further down, Della could see trickles of condensed air falling over Barbara's stomach and becoming lost in the soft down of her pubic mound, as she drew nearer to the tub. The girl felt the naked warmth of Barbara's ripe female body close to her, and then quivered slightly as she felt her fingers reach down over the inner swell of her breasts.

Her eyes filled with wonderment and awe, Della looked down at herself and watched as Barbara's fingers started to manipulate gently at her bosom. They cupped, and then raised the melon-shaped mounds, and Della felt their weight suddenly disappear as Barbara held them firmly in both her hands.

Her hands feel so good… so soft! Della thought to herself, delighting the renewed sensations of warmth that filled her yearning body. She stretched her legs beneath the water, luxuriously pulling her muscles to their fullest length, then with a deep moan, let them fall wide apart, feeling the warmth of the bath water rush into the narrow slit between her cunt lips. Pushing slightly but meaningfully, Della urged Barbara to step into the tub. And, with the more experienced lesbian still feeling her breasts and getting into the water with her, the girl let her body go limp, sinking up to her shoulders in the all-embracing heat of the bath.

Still embracing the fleshy mounds of pulsating titties, Barbara positioned herself so that she was kneeling in the water between Della's wide-spread legs, forcing the girl to draw her knees up and allow Barbara's own legs to press against her crotch. Della gasped aloud as tiny wisps of forbidden pleasure began to ripple deep down in her belly, and her pointed tongue began to flicker over the outside ridges of her parted lips as the exquisite sensations took complete power over her consciousness.

Taking up a large sponge from the glass shelf above her, Barbara methodically began to soap Della's right breast, rubbing her fingers over the left breast and pulling gently at the rubbery nipple beneath the underwater slipperiness. She worked up a generous lather on the sponge and then used it to coat the rest of the girl's skin with foamy suds until the water grew cloudy and frothy with bubbles. Della leaned slowly forward in a dreamlike haze and rested her cheek against Barbara's thigh. The firm sleek muscle, already wet with splashes from the water, felt intimate and inviting.

The older girl was now soaping Della's left breast. She dipped into the water with her sponge and gave the lithe curvature a long, lingering massage with the soft appliance, until the nipple rose again to a magnificently erect stature. She let the sponge slide slowly back into the warm water and worked the suds around the surface of Della's smooth flesh with her fingers, caressing and washing each individual area in tiny rotating movements.

After completely saturating the upper half of Della's lush body with suds, Barbara gently urged her to stand up in the tub so she could get at the even more exciting lower region. Della obediently climbed unsteadily to her feet and stood with her legs well apart, reaching out to the wall to keep her balance.

The heavy steam that rose steadily from the bath water tickled her nostrils and made her head feel limp and heavy with a slight dizziness. Della closed her eyes and nibbled unconsciously on her lower lip as Barbara's hands moved to her legs, her fingers resting just above Della's knees, on the first fleshy swell of her seductively open thighs. She washed the outside of Della's legs first, caressing her hands slowly up the tanned, splayed limbs, allowing them to rest momentarily on her lush, curvaceous hips.

When the girl's thighs began to shudder involuntarily under this tormenting caress, Barbara transferred her fingers to the softer, more voluptuous inside of Della's legs and, with her thumbs stretching as far to the rear as possible, began to fondle and arouse the quivering, faintly moaning girl in earnest.

Barbara's probing fingers worked themselves slowly inside the pink edges of Della's contracting cunt, slowly widening the lips. She slipped her index finger in and out smoothly between the lubricated opening, as Della stood there, hypnotized into immobility as the sensuous movements of the older girl's manipulations drove her upwards to a higher peak of yearning excitement. Della's facial muscles suddenly tightened in welcome painful pleasure, as Barbara joined two fingers with the first and pushed all three into the hungry pink folds. They disappeared with a soft, sucking noise as a soft moan of pleasure purred from the young girl's lips.

Della's eyes and teeth were clenched tightly together as she writhed beneath the driving fingers fucking into her open pussy in uncontrolled passionate thrusts. Barbara, her eyes wide with excitement and lust, repeated this tormenting act of love until Della cried out for her to stop, fearing that she would faint from the exertion of the intense pounding. Then, relenting, she brought her thumbs to Della's quivering pussy and gently pulled the wet, dripping lips widely open. From her vantage point, staring right up into the young girl's crotch, Barbara was able to see directly into Della's brazenly exposed vagina. Della leaned her weight against the tiled wall, whimpering softly as Barbara snaked her pointed tongue out and made contact with the soft, down-covered moistness of her vaginal lips. She licked wetly up and down the crevice around it, the tip of her tongue burrowing slightly into the outer fleshy anal ring. Barbara kept the pouting red slit wide apart with her thumbs, as she slowly worked her mouth back to the inviting spot around the standing girl's clitoris.

Della's eyes were tightly shut, though she could hardly avoid being completely aware of everything that the wily Barbara was doing to her trembling body.

"Oh... Oh... Ooooooh!" The cry was wrenched from Della's lips as she felt the most tender, the sharpest, the most delectable sensation that had ever possessed her, drive like an electric shock through her genitals.

"OH! BARBARA... I CAN'T STAND IT!" Her thighs were jerking helplessly, wedged open by Barbara's upraised face. Della thrust her hands down on the girl's head and began to beat her palms in helpless frenzy on her tormentor's hair, vainly trying to dislodge Barbara's teasing, rapidly, licking tongue from the hot pulsating opening between her legs.

Della tried to squirm away, but Barbara grimly continued to jab her pointed firm tongue at the hard, erected clitoris, which was now provoking Della into an uncontrollable feeling of ecstasy. She released her nibbling teeth from the lips of the girl's cunt, letting the fleshy folds fall back around her mouth, and passed her hands around Della's hips until they descended upon the rigid firmness of her tightly clenched buttocks.

A few professional caresses at the warm, slippery wet cheeks and Della's muscles slowly began to loosen, making the globes relax and flexible. As if in a hypnotic trance, Barbara coaxed her fingers into the crease of her buttocks and started to fondle her forefinger into the sensitive centre of the girl's anus.

From where she squatted, Barbara could clearly see the tiny, tight ass hole nestled in the crevice, throbbing as it anticipated her next move. Her fingers began to probe at the puckered little brown inlet like teasing needles. The hole was so wet from its immersion in the water that soon Barbara was able to penetrate it, her slim finger sinking easily into the wall of the tight inner muscles, until her middle finger was burrowed deep within the cringing girl, and could go no farther.

Della strained back at the intruding finger as the rubbery flesh closed over it in final acceptance. A flicker of surprised pleasure passed over her straining face as the probing finger reached its apex far up inside her straining rectum.

This bold and rude penetration seemed to relieve Della's torment to some extent. The girl stopped her desperate pounding at Barbara's head as she gave the inflamed clitoris one last, loving tickle with her tongue.

Della was exhausted from standing in the awkward stance, and wanted desperately to get out of the bath and adopt a more comfortable position. In reality, her main concern was to place herself so that Barbara's body could press against hers; she wanted so much to feel the feminine closeness of the girl's breasts, loins and thighs on her own.

She gently disengaged Barbara's mouth from her cunt, and slipped her hand behind her back, drawing Barbara up to a standing position. For a moment that really seemed like an eternity, Barbara looked deeply, lovingly into Della's smouldering eyes, and then pressed her wet, warm body against hers in a lingering love hug. When she released her hold the parting wet flesh made a loud sucking noise.

Leading Della, she stepped from the tub, then the two girls quickly rubbed each other down with a pair of fleecy bath towels. When they were both thoroughly dried off, they sprayed each other with a spicy scented perfume, rubbing the cool liquid into the soft fleshy areas of their inner thighs, under their armpits, and on the brown still-erect buds of their breasts.

Moments later, the girls now eagerly willing to continue their lovemaking in a more comfortable position, scurried back to

the bedroom and fell upon the soft mattress, looking into each other's eyes expectantly. Della could see nothing but Barbara. Her eyes shone with obsessive, single-minded purpose as she undraped her own towel and stepped quickly into Barbara's waiting arms.

Her arms enfolded Della's softly firm flesh, and the younger girl responded quickly to her embrace. Bodies pressing, hugging each other tightly, their lips met in a long, shameless kiss... their tongues stealing in and out, mixing with each other's saliva. Della clamped her lips greedily over Barbara's, her mind drifting helplessly in a dreamlike fantasy, she felt as if her body was suspended in limbo... somewhere between heaven and earth. Her luscious body was now pressed beneath Barbara's, her thighs had opened and she could feel Barbara's fingers plucking insistently at the moist slit of her pulsating cunt, working patiently into the open, waiting hole.

Della began to run her trembling hands over the white globular mounds of Barbara's buttocks, smoothly stroking at them with long, loving caresses. She moved her other hand gradually between the small valley of Barbara's tits and softly milked at the spongy muscle closest to her grasp, unconsciously arousing the older girl to new and more pronounced heights of lustfulness.

Barbara's breasts responded immediately to the soft petting and the brown pointed buds of her nipples sprang to life, peaking and ebbing with each gasp of air that rushed from her lungs. Her tongue pierced the hot moistness of the small puckered lips beneath her with rapid in and out thrusts, exploring every nook and crevice and running it over the hard enamel surface of Della's sharp tiny teeth. She slowly inserted a finger into the soft, tight opening of Della's cunt that nestled between her widespread limbs, and began moving it in and out of her as if it were a miniature penis.

Unconsciously, Della moved her fingers down Barbara's tummy until they closed around the ripe protuberance of the gaping cunt that poised expectantly over her quivering body. Her knuckles pressed urgently against the hairy mound as she sought the opening of her lover's hole, first fondling the thick lips, then easily sliding her middle finger deep into the well-lubricated passage. Barbara's insides were warm and deliciously soft, her cum fluids flowed around Della's long finger like hot melting butter.

Gasping, their tongues continued to lick furiously in each other's mouths, following the rhythm of their stiff, ramming fingers, now thrusting in and out of each other's sexes. There could be no gentle caressing, for both girls were far too aroused and sexually excited to think of prolonging the love play. Together, they separated and plunged into each other as wildly as they knew how, and neither girl tried to hold back the mutual lust and hot passions that burst from their straining bodies.

Barbara thrust her forefinger as far as it could go... deeper and harder into the womb of the writhing girl beneath her. Then, as the walls of her vagina slowly stretched to the pushing pressure, she inserted her middle finger in with it, continuing to fuck wildly down into the marshmallow softness in lustful abandon. Della lolled limply beneath her, allowing herself to be used and plundered, sucking back in grateful homage to the lesbian that was working over her. Sinking into helpless delirium, she felt Barbara's fingers penetrating the depth of her cunt, bringing her to a pitch of nervous tension. Tension that demanded release with every thrust, from every particle of her body!

Barbara began to urge her loins up and down in an instinctive, mindless tempo of lust, her excitation focused entirely on what Della was doing to her cunt and ignoring the pitiless squeezing of Della's other hand around her breast and nipple.

Della's beautiful face was contorted and twisted into an expression of pain-filled elation. A low muffled moan came from her lips, distorted in sound from the loud sucking noises of the hard long fingers now pounding into her gaping cunt. Barbara swished her dark tresses from side to side as she rammed her fingers in and out of the young girl, as her firm tits danced and shook below her heaving chest.

Della was almost out of her mind, now. Her whole torso quivered under the blows of the impaling fingers, but she clenched her inner muscles against them tightly, fearing that they might escape and end her ecstasy before she had reached her climax. Then, she started to cum almost before she realized that her orgasm was welling up inside her. The completely unnatural occurrence of being fondled and kissed by a member of her own sex had triggered the spasm in Della much more quickly than normal...

"Oooohhh, ooohhh," Della moaned, all the inhibitions drained from her mind, "Give it to me! Quickly... or I'll die!" Barbara obediently increased the maddening probing until Della felt the fiery hot ball deep in her belly start to release its agonies, and she began blurting out incoherently all the vile words she knew, pleading with the older girl, as the lust in her desire-wracked body deepened her wild frenzy.

"Oh God," she moaned. "Fuck me, fuck me

faster... Go on, do it!" Biting into Barbara's lower lip, and shaking her head from side to side, forcing the older girl to move with her, Della trembled out her climax... the plentiful ooze of her hot cum spilling over Barbara's fast-working fingers.

Groaning aloud, the newcomer to lesbian love shuddered finally to exhaustion, unable to move, scarcely able to open her eyes, Della with sudden stabbing of shame and regret jolting through her whispered, "I'm sorry, Barbara, truly I'm sorry! It'll be better next time, I promise it will. I didn't... I couldn't help myself..."

Her voice trailed off helplessly. What could she say to the girl after all? What could she really say to her?

Just like all the other lovers Barbara had gone to bed with, she too had failed her! Even if she made it up to her later... even now, when she had regained her breath... she would still have shown Barbara that all she really cared about was her own satisfaction.

And perhaps that was all there was to sex. Ultimately, you only wanted to be sure of your own release... your own pleasure. If you could achieve this and at the same time bring your partner some degree of bliss... fine! But that was only a by-product of sexual union, a something extra that rarely came true. Lying there and thinking about it, Della silently thanked Danny for the brief joy he had brought into her life, and wondered sadly if she would ever meet anyone like him again.

Looking briefly into Barbara's frustrated eyes, Della could see that the girl felt she had been betrayed yet again.

It's not really my fault, Della wanted desperately to tell her. Honestly, I couldn't help myself. I got so excited thinking about my love for Danny, that I let myself get lost in your love through the sheer misery of being alone.

Della let her head fall back onto the pillow in weary resignation, the words of her thoughts left unsaid. A moment or two later she felt Barbara ease her body out of contact with hers and lay silently by her side on the bed.

Barbara made a few more half-hearted attempts to arouse Della to her former hot passion, but with little success. Della found it almost impossible to respond to the other girl's pleading attempts now that she had been sobered with the thoughts of her own guilt. Self-recriminations persisted in tormenting her, echoing through her brain until Barbara finally started to get up and dress herself.

Della was inwardly relieved that the girl made no further attempts to force herself upon her, and listened to the sounds the girl made as she got into her clothes. Barbara would be friendly enough to her later when her emotions had cooled off, for she was far too sophisticated and cynical to take such a disappointment seriously for more than a few minutes… or was she?

But that wasn't the point. It wasn't the point at all. Instead of getting through to the girl as she wanted to, Della had merely widened the gulf… not only between her and Barbara, but between Barbara and anyone else who might try to get close to her.

Della lay motionless as Barbara finished dressing, unable and not wanting to move. Her legs were still spread wide, as Barbara had left them, and her loins wet and raw from her long merciless fingers. Oh God, she had failed Barbara when she had most needed the love and understanding that she had promised to give to her!

She moved, pulling her limbs together experimentally to see if she could still control them. The pain and ache of her collapsed muscles shivered through her body, causing her legs to tremble spasmodically as she clasped them tightly closed, now, once more feeling deep embarrassment of her own nudity.

But Barbara barely glanced at her as she slipped the loose sweater over her head and quickly left the room. When the door clicked softly shut behind Barbara, leaving Della now truly alone to her own thoughts, she let out a deep tormented moan, clenching her fists in frustration until the knuckles stood out white and tense.

She could see her pitiful reflection in the dressing mirror across the room, showing the bruises and welts that now marked her smoothly tanned skin. Still sobbing softly, she reached up and hesitantly touched her breasts, feeling the dull throb from the marks surrounding her tender nipples, aching all the way through her chest as if to punish her for her rude failure with Barbara.

Della lay propped against the pillow, and stared back at her forlorn body in the mirror, suddenly understanding with all of her being the loneliness of incomplete love.

"Oh God, I'm sorry Barbara," she whispered to herself, "I'm so sorry... and I pity you. Dear God, don't ever let me end up like her!"

Then she buried her face in the deep, soft pillow and tried to loose herself in the blessed peacefulness of sleep.

Chapter 4

Steve Albright awakened refreshed and rested after his long night of work in the studio, selecting and rejecting the latest stills for the new pin-up magazine, due out on the first of the month for publication. If he had a choice, he would have gone to that Hollywood party with Ginny last night, but he reneged at the last moment, knowing that the deadline would not be met if he did. Now that his work was completed and he could safely assume a large profit for his toils, he considered the new day with a feeling of optimistic adventure.

He quickly showered and dressed, then made his way down to the sunny kitchen overlooking the ocean, hoping that Ginny would be up and preparing breakfast.

The kitchen was empty and the rest of the house was still quiet. Apparently Ginny had another rough night of it, he chuckled to himself as he turned on the electric range and plugged in the coffee pot. It was a well-known fact that his sister had one of the busiest cunts in town and would take on anyone – man or woman – if she felt inclined to do so. That was the beauty of sex, he thought, the more you used it, the more awakened your senses became, until like Ginny, you prowled around other unsuspecting civilized people just waiting for a new conquest, always horny and hot and never satisfied with the new encounter after it had been used.

He had his usual hearty breakfast of fresh fruit, two boiled eggs, Danish pastry and coffee, which he consumed in rapid gulps.

Now he was ready for his first cigarette of the day, smoked in a holder with a filter in it to soften the harsh bite of the tobacco. He poured himself a second cup of coffee and sat down at the table again to study the contents of the manila folder that Ginny had left out for him the night before. The cover of the folder was labelled in bright red ink, "New Inventory."

Steve opened the folder and smiled approvingly down on a glossy photo of Della Wilkins, one that Barbara had taken from her portfolio when she was out of her room. He reread the name attached to the picture, and recalled his conversation over the phone with Barbara a few days back.

Barbara really was a very good agent, he thought, tracing the outline of Della's body with the tip of his finger. He and Ginny had reason to be extremely grateful to the girl, for without her a large proportion of their amatory adventures could never have happened: she seemed to have a special talent for picking out the most exciting, the ripest girls that were available...

He closed the folder and took a deep drag on his cigarette, letting the smoke completely fill his lungs, then slowly exhaling it into the air forming his lips around it in a tight oval ring. Steve's expert eyes correctly identified Della as a relatively innocent young ex- suburbanite who wanted to make it big in the city. He had met the type on many previous occasions and they were invariably the most exciting, the most adaptive of lovers. But lately the supply of such girls appeared to be dwindling. Perhaps Hollywood was losing its appeal for them; the myth that the movie capital was a Mecca of golden opportunities was possibly in the process of being shattered.

How ingenious of Barbara to find one of this fast-dying species! She was worth every penny of the large fee she charged him for such rare and captivating girls. Steve smiled as he thought of what a delicious encounter it would be to have a fresh new body under him again... there was no doubt in his mind that he would have her, and soon.

The kitchen door suddenly opened, breaking his reverie, and a magnificently proportioned girl entered the room. She looked as if she had just stepped out of the shower and was clothed only in a scant transparent negligee and panties.

Her glittering blonde hair was swept up on top of her head, its freshly shampooed tresses reflecting light as if she possessed some inner form of illumination. Her lightly tanned body peaked and curved beneath the sheer material as if it were going to burst forth with every step she took. The white pair of nylon panties that were stretched as tightly as possible over her loins accentuated the tan-ness of her rippling, full-fleshed thighs, as she ambled towards her brother with the agility of a stalking panther. Ginny carried herself with an air of complete self-assurance, her head high and her lips perpetually pursed in a promise of moist-mouthed sensuality.

Her movements embodied sexuality in every fibre of her body, and her smouldering eyes clearly showed their inner desires... her sole purpose in life was to seek the gratification of the senses. Ginny's body was a wonder in itself, considering the fact that she was thirty years old. Her breasts, though large and generous, were as firm as a young girl's of twenty, they proudly jutted out from her slim limbs in two huge mountains of flesh, promising fulfilment of her womanly charms to anyone that ventured to try their luck.

Steve was amazed that the fast pace of her party life left no trace of wear on her face and body and he smiled at her appreciatively, acknowledging to her that she was at the peak of her animal magnetism, even to him, her own brother. When she walked into a room, she dominated it utterly, always drawing looks of envy from the other women that came close to hatred, and completely hypnotizing the males with her exquisite beauty and charm. Her lovers, of both sexes, had been so numerous that she would have lost count of their number had it not been for the fact that she kept a carefully-detailed record of their particular methods of love-making...

This dossier, to which her brother Steve contributed as well, took the form of a neatly indexed, cross-referenced file of papers; with a separate sheet for each person either Ginny or Steve had slept with. Details of their physical appearance, their age, sex, colouring and... most important of all... their individual preferences and idiosyncrasies in regard to sex. This was merely one of their hobbies, though. Neither Ginny nor Steve had any intention of using their dossier for any other purpose except for a permanent reminder of their most pleasant hours.

How lucky it was for them that their career in the photography business afforded them every opportunity of practicing their desires! Their parents had both been killed in an automobile accident when Steve and Ginny were in their late teens, leaving them with a generous amount of money and a successful family portrait studio. A few years after that, Steve had gradually made the transition in clientele, dealing exclusively with pin-up and "artistic" pictures. This change was a huge success because their models were carefully picked for each special effect, and their poses were in the most lewd positions imaginable.

They sold their material (sets of photos, three regular monthly magazines) entirely through the mails. Slowly, with the minimum of advertising, they had built up a faithful clientele both in United States and Europe.

In addition to the separate stills, Steve and Ginny also published a regular series of undeniably pornographic magazines, and it was from these latter activities that they both derived their greatest pleasure and satisfaction. The high salaries paid to the publishers of their materials ensured that they were safe from official interference. Their only major problem was in keeping up the supply of fresh and unknown models, for Steve knew it was of utmost importance that his models appear innocent and youthful to the eyes of his clientele, otherwise they would go to other magazines that offered them what they wanted.

He depended heavily on agents such as Barbara, an ex-model herself, to supply him with the girls who were the exact image of what Steve and Ginny needed: unprofessional and inexperienced young girls who longed to break into fashion or photographic modelling.

Steve had been highly successful in seducing the majority of this youthful crop of females... apart from his powerful position in relationship to their ambitions, he was strikingly handsome in a healthy, boyish way. His tall, slender frame was tanned a deep bronze from the generous southern California sun, and he had an easy wit and natural charm about him that affected almost every woman he met with an instantaneous and powerful magnetic attraction. His sandy-coloured hair was styled in a brush cut neatly framing the even features of his face in perfect symmetry.

Now, his steel grey eyes gloated openly over the stalking figure of his sister as she went straight to the counter and poured herself a steaming hot cup of black coffee.

"Good Morning, Love," he greeted cheerily, now focusing his complete attention on the beautiful body standing so near to him that the fragrant scent of her body odours caused him to sit erect with excitement.

"What's so good about it brother dear?" she answered dryly, carefully sipping at the hot liquid, not quite alert yet after the previous evening of excess drinking and sex.

Steve ignored his sister's outwardly distant manner, because he knew that Ginny secretly enjoyed appearing in her underwear for him; about the house she rarely bothered to put a dress on and the constant sight of her underdressed body in its high-charged and sexy underwear provided Steve with a great deal of inspiration for his photographs.

"Well, pussy cat," he chided, "it might

be a lot more pleasant, if you would refrain from some of your nocturnal wanderings. By the way, who wound up your partner last night?"

Ginny came over to the table and stood beside Steve, leaning her curvaceous thighs against his arm, and then squeezed her lush body into the chair beside her brother.

"I'm a big girl, now... remember?" she said softly, not in the mood to start an argument."

"Ok, Ginny... Forget it. I just wanted to find out how the party went last night."

"Oh, the same as usual... no new modelling material, if that's what you mean."

"What do you think of this one?" Steve opened the manila folder, and handed the glossy print to his sister.

"Very, very nice," Ginny purred, staring at Della's picture with open admiration.

"Barbara's sending her over here Monday. I think she'll fit in just right for that special edition that we're preparing for this winter. You know, the one we were going to set up as a snappier edition of '*Fashion Shots*'."

Steve was referring to a project that Ginny and he had planned for several months. It was to be a definitely pornographic translation of their monthly glamour magazine '*Fashion Shots*' in which girls were usually posed trying on various items of sexy underwear and lingerie.

For the newer version, a "sales lady" was to be included in the photos, assisting the girl to get into the bras and panties. Ginny was going to take this part, but so far they had been unsuccessful in finding a suitable girl to play the role of the buyer.

They wanted someone who could appear to be a regular girl, outwardly shocked at the indecent fondlings of the extremely forward "sales lady." It had been difficult to find a girl with just the right expression… and Steve wanted this particular magazine to be his best: he wasn't prepared to shoot it unless the model came right up to his preconceived ideas.

"She looks wonderful!" Ginny commented, "I only hope she can play the role." When she spoke, she teasingly let her long tapered fingers caress the inside of his thigh, knowing that this fondling could drive her over-sexed brother up the walls if she persisted long enough without giving in to him.

Steve put his hand around her and rested his palm affectionately on the smooth flesh of her buttocks… feeling the warm, semi-nude flesh of his sister's bottom under his fingers. At the contact, his penis gave an involuntary twitch inside his tight-fitting slacks, stirring uneasily and uncurling slightly as the softness of Ginny firm-fleshed bottom moved against the light pressure of his hand.

Ginny nuzzled her face against Steve's,

her lips brushing his cheek.

"Of course, even if she's just what we want, we'll have to bring her along very carefully before we suggest that she poses in that way," Steve warned her. "I think we rushed that last girl too much, remember? I told you she was getting nervous about what we were asking her to do! We should have played her more carefully, more slowly..."

"Oh, don't be ridiculous!" Ginny interrupted. "I've told you hundreds of times that most girls love posing for sexy pictures. It inspires them to show off their womanhood. And once they've done a few ordinary ones it doesn't take very much to persuade them to go a little further." She teased him again, letting her fingers stray right over the growing thickness of his cock, and gently squeezing it until it burst forward against the material of his pants, ripe and hard.

"I know that dear," Steve told her patiently. "But when it comes to the extra special photos you've simply got to be subtle about it. It doesn't do a bit of good plunging in at the deep end, everything should be relaxed... natural. Besides, I feel we've been too careless with the last couple of girls that posed for us. Remember how Gloria took off like a startled fawn when you started to fondle her?" Steve traced his fingers along Ginny's shoulder, watching as his nails raised momentary red marks on his sister's flawless skin. They faded rapidly and returned her flesh to its normal white and tanned beauty. He stared, fascinated, as the welts appeared then vanished under the pressure of his manicured fingernails.

"You really do have the most exquisite shoulders," Steve whispered, caressing Ginny's youthful skin, and trying at the same time to focus his attention back to the matter at hand. But it was very difficult to concentrate now that Ginny's fingers were brushing so insistently over his covered loins. The bitch knew exactly how to touch him there! She was deliberately arousing him to cut short their argument!

"All I'm saying is that we should be extra careful with this new girl," Steve finished weakly. Ginny had lifted her legs over the far side of the chair so that she was sitting in his lap. The voluptuous weight and heat of her thighs burned through the thin material of his slacks and Steve could feel his sister's fire spread from between her legs and melt down on his hardness, sparking it with renewed life.

"Let's play it safe with Della, shall we? Let's be slow and easy with her, OK? That's all I'm asking. I've waited a long time to find a girl to do this magazine with us, why spoil things by scaring her off. Especially since she looks so perfect for the role."

Ginny wound her arms lovingly about Steve's neck. "You're the boss, big brother!" she whispered sexily. And Steve, feeling the pressure of his sister's breasts against his chest, feeling the sweet fragrance of her breath and her skin so intimately close to him, gave up the struggle.

Steve slid his trembling hands around her body until they held his sister possessively around her bare midriff. She leaned more closely to him, taunting him with her almost naked femininity.

"Here?" he whispered, a catch of desire in his voice.

Ginny stood up slowly in front of the ocean bay window, scanning the horizon with smoky lust-filled eyes. Why not, she thought, they should take more advantage of the expensive privacy they both worked so hard to maintain. She reached down without a word, removed her panties and threw them on the back of the kitchen chair. Then, she lifted her thin negligee high above her head and straddled him, the whiteness of her rounded buttocks poised directly over the hardness of his long thick cock.

"Here!" she breathed into his mouth. "Here, my darling..."

Steve, still sitting in the chair, moved his hands around his sister's back, half-supporting her, raising her so that her body lifted slightly above his.

"Help me get it out," he pleaded, almost breathless from the delicious nearness of her.

He slithered the pointed tip of his tongue around the sensitive outline of her full mouth, as she eagerly unzipped his pants and pulled out his erect cock, momentarily holding it in her hands like it was a valuable art treasure. Her large pulsating breasts pushed forward as she raised her body even higher, breaking contact with his mouth and almost smothering him as he leaned her tits against his face to gain support in her awkward position.

Still holding her brother's pulsating cock firmly in her hands, she leaned back and positioned her buttocks on the edge of the table, pulling him to a half-standing position as she moved. Steve's pants fell loosely to the floor and his fingers ran down both sides of her curvaceous hips, caressing them with loving adoration.

Ginny, with a small gurgling noise, continued to run her cool, slender fingers up and down the underside of his prick, teasing it until the long thickened rod jumped and pulsed in front of her. She knew every inch of her brother's body, but each time she touched Steve's cock she felt the same terrific thrill – it was as if she could never quite believe that she was being so daring... so outrageous as to enjoy her brother in this incestuous and

taboo fashion...

Their half-nude bodies were clearly exposed in front of the large bay window, but neither of them cared... the only thing in their minds at that moment was to somehow quench the hot fire that now burned deeply in both of them. As she played with him, Steve dug his fingers into the soft flesh of her creamy white titties. He fondled her nipple until it grew large and stiff beneath his touch, the jellied flesh of her well-filled breasts exciting him beyond belief.

Ginny liked nothing better than to have her breast manhandled as roughly as possible, he knew that: the fiercer, the more violent the caress, the greater her pleasure. He squeezed his fingers around the firm, white globe, digging them ruthlessly into her, pulling and stretching them like a large piece of baker's dough.

His manipulations thoroughly delighted his sister, and she flicked her tongue deep into his mouth and started to French kiss him slowly, allowing the moist saliva to dribble from her mouth and onto him. She kissed him urgently, rubbing her mouth sideways on his, at the same time gripping his cock with fierce desperation... squeezing it so tightly that Steve feared his blood would cease flowing through it. With her free hand, she strayed her sharp fingernails softly over the sensitive tip of his cock, provoking her brother into a deeper frenzy of passion through the tortuous manipulations.

Steve brought his right hand down to the soft waiting pubic mound nestled seductively between her lithe thighs. He parted the soft fleece gently and worked his finger slowly into the warm moist crevice, gently massaging her there, and softly squeezing his fingers open and shut around the spongy softness of her slightly quivering vaginal lips.

Ginny began to softly moan and twist her body from his delicious massaging, and continued to stroke her fingers rapidly over the sensitive tip of his cock, coaxing a single premature tear of pre-cum from it. Lubricated by this droplet, Ginny's finger moved down further to the tight elastic pucker of his anal ring, fidgeting tenderly around the opening and giving Steve a delirious feeling of sheer, obscene delight. She moved her other hand up to the nape of his neck, caressing the sensitive bone there, which she knew only too well brought Steve to an almost unbearable pitch of nervous excitement.

These dual manipulations ignited Steve to a higher feverish pitch of excitement and lust, and his hands began to move furiously, massaging and probing at her trembling cunt, until she too was a complete bundle of raw nerve and unreleased tension. Ginny uttered a low gasp, and spreading her long tanned legs wide apart, proceeded to prop her feet on the window ledge behind him. Her loins were now completely open and exposed to his staring gaze, with the moist pink opening secreting tiny drops of warm wet fluid, so ready was she for his immersion into her.

Steve moved his hands upwards and placed them back on her thighs, then rubbed them firmly upwards, letting his fingers mould and shape the yielding texture of his sister's buttocks. The cheeks tilted whichever way he chose, moving in docile obedience to the pressure of his hands. He fitted his thumbs into the deep crevice which curved beneath each cheek while he kept his remaining fingers splayed over the glossy surface of Ginny's ass and pressured his thumbs upwards...

Generously, the placid globes opened under his fondling, revealing Ginny's neat brown anus just below the pink slit of her moist and ready cunt. Still holding the cheeks so that the cleavage between them was a clearly revealed, he gently pushed his sister down on her back across the kitchen table and began to kiss into the warm, slightly moist opening between her wide-stretched thighs.

His tongue licked forward, the tip teasing wetly against the tiny bud of her clitoris, while small mewls and gasps of pleasure escaped from her slightly parted lips.

"Mmmmm… that's it darling," she coaxed him on. "Don't stop sucking, dear… Oooooh… Lick it! Lick it!"

She moaned again through the sensations of desire building up deep within her belly, as his tongue circled around maddeningly inside her, with the tip flicking against the wet sensitive walls of her pussy in wild frenzied motions.

The odour of her flowing fluids filled his nostrils with a sharp pungent aroma, and they flared out in two small circles above his licking tongue and sucking mouth. With the tip of his tongue, Steve licked tentatively lower into Ginny's anus. The tiny, tight orifice seemed to quiver and clench tight against the wet intruder… but Steve persisted, holding the girl's anus well open, and eventually succeeded in worming an inch or so of his tongue into her back passage.

While he explored orally the exciting, erotic zone of his sister's anal ring, his thumbs were at work on the trembling lips of her cunt, playing with and fondling the two wet folds of flesh, then plunging them down deep into her vaginal hole, which now was a steaming gate of fire.

His back was aching slightly from bending over his sister and so, without altering the close intimacy of their connection, and without losing contact for one precious moment, Steve

managed to wriggle his body down so that he supported himself by his elbows, using them to force Ginny's legs even further apart.

By now, his sister quivered and her entire body shook in a jellied mass of uncontrollable spasms. Her head hung back down over the table's edge, with her long blonde tresses swishing from side to side, gently brushing against the seat of the upholstered kitchen chair and knocking her soft, silk panties unnoticed to the floor.

The hot smooth flesh of the girl's loins was so delightfully soft and tender that her brother lost momentary control over himself and a small dribble of cum spilled prematurely onto the cool kitchen floor. But he closed his eyes tightly until the urge had passed, finally managing to fight back the spasm that had so nearly brought about an ejaculation. Then he concentrated his full attention on Ginny's hot moist opening, thinking how strange it was that his sister, after countless intimacies, still was able to arouse him more rapidly and more violently than any other girl he had ever known.

His tongue worked around and around once more in the warm opening just behind her swollen, quivering labia, until he felt another sudden small rush of liquid escape from the orifice and run teasingly into his mouth. This eruption meant nothing. He knew this from prior experience. His sister frequently came, bit by bit, during their preliminary fondling, and she had scarcely so much as stiffened and clenched her buttocks. When her real orgasm came, it would be as much as he could do to hold her down.

Steve continued to lick and suck at her vagina, almost deriving as much pleasure from the lewd act as Ginny herself was obviously getting. She had started to revolve her buttocks in a steady, grinding rhythm... trapping his nose tightly between the cheeks and rubbing them lewdly and sensuously together.

When he had cunt-sucked her for several timeless minutes, he returned his tongue to his sister's anus and briefly licked teasingly up the warm, soft divide... as if to bid a temporary farewell... he could wait not a minute longer to sink his pulsating cock into the depths of her hot, hungry cunt.

He raised himself from his squatting position, and stood up straight, his cock sticking rudely into the air like a flagrant missile ready to be shot from its launching pad. Gracefully, Ginny positioned herself under him, still bracing her feet against the hard surface of the window ledge.

Steve threw himself over her in a silent gasp, levering up on his hands into a push-up position above the slowly undulating body of his sister. Her face was now contorted in indescribable rapture and her lips were pursed in a wet rounded oval shape, with tiny, wispy groans of pleasure escaping from around the soft pinkness of the inside of her mouth.

No matter how frequently she was fucked by her brother, Ginny could never avoid the brief but electrifying moment when she visualized herself defying the Gods and the entire universe itself. The most primitive societies in the world would condemn this behaviour, for it was viewed with horror and fear by every civilization on earth. Now, here on the kitchen table, she and her brother Steve were defying them all! It was a terrifying, yet a uniquely and profoundly exciting concept. Each time they coupled, they were challenging the world! Ginny's body thrilled to the idea, deriving an intensely powerful sense of importance from their lewd and wicked perversion.

She lifted her head, the cords on her neck standing out and turning white from the strain, and looked deeply into her brother's fiery eyes.

"Oooooh, fuck it, fuck it hard, hard!" she commanded, her voice in the high pitch of a shrill scream.

Steve grunted over her and began to work his cock into the hot interior of her clasping cunt. He loved to hear her begging him like that, so abandoned and yearning with a hot, helpless passion for every inch of his rod. His tortured prick slid easily into the slippery, yielding cavern of Ginny's cunt, and she in turn, eagerly absorbed it, loving the feeling of the muscular rod slipping tightly up into her throbbing pussy.

A surge of immense gratification pulsed through Steve's body as he slowly penetrated his sister's opening. They fitted each other so perfectly; in every possible way they were a wonderful match. Ginny swallowed his long rod deep into the hot passage of her vaginal walls, the muscles clasping and releasing at it, stimulating his senses with indescribable sensations of joy. Her hands caressed the hair on his chest lovingly, stroking his nipples as her eyes looked up into his face, hot, flushed and excited with a wild, burning desire.

She twisted her lust-gyrating hips sharply against his pounding loins, wanting to feel the penetration in every inch of her demanding hole.

"Oooh... My God." Steve groaned, feeling the exquisite softness of his sister's inner pulsating muscles. He looked down between them, the sight of his hard shaft of flesh sunk deep into her like that increased his sensitivity a thousand-fold. He could feel the warm slippery juices inside her flowing around his rock-hard cock like melted butter, as she expertly contracted her muscles around it, stroking and pulling on it with her inner thighs locked around his waist in a tight death-like grip.

He flexed his muscular buttocks; his head still raised, he watched her as her head lolled limply from side to side, her eyes now two burning-hot coals of lust. Ginny could feel his throbbing reaction and began to bounce her crotch more furiously against him, her teeth tightly clenched together from the tremendous strain of the delicious, obscene coupling. She lifted her feet from the window ledge and locked them around his ankles, then reached up around his driving buttocks and cupped them greedily in her palms, pulling his loins down tighter into the hot opening of her rampaging cunt.

"Oooh Shit! It's soooo good... sooo good," she chanted, not caring that their lewd incestuous fucking was happening in the bright daylight in front of a huge glass window where anyone who chose to stroll by might see them.

Steve, his eyes dilated as if in a hypnotized trance, slid his hands under her buttocks, cupping them in his hands, and drove his cock rhythmically into the wetness of her cunt. His hands dug deeply into the two globular spheres as he kneaded at them and stretched them apart with each in and out thrust as he plunged wilder and wilder into her.

He worked his middle finger in between the crevice of her buttocks, searching with the tip of it for her tight throbbing anus. A small rivulet of warm moist liquid was running down the widely split crevice from where he could feel his hard rod of flesh sawing into her. It moistened the tight puckered little hole, lubricating it slightly and he probed experimentally for a moment with the tip of his finger. He pushed hard, feeling it give a little, and then suddenly the tight elastic nether ring gave way completely and his finger slid in with a pop up to the first knuckle joint. She lurched forward, almost crawling on her back across the slick table to escape the first unexpected pain.

"Steeevvvee!" she screamed, "Oooooh! Yessss, yesss! Hurt me, hurt me, hurt me!"

In spite of the pain, he felt her suddenly begin screwing her buttocks back on his finger until it was sunk to the palm of his hand. He jiggled it inside, rotating it around in the fleshy depths of her rectum. He could feel through the thin wall of flesh separating her two passages the underside of his cock sliding in and out of her and began skewering her between them, maintaining the same rhythm for both as she groaned on under him. His nail caught the flesh momentarily in her asshole, scraping her and she jerked, but then caught up the rhythm again, opening her legs wide out over the table to give greater access to the ravishing of her loins.

Steve could feel his cock growing and expanding inside her until it felt as though it were going to burst from the exquisite pleasure building in his testicles as they slapped heavily against her buttocks below. It wouldn't be long he hoped, he knew he could not hold it back much longer.

She had to cum, and soon, or else!

He began ramming it into her with long hard strokes in time with his finger skewering into her asshole to excite her more. Ginny suddenly brought the flat of her palm against his bucking rear, slapping down on it like a jockey, urging his horse down the last lap of the track.

"Faaaasster, Faster!" she shrieked up at him, her eyes rolling up underneath her fluttering eyelids as if she were in the throes of a wild uncontrollable epileptic fit.

Steve jerked his sweating loins harder and faster down into her hot clasping cunt. He could tell she was near completion as she gripped him tight between her thighs, opening and closing them around him in time to his long hard thrusts into her. She gurgled beneath him, the sound coming from deep within her throat as though she had no control over it. He knew she was near and he continued to thrust down on her with a merciless in and out fucking movement... with all the strength he could muster.

Ginny scratched at her brother's chest like an unleashed tiger, her long fingernails leaving a series of jagged red trails on his skin, as she fought to reach the zenith of her excitement. She jack-knifed her legs up tight, pressing her knees back hard into her heaving breasts and offering him the full opening of her upraised crotch. Her eyes rolled uncontrollably in her head, her face contorted and straining for the final explosion that was so near now...

"I'm cumming," she coughed suddenly, her mouth gaping wide open in an ecstatic abandonment. She pulled back her thighs tighter until the whole of her stretched pink vaginal slit was presented up to him to batter and use as he willed. Her ankles locked over his shoulders, her crotch squirming beneath him in a wild uninhibited dance of abandoned ecstasy. Her mouth hung open wide, unseeing eyes gazed blankly at the kitchen ceiling.

A silent scream suddenly formed on the edges of her lips, with her teeth clenched tightly together in pain-filled ecstasy. Tiny muffled grunts erupted from deep within her, punctuating the rhythm of her brother's wildly fucking loins. Her nostrils flared out rigidly as she screwed herself up on his thrusting cock and locked herself to him with all the strength of her thighs while her loins jerked spasmodically against his sides.

"Eeeeehhhhh!" her loud shriek pierced through the screened windows and floated out into the bright light of day.

After the initial explosions, she held her breath for an interminable moment and then expelled it as though she had been trapped under water, her lungs bursting from the prolonged pressure. Then, she lay still, except for the uncontrollable quivering of her pussy still locked tightly around his tortured prick. He pushed it deep inside her gaping hole, and then lay quiet over her, allowing her to rest for a moment.

Ginny's lush body had slowly inched its way across the slick table, until now her entire head was hanging back over the edge of the kitchen table. Her mouth hung loosely open as she sucked in greedily at the air around her, trying once more to catch her breath. Steve slowly withdrew his hardened cock from her lust-stretched cunt, watching it easily slide out, making a soft sucking noise as the head slipped from the satiated, quivering cunt-lips like a foot withdrawing from quicksand.

He stood up straight, stretching his tortured muscles as his rock hard cock sprang out and stood away from his body in stiff erection.

Running his hands over the gorgeous curves and peaks of her body, he edged around to the side of the table from where her head still dangled in helpless exhaustion, her lips still parted, tempting mewling sounds rolling aimlessly from them.

His eyes locked on her full red, sensuous lips, still muttering nothings out into the air from her tremendous climax. They were wet and moist from her tongue swirling around them as she lay suffering, yet not suffering, from her awkward position on the table.

He tangled his strong fingers into the long blonde tresses of her hair and pulled her parted lips up to the hard swollen head of his organ. He wanted to shove his cock all the way down between them and shuddered at the thought of that moist, warm cavern closing around it caused it to jerk and almost ejaculate down onto her upraised breasts.

Ginny's eyes grew wide with excitement as soon as she realized her brother's intentions. She knew this was his favourite part of fucking her, and secretly, she enjoyed the lewdness just as much as he did. Her lips were a bare inch away from the tip of his swollen instrument, and she opened her mouth and breathed softly against it, allowing her hot breath to flow over the cool tip with a maddening slowness.

"Ooooh God, suck it now, baby," she

heard him groan above her. Her brother's words excited her as she knew his eyes were hungrily taking in the nudity of her helpless, battered body as he spoke.

Her tongue flicked out, the tip coming into warm wet contact with the head of his cock. She circled it about the smooth, rubbery flesh as he groaned and twisted above from the cruel teasing she was subjecting him to. Her tongue continued to flick at it hungrily out from between her small white teeth, licking rapidly at the tiny opening in the head. A thin string of his cum seeped from it and stretched across her open mouth. She strained closer to him, the cords of her neck standing out, trying to suck the teasing instrument into her mouth, and when this movement failed, she frantically reached up grabbing his balls, and pulled the thick rod deep into her sucking mouth until it pressed tight back against the tips of her tonsils.

She closed her eyes to keep from choking. Her brother's thick spongy cock was now rammed deep inside her mouth, and she could feel the rubbery head rub the full length of her tongue imbedding itself deep in her throat. Saliva seemed to fill her mouth, all of it, except that filled by Steve's great cock, now protruding like a giant, impersonal tree trunk from her oval shaped lips.

He began a slow rhythmic undulation of

his hips down into her face, as she in return, sucked like a demon, swishing her tongue with wicked vengeance, around and around the throbbing head sliding in and out of her ovalled lips.

Steve groaned incoherently above her flailing head and pushed his hands tight against her bloated cheeks. He had waited for this precious moment long enough... now he wanted her to make him cum so he could let his hot, impatient juices flow freely down her hungry gaping throat. As he flexed his loins in and out at the rounded open hole formed by her sensuously sucking lips, he could feel all of himself, every nerve he possessed, pulsating and throbbing between her teeth and into the moist cavity and warmth of her saliva-filled mouth.

He could feel the pressure building in his balls slapping against the bridge of her nose as she worked away on him in hot passion, inflating and lengthening his cock to a dimension he never thought possible. Then, he suddenly jerked his powerful loins forward and let out a low, tortuous groan as the hot, white cum lying in wait inside him spurted up from his aching balls and out the tip of his jerking penis. He gripped her head tight between his hands and shoved his cock deeper into her throat.

Ginny groaned beneath him as the first

hot spurt of fiery liquid flooded into the back of her mouth, filling the warm sucking cavity and bloating her cheeks into twin mounds of puffed-out flesh. Her throat contracted greedily, swallowing and sputtering to keep from choking on the white sticky semen as he emptied his balls relentlessly deep into her throat.

He collapsed over her in complete exhaustion, starting to ease his deflated cock away from her, but Ginny continued to suck at it gently, licking the last of his hot, remaining sperm from it... washing it down thoroughly with her glistening voracious tongue.

He stood up with snaky knees when she had finished her task, and gently lifted her off the table and into his arms.

"I love you so much," his sister whispered to him as she buried her head against the wide expanse of his chest.

Steve squeezed her shoulders gently and lifted her chin up with the tip of his finger, looking steadily into her still smouldering eyes.

"And you're the only girl for me... You know that don't you?"

She smiled up at him, feeling wonderfully secure in his love. Their forbidden relationship was wicked, of course, but to her it was the only thing in her life that had any real substance.

Ginny stepped back, still smiling up at

him, then winced as a sharp pain cut into the bottom of her foot. She looked down to see the shattered remains of their coffee cups that had smashed unnoticed to the floor during their passionate lovemaking.

Their eyes met again and they both burst out into spasms of uncontrollable laughter.

"Let's clean this mess up and then go for a quick dip in the pool," Steve said, tears still pouring from his eyes over the ridiculous glee he felt from the wreck they had made of the kitchen.

"Oh, Steve," she said, "I love you… I truly do, you always have such fun ideas!"

"That's because I love you so much, baby," he said. "You inspire me… Come on now, be a good little girl and tidy up the kitchen. If you do a real good job of it, big brother will take you swimming in his birthday suit. The hell with the neighbours," he chuckled. "They'll never know the fun they're missing!"

Chapter 5

The ocean shimmered in glistening yellows and pinks as the afternoon sun slowly sunk into the watery horizon outside of Barbara's beach cottage. Barbara moved restlessly across the living room, standing for a moment by the tray of reefers she had so carefully prepared for the party that night, counting them again to be sure there would be enough for her guests.

Her eyes slowly scanned the rest of the room and spotted two mugs on the window ledge half-filled with cold, black coffee. Taking them into the small kitchen, she rinsed the cups off with warm water, carefully rubbing the lipstick marks away with her thumb, and then turned them upside down on the draining board.

She walked back into the living room and inspected it once more. Everything seemed tidy enough, though she didn't know why she was going to so much bother for the party tonight. The people she picked out for her friends could really care less about such trivial matters as a tidy living room. All they cared about was getting high and tuning in to the wild music from her stereo collection... that, and of course the exchanging of ideas, and getting into heated arguments about the passing scene.

Most of this group consisted of the liberal faction as far as politics go, and they all insisted that the way to live your life was from a day-to-day existence, taking each minute and hour as it came.

They professed to love everyone, even

their enemies, just as the Old Testament directed... of course they didn't follow it exactly, for they practiced "free-love" as though it were a religious inspiration.

Barbara reached down and picked up one of the reefers from the tray, lighting it and taking a deep drag, letting the sweet pungent smoke fill her lungs completely until she could feel a painful burning sensation at the back of her throat.

"Christ, this is good strong stuff," she muttered, pulling on it again and taking a longer, more prolonged drag.

Already her head began to feel deliciously light, as though she were slowly drifting into a fantastic dreamy world of pleasure. She giggled to herself and turned on the stereo, sexily undulating her loins to the Latin beat of the music, now permeating the room with the pulsating beat of bongo drums.

She danced across the rug in delightful abandon, swinging her arms loosely out in front of her and turning in fast, rapid circular motions, freezing suddenly as the drums came back on and jerking her hips from side to side in time with their pounding rhythm.

The slowly burning reefer, now dangling loosely from her mouth, sparked and glowed from the swish of air that played across it's burning ember... as Barbara whirled and twirled herself into absolute dizziness, then finally collapsed onto the rug in complete exhaustion.

Her entire body felt light and free from any weight, even the pull of gravitation. Her thoughts were all good and everything, even her most disturbing problems seemed minuscule and unimportant, now that the hashish had absorbed itself into the deep recesses of her mind.

She lay there momentarily, completely enjoying the familiar lifting sensation in her head, a sensual heightening of her mind as her thoughts spiralled beautifully around in her brain... the colours she saw and the things she touched, taking on a new and intensive perspective.

Della would be down in a few minutes, for it was almost time for the guests to arrive. The girl was deliberately delaying her entrance until a few people had arrived... Barbara smiled to herself as she thought about Della's reluctance to be alone in the same room with her.

Ever since yesterday morning, when she had so skilfully conned the younger girl into going over to the studio and offering her services to Steve and Ginny, they had scarcely exchanged more than a few words to each other. Obviously, Barbara knew, Della felt shy and embarrassed at what she thought of as her *faux pas*. She was not in the position now to suspect that Barbara had engineered their intimate affair in the bath, and the even more sensual love-play that had followed.

The whole episode had been nothing more to Barbara than a sort of softening-up of the girl for Steve and Ginny. They wanted to be sure that the models she supplied to them didn't possess too many inhibitions, and what better way could there be of insuring that the girls would finally end up stripping and posing for them as sexily as possible?

All of her detailed preliminaries with the new models usually saved a great deal of time for the brother and sister, and Barbara got a 15 percent increase on her commission if she succeeded in seducing the girls before they kept their first appointment. All the same, Barbara did feel a slight pang of regret for the way in which she so cleverly deceived Della. Not that this girl was any different from the others, but Barbara kept seeing her big hazel-green eyes, so sad and compassionate, and so filled with unvoiced dismay because she thought she had hurt Barbara by her sexual performance. Of course, everything Barbara had told her about the older girl seducing her was completely true. The episode had really happened in exactly the way she had related it to Della, but she had narrated the same story so many times, and to so many different girls, that it had long ago stopped seeming real to her. It was as if she had rehearsed the lines of a play so intensively that they no longer had the power to move her any longer, no matter how poignant they had been at the beginning.

She reached the final draw on her reefer and crushed the tiny butt into an ashtray, sighing regretfully as the thought of the whole messy affair lingered deep in her conscience. The hashish was increasing her self-pity gradually, until waves of misery began to steal through her tormented mind. With a determined effort, the girl swung her legs to the floor and forced herself to stand up. Movement of any kind seemed to disperse the effect of the drug, and feeling more in control of herself now, she walked back into the kitchen and poured herself a foaming glass of beer.

Greedily gulping down the frothy liquid until she could see the bottom of the glass, she heaved a sigh of relief and wiped off the sides of her mouth with the back of her hand... she felt better almost at once. There was really no sense in letting morbid feelings like this persist, she thought, besides, there was nothing that could be done about them, anyway. They were best ignored or suppressed.

Thinking of Della again, Barbara giggled as she remembered that she had a further surprise in store for her Monday… Steve and Ginny were fast movers, and Della would soon learn plenty under their tutorship.

The ringing of the doorbell brought Barbara back to the present, at last the party could get going, she thought impatiently, as she hurried to answer it. She opened the door with a set smile on her face, and then gasped in amazement as she stared at her unexpected visitor. Before her stood Danny Ritter, an old boyfriend that she hadn't seen for months and months! Barbara stood there speechless for a moment, not knowing quite what to say to him.

She had met Danny Ritter over a year ago at one of those ultra-literary parties in Hollywood, and she took to him right away… he was handsome, charming, witty, and above all else, a rebel in every sense of the word.

During that first conversation between them, the young writer mentioned that one of his novels had been seized by the police and, after a brief court case, had been banned… after that Barbara had seen to it that their first casual encounter had been followed by a brief, but blazing love affair.

Barbara's strong animal attraction to him in the physical sense became even more poignant when she found that his basic social beliefs were almost identical to hers, although she found out later, unlike her he was a pure idealist and had a tendency to be a bit too romantic about sexual encounters. But he loathed authority of any kind; he was well-informed about the "hip" scene without being pretentious about it. One day he called her to tell her that he was going away to write a book, and that the LA scene was too distracting a place to concentrate in. That was the last time she had spoke to him, and often wondered in the months that followed what had happened to him... now as he stood there before her, all the old attraction for him was rapidly coming back...

"Danny! Where on earth have you been? It's so good to see you again!"

He laughed happily at her surprise, lifting her up in his arms, half-carrying her down the hall, and planted a warm kiss on her lips.

"Believe it or not I've been working, Jugs," he laughed. "Jugs" was the nickname he had christened her with the first time he got a look at her huge, firm breasts. He began to whirl her around and around him in a playful manner, still holding her helplessly in the air.

"Hey, put me down!" Barbara wriggled her breasts against him, laughing and pretending to punch his shoulders.

He ignored her pleas and buried his face in her neck, growling and biting her skin playfully, as they came to the entrance of the living room. Then suddenly, he stopped dead in his tracks! His eyes were opened wide in disbelieving amazement, staring past Barbara at Della, now standing at the foot of the stairway.

"I don't believe it!" he half-whispered, then gave a long, dry whistle, his face still contorted from the sudden surprise. As if in a dreamlike trance, his hands slowly left Barbara's body, lowering her gently to the floor.

Della was standing halfway on the last step of the stairway with her hand on the banister, looking at him as if she couldn't believe her eyes.

"Della!" He moved quickly towards her, caught both of her hands in his and gave the girl a broad, genuinely pleased smile. "This is fantastic! What on earth are you doing here?"

The touch of his hands on hers sent jolting electrical impulses whirring through her body, and she felt winded, as if she had just run for ten miles without stopping to rest. She blushed deeply, thinking that he could probably hear the pounding of her heart, thudding wildly inside her and pumping blood up to her brain so fast that she leaned slightly towards him to stop the dizziness.

Della took a deep breath and smiled up at him, determined not to let her emotions betray her, for she was not sure where she really stood with him now, or for that matter, just how much their brief affair had meant to him. When she finally spoke, her voice did not give away her inner feelings.

"I was just about to ask you the same question," she said, the initial excitement gradually ebbing.

His eyes were as warm and exciting as she remembered them, smouldering with secret promises of love and crinkling boyishly at the corners at the same time, as if he were laughing at his own burning desires.

"Friends?" he asked her quietly. And then Della suddenly remembered how abruptly she left the beach cottage that day, leaving no word of explanation.

She nodded; then she smiled. "I tried to find you later, I – I wrote you but..."

He cut short her apologies. "There's no need to say anything," he told her. "We were both very much on edge then... Anyway... let's just forget it, luck is with me today; I've finally finished that book, and found you again in the same week. What more could I ask for?"

"Oh, Danny, I'm so happy for you. I knew how much you wanted to finish it, that's why I..."

"No more about that," he said softly, increasing the warm pressure of his hand on hers. "Are you staying with Barbara now?"

"Y – Yes, I'm trying to find a steady job in modelling, and Barbara's sort of helping me along... my money's running a little low right now." She looked over his shoulder and met Barbara's eyes. The girl was staring at them with a puzzled, almost angry look on her face... as if she deeply resented their knowing each other.

Barbara, who had been watching this exchange with mounting impatience, now interrupted the couple's intimate reunion.

"Suppose you two lovebirds come downstairs and help me open a few bottles of beer. It's time we got this party moving!" she called. "You'll have plenty of time for tête-à-têtes later on."

Della released her hands from Danny's, and looked over at the other girl quizzically. Barbara was standing with her arms folded, now unable to disguise the anger in her voice and in her stance. What was the matter with her, Della wondered. Surely she wasn't jealous... Danny wasn't her lover too, was he? No, that wouldn't account for Barbara's bad temper. She knew the girl well enough to realize that Barbara was cool enough in her relationships not to be put out by an unfaithful lover. But something was clearly bothering her, and it obviously had some connection with Danny and herself.

Della shrugged her shoulders. Whatever

it was, it couldn't be helped now that he was with her again. She hadn't realized before just how much he meant to her until he had appeared right out of the blue, but the pounding of her heart and weak feeling at the pit of her stomach told her that she wasn't about to let him get away so easily this time...

After those first few uncomfortable moments with Barbara, Della noticed with relief the other girl gradually relax, becoming her old "cool" self again, laughing with them and telling Danny the latest gossip and happenings revolving around their inner circle of friends. It was not until much later when the rest of the people had firmly entrenched themselves in the living room, that Barbara slowly withdrew from them, becoming moody once more and talking little to anyone around her. She began to chain-smoke from the tray of reefers... and at a rough count Della guessed that the girl had gone through at least six of the homemade sticks.

Della also noticed that none of Barbara's "friends" seemed to pay very much attention to her withdrawal, for most of them were perfectly content to curl up on the floor and drink beer, talk and smoke an occasional reefer themselves. Della tried to join in the conversations, but despite the undeniably interesting topics that weaved patterns all around her, she was beginning to feel bored and restless.

Ever since Barbara's first interruption, she hadn't really had much of an opportunity to talk to Danny, because the boy had been led into conversation after conversation as each new guest had arrived at the cottage.

He was in another intense conversation now with a studious-looking man wearing horn-rimmed glasses and dressed in the tweedy, casual manner of a university professor. From his appearance and from the way Danny listened to him, Della guessed that he was someone pretty influential. This was confirmed to her when the man finally left the room and Danny came over to the fireplace where Della sat with her back propped against the wall.

"He's a reader for one of the big publishers," Danny told her apologetically. "They might possibly take a chance on my next book... It's been difficult to find a publisher for what I'm really interested in writing... ever since that court case."

The room was thick with the fumes of hashish, and Della, who had still not experimented with the drug, felt a wave of nausea slowly envelope her as she looked back up at him.

"Couldn't we sneak up to my room and talk about it, Danny?" she asked with a half-pleading look in her upraised eyes. "All this smoke and noise is making me ill."

The never-ending LP of sitar music was turned up to the highest volume on Barbara's stereo, with the plaintive, wailing sound of the weird instrument filling the room, its purpose mainly to enhance the setting of the drug-takers.

Without another word or hesitation, Danny pulled Della to her feet, quickly stealing a glance at Barbara who now seemed oblivious to everything happening around her. She lay with her head on another man's lap, eyes closed, her fingers tapping against her thigh in rhythm with the pulsating music.

As soon as they were safely inside her bedroom, Danny took her in his arms and began kissing her feverishly as if he were trying to absorb completely her voluptuous, young body by his ardent movements. He ran his trembling lips across the smooth skin of her forehead and down on her flushed cheeks, on the tip of her nose, then planted them firmly on her slightly parted lips. His mouth felt both familiar and strangely exciting to Della, as if she were tasting sweet water from a trickling fountain that would never be able to quench her thirst.

She pressed her body tightly against his, squashing her firm full breasts against his hard expansive chest, remembering the heated passion they both had shared months before. Della was wearing a dark green mini-skirt that ended just six inches above her well-formed knees. Beneath that, a pair of skin-coloured tights served as both stockings and panties, covering her bottom half in seductive sheerness and transparency. A cool, crisp blouse tucked neatly below the narrow band of the skirt bristled its starchiness against the rough texture of his sports coat as their bodies rubbed and twisted against each other with mounting passion.

Danny worked his mouth over her parted, gasping lips, gradually slipping his tongue between her teeth and then slowly swirling it around the wet moistness within. He moved his hands down her body, drew her brief skirt up over her ripe buttocks and began to massage the firmly tensed cheeks through the sensuous feeling material of the girl's tights.

He moaned softly as he continued to massage them lovingly... they were so soft and supple, so easy to pull, first this way and then that... He pressed them tightly, straining her body even more against his own, his fingers curling so that they fitted snugly into the twin curves of her luscious buttocks.

Della's short skirt slowly began to creep up in front as she pressed against him tightly, and Danny could feel the hot coal of passion from deep within her loins burning against his leg. The warmth felt good on him, proof beyond a doubt that her cravings matched his own, and he gently nudged her legs apart with his knee, nestling the side of his thigh tightly against her open crotch.

Della responded rapidly to this fondling by placing her hands firmly on his buttocks, rubbing and caressing them sensuously as she jerked and twisted against him, her whole body now begging to be fucked again by him as she had been before. Her tongue worked violently inside his mouth, taunting him with its liquid, incessant movements. She made tiny little muffled cries, wrung torturously from her lips each time he pressed his thigh against her hot, open crotch.

Danny could feel his growing cock reaching full erection as Della writhed and squirmed her cunt shamelessly against him, and tried to hold himself in check now as he felt several small droplets of cum oozing from his throbbing gland. Two of his long fingers crept into the globular mounds of her ass cheeks, pushing the material of her tights well into the crease, rubbing greedily up and down the warm hollow until he could feel the tight, resilient hole of her tiny puckered anus.

She grunted in sharp surprise as his probing fingers tried to push into the tight elastic ring, and opened her legs wider, raising herself at the same time on tiptoe to press her hot, sweltering loins more intimately into his rising passion. She strained and squirmed her whole pelvis against him, feeling his penis slide to the left and right as she worked her crotch desperately into his rising maleness.

Breathing heavily, Danny ended their long kiss, and started to walk the lust-drunken girl backwards to the softness of her bed. They moved dreamlike as if in a trance for a half-dozen paces until the backs of Della's knees bumped softly against the edge of the mattress. Then he lowered her, his hands never leaving the hot, quivering cheeks of her bottom, until she was lying flat back on the bed... her feet still resting on the threadbare carpet.

He manoeuvred himself down beside her, his fingers still securely entrenched in her protesting anus, taking lustful pleasure in her small mewls of pain. He brought his mouth down to her open thighs and pressed his lips along the soft silky inside of her leg. His mouth sank firmly into the resilient flesh, and she parted her thighs even wider, enabling him to see the quivering lips of her vagina, completely visible through the transparent nylon of her tights.

Della could now feel the pressure of his strong hands gently urging and pushing against the softness of her inner thighs until they were slowly spread wide apart in a

V-position. She looked down on him, eagerly awaiting his next move, her secret treasure open to him to do as he willed. She watched with bated breath as his head lowered slowly then made firm contact with the target.

"Ohhhhh!" She jerked, as his hot moist lips closed over the soft hair- covered mound at the base of her belly. His hazy face disappeared from her view into the curly soft fleece as he planted wet tickling kisses on the nylon-covered mound, his tongue flicking lizard-like at the tight throbbing opening of her cunt.

With trembling, barely controllable hands, Della quickly unbuttoned her blouse and, arching her body and pushing her screaming loins hard against his face in the movement, she desperately reached back and unclasped her bra. Not wanting to lose the urgency of the moment, she moved her own hands sensuously down over her throbbing breasts and slid them slowly down her smooth flat stomach, coming to rest on either side of his lips. Her fingers stroked softly for a moment at the flexing hollows of her inner thighs moving her legs open and shut against his ears and allowing him as much access as was possible through the straining nylon to her hot, moist pussy.

Through the thin-stretched material of her tights, he tasted the warm secretion now amply flowing from inside her into his sucking mouth, the thin, veneered hose totally inadequate to hold him at bay. His tongue pushed hard into the tense stretch of the tights pressing them wetly into her pink, open slit, and licked rapidly at the pulsating clitoris between her thighs. His thumbs pressed firmly on either side of it, causing it to bulge out more prominently than before.

Della strained her body, making a tremendous effort of will power to keep her hips relaxed and her buttock muscles slack. She closed her eyes blissfully and moved her hands back up to the twin globular mounds of her titties. The nipples had started to throb lewdly already, and it required only a brief manipulation with the tips of her fingers for her to feel them grow more stiff and erect. The wonderful tongue darting lizard-like between her splayed legs seemed to be causing her already ballooning breasts to inflate much larger than their normal size. They seemed so huge now that Della was getting almost as great a thrill from touching and fondling them as she was from the sensuous licking tongue thrusting between her legs below.

The lust-inspired Danny had now rested his nose gently against her pubic mound and was inhaling deeply through it, making it plain to her that he no longer controlled himself. He was sniffing animal-like at her sex and enjoying every intake of her rare and mysterious bouquet. He rubbed his flared nostrils from side to side, the transparent material becoming moist with the flow of excited secretions.

Della was beyond the point of controlling her inner muscles now, and she throbbed helplessly inside under the probing of his nose and mouth, even though their violent lovemaking had only begun a few short moments before.

As he felt the uneven and desperate jerking of her crotch against his face, Danny brought his other fingers from beneath her buttocks and quickly pinched up two folds of the pantyhose between his forefingers and thumbs. He ripped at the material as hard as he could, deriving a savage pleasure from the way the soft, flimsy material shredded suddenly in his hands.

No sooner had the tight material been torn from her crotch, than the swollen lips of her tortured vagina burst free and open to his touch, like the sudden blooming of a hothouse flower. Danny ran his tongue teasingly into the soft-rimmed flesh, flicking softly at it for a moment, and then quickly withdrawing it again to tantalize cruelly around the ragged pink edges.

Della moaned softly and reached her eager hands down around his ears, gently urging him to continue his maddening manipulations. He paused and let her force him this time, pressing his mouth directly over her tight little hole as she frantically squirmed her crotch back up against his face. As his lips rounded and covered the contracting opening, he thrust his tongue deep down into it, bringing a low guttural groan from the girl whose soft warm thighs closed convulsively around either side of his jerking head.

He could feel the wet flesh slip moistly around his long extended tongue as the walls of the invaded vagina opened and closed in a desperate sucking motion, attempting to pull it deeper and deeper into it. It felt as though the nibbling hair-lined mouth would pull his tongue out by the roots, devouring it alive.

Her heels pushed down against his back pressing his body into the hungry flesh trap between her legs until he couldn't breath, his nose was smashed tightly against the tiny hard clitoris above, breathing the pungent odour of the lust juice that was now flowing in abundance from it. It incited his penis to a hardness that he could no longer control... he knew he could wait not another minute to plunge his hot, impatient cock deep into her warm, soft pussy.

Della's body was lost in a furious hot passion that she had never felt before. Every muscle in her body was tensed as she strained her hips upward toward the maddening fleshy probe between her legs. Her love for Danny incited her further, and the cords of her neck stood out as she pulled with all her strength against the tangled hair of his head. She had never expected it could be like this, that he or any man could bring such hot primitive passions from her body. Her drawn-up legs opened and closed around the tormenting head that was licking gluttonously at her flame-seared hole.

"Oh! Ohhh! Aggghhh!" she moaned, throwing her legs wider and wider apart to give him greater access.

Then, he could stand the prolonged torture no longer! He reached out for her flailing legs and grasped them behind the knees, shoving them back against her shoulders, while slithering his cock up against the juice-soaked opening between her wide-stretched legs at the same time. His rigid stiff cock brushed against the wet dripping pubic hair. In obedient servitude, Della locked her ankles tightly behind his neck as he planted his hands on either side of her shoulders, pressing her back against the soft, giving mattress. As he looked down between their bodies, he could see her upturned ass completely exposed to his staring eyes.

The expanded narrow cunt-slit was visibly

throbbing its lips in open invitation, the wet, moist furrow held wide apart by the pressure of his thighs pressed tightly up against hers.

As he hovered over her pleading body, Della could feel the hugeness of his fleshy hardness laying the full length of her open, quivering slit. The jerking head of his cock rested throbbing between her wide- spread buttocks, insinuating itself up and down, up and down, in a maddening tease that caused her to twist her hips down toward it, her hungry cunt searching desperately for its hard blood-filled tip.

And then he entered her. His long hungry penis drove and burrowed its way through the soft cushions of moist flesh until it was nestled solidly at the bottom of her waiting vagina. Danny paused, trying to catch his breath now from the floating, almost breathless feeling of ecstasy that charged through his body. His hot, pulsating rod lay still in her deepness, feeling the warm, moist walls of her cunt tightly clasped around it, as if it had been custom made for his hardened cock.

"Oooooh, Baby," he mumbled, struggling to force her into a better position. And, although his knees felt weak and shaky he managed to slide them up on the soft mattress against her soft, flaccid buttocks, forcing her legs up tightly around his waist.

Della responded eagerly to this position,

trapping his body in a vice-like grip between her strong, flexing thighs. Her loins were now twisting and turning crazily, screwing tight up the full length of his cock to the chant of the Indian LP's that drifted up to them through the wooden planks of the bedroom floor. The full moon filtered through the bamboo curtain, throwing horizontal bars of light across her solid body and partially illuminating her lovely face.

She continued to work her body against his, her eyes in the seraphic smile of the Madonna, slightly parted in a mysterious smile. Her body seemed extraordinary light and gauzy and he reached down and kneaded his hard fingers into the softness of her breasts as if testing to see if she were really there beneath him, letting him fuck her like that.

Her tits gave way beneath the pressure of his hands in marshmallow softness, except for the two hard pulsating peaks of her nipples which rose and fell, then stood hard and erect on their own, cresting the two snowy mounds of flesh with the colour of baked earth.

Outside her bedroom door the endless trod of feet could be heard making their way clumsily to the bathroom at the end of the hallway. Downstairs the party seemed to be building up in momentum, gleeful shrieks punctuated the low drone of conversation and the stereo was now turned on full blast with the erotic sounds from the L.P.'s now completely satiating the room around them.

Danny pulled his rock hard cock slowly in and out of her hot, throbbing pussy to the erotic rhythm of the Indian music as Della's body ground in slow motion around it, her head turning listlessly from side to side as if she were caught up in the throes of a heated, primitive dance. Her heavy-lidded eyes stared past his passion-contorted face and up to the ceiling as if she didn't realize that he existed.

He worked the hard, throbbing head of his cock slowly outwards to the tip of her quivering vulval lips, massaging it over and over against the bud of her clitoris. The tormenting caress of his cock against the hot, sensitive area between her thighs inflamed Della back to conscious awareness, and she jerked her heels against his back, pulling his penis deep down inside her again.

"Oh... God! Don't take it out again," she pleaded, her eyes now widened almost in fear. "Don't ever take it out of me again! I want you to fuck me and fuck me... foreeeever!"

Della slid her fingers lovingly through his hair and pulled his mouth down onto her breasts, at the same time arching her body so that they thrust themselves against his face, almost smothering him, with their softness.

He sucked down on them gratefully, moving greedily from one firm, pulsating mound to the next, taking a portion into his mouth each time and fastening his teeth securely on it as he continued to suck at her in greedy, desire-filled abandonment.

Two scuffling pair of feet could be heard just outside the bedroom door, and the soft plywood creaked and gave slightly as the weight of a body was pressed against.

"Not here, Rob," Barbara's slurred voice could be heard on the other side of the door. "My room's down the hall... stop that! Oh my God! Someone will see us!"

"What do you care, baby... You've got me so hot that I can't make it that far."

Danny and Della froze momentarily from the sound of lewd voices on the other side of the door, but then renewed their rhythmic fucking, now unable to fight against the tide of passion that completely enveloped their lust-consumed bodies.

He slipped his hands down to the soft curves of her small waistline and slid them under the smooth globes of her moving buttocks, grasping them harshly, one in each hand. They were flexing and unflexing, oozing foam-like around his fingers as he pressed his hands tightly into them. He jerked her harder to his loins and felt her pulling her thighs back a little more, the moist wet hole of her cunt flowering open to receive his cock to greater and greater depths than ever before.

Della raised her head and worked her tongue up into his gasping mouth as small mewling sounds of velvety pleasure rumbled from deep in her throat. The cords in her neck and thighs stood out hard and tense from the intensity of her feeling as she writhed and twisted beneath him. There was no longer any thought of anything but the delicious sensation of lying beneath this man who was fucking her as she would never be fucked again in her entire life! The sound of Barbara's pleading, yet lust-filled voice on the other side of the thin wooden door only seemed to add to the urgency and abandoned pleasure of the moment.

Barbara's body was trapped, standing against the firm, unyielding wood and in front of her Rob, now in a semi-daze from the hashish and her teasing manipulations against his loins, had already unzipped his pants and was pointing his hard inflamed cock at her wide-spread legs as though it were a gun ready to be fired.

He reached up under her short mini dress and pulled roughly down on her panties, not caring in the least if someone should happen to wander by and witness the lewd scene. Then, without ceremony, he forced her legs wider and putting his hands under her knees lifted up so that her feet were high off the floor, her back pressed tight against the wall. Her legs were wide apart, the whole of her naked crotch presented up to him. Then, he rammed forward, sinking his throbbing cock quickly into the moist open cunt between her thighs, now wet and open to his hot, lust-aching rod, making an easy but brutal penetration.

"Ooooooh," Barbara gasped, the sound bubbling from her half-parted lips as she felt his delicious hardness impale her like a stiff sword.

He pushed into it again with a sudden quick movement, feeling the soft rubbery flesh yielding butter-like before his attack.

"Agghhhhhh!" she groaned louder, at the same time grinding down at his hot loins using the door as a lever against her pushing back. Barbara put her hands up on Rob's wide shoulders as he tensed the muscles of his arms, to support her legs cradled over them, trapping her squirming crotch against the firm upward pounding of his hot, pulsating shaft. Her eyes were wide open and dilated from the hashish, her mouth parted and closed with each brutal upward thrust whose momentum lifted her body up and down the wall as though she were a yo-yo.

Rob buried his mouth in her shoulder and bit down hard on the tender flesh. His face was contorted with the savage anger of a man that had been teased too long and was now returning his previous suffering, blow by blow, brutally spearing into her hot, throbbing belly with lustful uncontrollable passion. There was no room for tenderness here because he knew the girl wouldn't accept it if it were offered to her, in fact she would probably laugh at his attempts to be civil. So now as he fucked into her for all passing eyes to see, he secretly knew that his brutal, uncaring rape of her loins was what she had been waiting for all night as she sat beside him in the dimmed living room, playing her fingers across his crotch until he was almost out of his mind from the excitement.

The crude rhythmic thumping against the door could clearly be heard by the churning, twisting couple inside as they slowly built up an intensified climatic peak within their grinding organs, driving and lunging at each other's body with suicidal frenzy. Danny strained forward and rammed deep into her as far as he could drive his hard, tortured cock, jerking the base of it tight up against her inflamed clitoris with each wild lunging movement.

Della grew so stimulated from these manipulations that she thrust herself forward dropping her legs until her feet once more touched the carpet, her thighs splayed out as fully as possible, Danny's body lying over her, with his toes just on the floor... his thighs locked together between hers. The slipping down of Della's feet forced his cock to penetrate the girl from a new and exciting angle. It was driven almost vertical, deep into her cunt, the thick stem twisted upwards and digging exquisitely against her clitoris with every forward spring. To better support her awkward position, Della gripped desperately at the sides of the bed for support, her hands holding tightly to the fold of the blanket as she levered herself up and down lewdly on his pistoning cock.

"Yessss... Yesss, I'm cumming darling!" she started to choke and gurgled up at him. "I'm... cummingggggg!"

And then suddenly he felt his loins jerk uncontrollably beneath him as the white flow of hot liquid rushed from his hard thrusting penis deep into her wet, gaping vagina. He gripped her hips tight between his hands and shoved his cock deeper into her as the first spurt of hot, fiery liquid flooded into the back of her womb, filling the hot moist cavity to the bursting point as her desperately clenching buttocks continued to milk his hot, jetting sperm far, far into her.

As Danny squeezed the last of his juices into Della's gaping pussy, he could hear the groans and moans of the couple outside the door as they too began to climb the peak, straining to fall into the delicious limbo of orgasm.

Barbara was bouncing off Rob like an electric drill, jerking and bucking her hot loins against his hard shaft like she was trying to feel and read every part of it in Braille. She ploughed her haunches against him like a wild she-animal in the forest, not a human word escaping from her parted lips, not a sign that she knew any language at all except the grunting and groaning noises she used to urge him on against her as if he too were a dumb animal... to be used for her sexual satisfactions.

"Go on... stick it up me... harder," she gasped, not caring that two other men from the party downstairs had roamed into the hallway in search of the toilet.

They both stood there, high on the hashish, watching the lewd fucking scene before them in the casual detached manner of viewing a pornographic film, chuckling mildly at the frantic bucking Rob was going through as he tried to spill his cum up into the wild female screwing her crotch down on him. Another man came up behind them and the three of them stepped closer to the writhing couple to get a closer look at the unbelievable spectacle taking place before them.

One of the men, apparently one of

Barbara's past conquests from the insinuating remarks he was muttering under his breath, lifted up her dress so they could all clearly see Rob's inflated cock ramming into hair-covered cunt. A simultaneous gasp escaped from their lips as they stood watching the swollen vaginal labia pull and stretch from the pressure of the cruel in and out thrusts.

Barbara leaned her body flat against the door, thoroughly excited by the looks of raw lust spread across the gaping faces of the men that surrounded her. The man closest to the right side of her grabbed her bouncing breasts and began to squeeze them through the thin material of her dress. The stimulating massage incited Barbara's lust to new heights, and she threw her head loosely from side to side, muttering lewd words at the group.

"That's it," she hissed, "Pull my tits! Fuck me... Fuck me... I'm just about to spill my load!"

No sooner had the words escaped her lips, when she suddenly bucked forward against Rob, her mouth open wide like a gasping fish.

"Ooooohhhhh... Aggghhhhh! Don't stop everrrr... !" Her words mixed and swirled out of her salivating mouth and her eyes bulged wide open shrilling out her climax while looking helplessly into the staring faces of the other men surrounding her.

Rob could feel his own hot cum shooting up into her as if the fountain inside him could not be turned off. He was glad he had an audience now because it made everything he was doing to her seem even more obscene and vile than it actually was.

When he had finished his job, his weak limbs collapsed beneath him and he fell to the floor on his knees, still groaning and muttering to himself through the haze of hash that clouded his mind. Barbara was caught by one of the men standing near them and carried off to her bedroom with the other two following, knowing that each of them would eventually get their turn on top of her before the night was over.

* * *

Danny pulled the soft wool blanket around Della's head, muffling out the lewd sounds on the other side of the door, and gently nuzzled the full length of his body against hers; the thrill from their lovemaking pulsed through his body even now as they both lay dry-throated in weary exhaustion. The ticking of the alarm clock by the side of the bed mixed with their deep breathing, and soon the lewd sounds outside were muted as if some giant hand had swept Barbara and her lover away... leaving Danny and Della alone in their exhausted satiation.

Danny had slipped his limp, moist penis from her and its red length gleamed in wet droplets of both his own and Della's orgiastic fluids. He felt it brush itchily over the sheer silk of her sexy tights, then droop a little as his body lost contact with her. Still nestled up close to her, he drew her head onto his shoulder and closed his eyes.

One thing was certain, he thought playing the tips of fingers over her curvy hips, he wasn't going to let this alluring and utterly satisfying girl out of his sight if he could help it. He had never found a sex-partner so incredibly attuned to his particular tastes. They both had reached a satisfying climax at almost the same time... and, even more important, they had a kind of intuitive understanding of what pleased the other.

He had written his last book after the inspiration she'd given him at their first meeting, and already he felt a strong emotional attachment to her... apart from his strong physical desire. She might turn out to be someone very important in his life, he thought. His eyelids began to grow heavy as he started to drift off in a light sleep... someone very important... kept running through his foggy mind, and then he was asleep.

* * *

"What kind of modelling job?"

An hour or two had passed and they were sitting up on the bed now, smoking and talking. Danny repeated the question, since Della hadn't replied and a small but uncomfortable pause had settled between them.

"It's... it's for pin-up photos," she said at last. "You know... nude, lingerie, swimsuits..." Della turned a suspicious eye on him. He seemed to have received the news of her first important job with a kind of ominous apprehension.

"Why do you ask?" she said, "Surely you don't think there's anything wrong in that sort of thing?" She put a finger under his chin and tilted his face towards her. "Or do you?"

He smiled, bent his mouth and kissed the palm of her hand.

"Of course I don't," he replied, "As long as that's all there is to it." He took Della's hand and stared down at it, caressing her fingers lightly.

"You say Barbara arranged this appointment for you?" he asked casually.

Della nodded. "That's right. Why... do you think she's got some dark, ulterior motive?" She was teasing him again. Danny started to say something else and then changed his mind.

"I don't think she's really that much of a

friend to you, Della, and you might find out later that Barbara is not as loyal to you as you wish to believe right now."

"Oh, really, Danny!" Della stood up and started to adjust her clothing. "For God's sake let me use my own judgment about this job, it's the first chance I've had at it for months and months. I want to find out about things by myself for a change. I'm sick and tired of having people tell me what's best for me... pointing out all the pitfalls. I put up with it for 21 years from my parents and now I want to be free of it!"

Della's voice and words were much angrier than his mild, tentative advice called for. And she knew this, but she hated the idea of people treating her as if she were still a small child. Whatever Steve and Ginny were like, she felt confident that she could handle them... Why did Danny have to try and spoil things for her now, just when she was beginning to feel sure that she could make a go of it in modelling?

He got up from the bed and lit another cigarette, taking short, quick puffs on it, unconsciously showing his mild irritation with her stubbornness.

"It's getting late... I'd better be going," he said. He turned back to look at her but Della deliberately kept her eyes on the floor, determined not to give in to his wishes now.

"Let's talk more about this matter when you've cooled off," he relented. "I can understand your thinking that I'm trying to run your life for you, but there's more to this than that. I'd hate you to get involved with something you're bound to regret later on."

There was real concern in his voice now and Della was tempted to apologize and listen to what he had to say about it. But something inside her insisted that she continue to run things her own way.

After Danny left, she lay thinking of what he said to her, weighing the pros and cons of the matter in her mind, until her eyes grew heavy with sleep again. Her whole body felt like a sack of cement... weighted and clumsy. She knew she should attempt to get up and change into her nightie but her physical weariness overcame any willpower she had left in her body. Sunday she would think the matter over again, but whatever she finally decided, she would at least go and see for herself what her potential employers were like... Tomorrow was another day and after that Monday and her appointment with Steve and Ginny would settle the matter... once and for all...

Chapter 6

Della was dressed and out of the beach cottage by ten o'clock on Monday morning. She steered her MG convertible along the hot black asphalt highway that led to the Santa Monica turnoff, grateful for the openness of the car... as usual the day was heavy with smog and humidity. The sweltering morning had been in the nineties and would probably go much higher before noon. She drove leaning slightly forward in the seat, so that her back would not touch the hot leather of the car seat; but even so, she could feel sweat gather at the back of her neck and run down the ridge of her spine.

The skirt of her dress was pulled up around her hips to take advantage of the air rushing through the ventilators, but the air too was scorching, like the day, and gave little relief. Vehicles jammed the wide highway, even though the morning rush hour had long past, and Della tried to concentrate on her driving, deftly switching lanes to keep up an even speed so that she would not be late for her appointment.

She had deliberately spent Sunday down

on the beach, cultivating her tan in a state of blank-minded apathy, refusing to speculate on the experience that was in store for her. It was best to go into it with a completely open mind, she had decided. The important thing to remember was that she was conducting her own life now, moving of her own free will into a possibly exciting... and certainly financially rewarding modelling job.

* * *

At the studio, Ginny impatiently checked her watch for the third time, any second now the new model should be turning in at the gate. She was alone that morning because Steve had been forced at the last minute to go down to the printing company and straighten out a few technical problems, leaving Ginny to interview and appraise the now eagerly anticipated Della. He had left her alone with the new model with great reluctance, warning his sister repeatedly that she was on no account to make advances that would scare the new girl off.

She lit up a fresh cigarette and poured herself a tall screwdriver, adding a double shot of vodka to calm down the excitement building up in her stomach in anticipation of the new arrival. She was aware that for the last year her "afternoon cocktails" were starting earlier and earlier in the day, until like this morning, she usually began her drinking right after breakfast... sometimes she would even skip breakfast and start her daily liquid diet soon after awakening. She still managed to preserve her fresh beauty by eating expensive health foods and getting plenty of exercise before the fattening alcohol could build up in her system.

For her birthday last year, Steve had a sauna bath constructed out by the pool where they both frequently perspired in the nude, jumping back in the cool chlorine water when the heat had been more than they could stand. Twice a year, Ginny spent a week or two, depending on her time schedule, at a luxury health spa near Palm Springs. Here, she was pleasantly starved on a diet of lean meat, broth and vegetables, most of them raw, for the price of four hundred dollars a week.

The amazing thing about the Spa and its sublime dietary tortures was that she always felt so fit and relaxed when she left. The warm circulating baths, massages, and daily exercises were conducted on a rigid schedule, toning and trimming every muscle of the body into a supple firmness. Now, as she studied her well-toned body in the full-length mirror, she decided the money was a good investment after all, for one of her greatest fears was that someday she would lose her attractiveness to other people.

She took another sip from the tall, chilled glass, and quickly pushed the ugly thought from her mind. The present... the here and now was what really mattered to her... and right now Ginny could safely state that she was probably one of the most attractive women in town. She almost purred with self-satisfaction as she continued to pose in front of the mirror. She knew her body and beautiful face could be used in a position of power to obtain just about anyone she desired, man or woman. And right now her thoughts were fully concentrated on the luscious new model, whose arrival she had been looking forward to with mounting expectation... Not only because she wanted the new magazine to be a success, but also because she had a yen in her sex life for something new and exciting.

From time to time her sex life required the extra stimulus of an innocent young girl. One who could be seduced without too much difficulty, but who could play out her participating role with a certain enticing amount of reluctant hesitation. Ginny smiled to herself again, feeling sure that she wouldn't spoil anything by gently indulging in a few harmless fun and games with the new girl. Besides, if the new model turned out to be genuinely reluctant, Ginny had a tiny pill that was guaranteed to shed the girl of any remaining inhibitions she might possess.

The melodic electric door chimes interrupted Ginny from her sexual plotting, and she quickly set down her drink and walked briskly to the door, opening it and viewing Della with open admiration.

"Della?" she asked hesitantly, knowing full well who the girl was from the picture in Steve's portfolio.

The young girl nodded, outwardly nervous and suddenly shy in front of Ginny. She had never expected her new employer to be so beautiful and glamorous looking. Standing by her now, Della felt drab and unattractive… surely they would never be interested in her unsophisticated looks and inexperience… Barbara must have exaggerated her abilities to Ginny and Steve, she thought, and she felt like turning and walking away before facing the inevitable rejection, but Ginny's manner seemed warm and friendly enough and she was talking to her now as if she had been a long-time friend, stopping by for a visit.

"So nice of you to come down," Ginny beamed at her, opening the door wide and ushering her into the house. "I'm Ginny Albright… unfortunately, my brother Steve has been called away on business. He won't be back for an hour or so." Ginny followed Della into the house running her eyes professionally up and down the girl's figure as Della looked around her wonderingly at the beautiful luxurious interior of the sprawling ranch home.

Ginny steered Della into the spacious, sunlit living room and invited her to sit down on the large custom-built couch situated before the ocean-view windows.

"Even though Steve's away right now," Ginny said, "I can fill you in on what type of modelling we'll expect from you... but first – how about a tall, cool drink? I know it's still early," she added noting Della's surprise, "but it's the only civilized way I can find to beat this ghastly heat."

"Yes... please," Della accepted. She was desperately trying to act casual and aloof in front of Ginny, and the drink would serve to steady her nerves a bit.

"Screwdriver?" Ginny asked.

"Yes... fine."

While Ginny was in the kitchen preparing the drink, Della took time to survey her luxurious surroundings. The living room was a spacious, superbly furnished and decorated room, and Della felt suddenly overawed by the setting. She realized that the couple must be extremely wealthy to afford such a beautiful home. In the corner of the room was a large grand piano, the wood dark and gleaming in the morning sun. She walked over to it, inspecting the dustless keyboard and running her hands over the smoothness of the polished wood. The lid on the piano was closed and on the top of it was a small statue, of a jade green reclining cat. The oriental design of the intricately carved face aroused her curiosity, and she picked it up to examine it more closely. The heavy weight of the statue surprised her, for at first she thought it was porcelain enamel... she gasped in amazement upon suddenly realizing it was made of solid jade, and quickly placed it back on its velvet cushion.

Ginny came back into the room carrying two fresh drinks in her hands, secretly amused at the awed expression on Della's face.

"Do you like my cat?" she asked, handing Della the vodka drink.

"Yes... it's beautiful, I've never seen anything so delicate and lovely in my life. It must have cost a fortune," Della added, and then was suddenly embarrassed because she had crudely brought up the price.

"It was very expensive, my dear," Ginny acknowledged. "However, if you have a taste for such things and also have a strong determination to be a successful model... it won't be long before you too can afford such frivolous *objects d'art* for yourself."

"Oh, yes I am determined," Della replied, eager now to please the lovely, vibrant woman beside her. "I haven't had much experience, Miss Albright, but I'm very quick to learn... I'm sure you'd find me suitable for the job."

Ginny patted her on the hand. "Please... no formalities," she insisted with a friendly gleam in her eyes. "You must call me Ginny, and I'll call you Della... OK? After all, if we're going to see you in the nude and in your underwear, we can hardly use those polite, distant forms of address... now can we?"

Della smiled and nodded her head. She already was beginning to feel at ease with this beautiful woman, even if she did belong to a different class from herself. Ginny seemed to be completely aloof from the wealth that surrounded her as if she had known it every day of her life, and even though her speech was a trifle pretentious, her warm and friendly manner convinced Della that Ginny wanted to be friends with her.

"How would you like to go down to the studio with me now, and I'll show you around before Steve gets back," Ginny suggested, noticing gleefully that Della had quickly gulped the drink down in her nervousness. While in the kitchen, Ginny had dissolved the persuading pill in Della's drink, and she knew now that it wouldn't be long before it's aphrodisiac stimulation would take hold of the young girl.

Della stood up, swaying her body

slightly, and the room seemed to dissolve momentarily in a shimmering rush of bright colours. What's come over me, she thought dizzily, the excitement of meeting Ginny and the summer heat was too much for her body to take all at once. Ginny took her arm, apparently not noticing her shaking limbs, and led her down a winding spiral staircase.

As they walked together, Ginny still holding her hand and chatting about the photography business, Della felt strange and warm sensations pulsating through her body. Ginny's face seemed to be uncomfortably close to hers, and she could now smell an intoxicating perfume emanating from the older woman's skin. It made her feel very warm and sensually aroused, as though the scent's aphrodisiac qualities had penetrated quickly to her own bloodstream and stirred up a deep and very sweet sexual urge.

They entered a large basement that had been converted into a staggeringly well-equipped photographic studio. Spotlights, floodlights, an impressive array of still and moving picture cameras, a variety of tripods, beautifully painted backdrops; armchairs and couches; various "props," such as giant teddy bears and an imitation shower... all of these were neatly in place, leaving plenty of room for rearrangement of scenes.

Ginny walked over to the far wall and

turned on the main overhead light. "That's the changing room," she said, pointing to a door close to where Della stood. "And over here," she continued, "is the various equipment and film that Steve uses while he's in a shooting session." Ginny guided Della around the studio, showing her how everything worked and explaining that it was important for a model to understand these basic principles in order to attune herself to the photographer's commands.

As Ginny completed the tour of the studio, Della was growing increasingly aware that her body felt the unmistakable yearnings of sexual desire. She tried to fight back the tense, prickly longings, but the thought of all the naked and semi-naked girls who had posed here in the studio, in alluring and abandoned positions, only served to heighten her itchy, hot-blooded feelings.

Ginny, all too well familiar with the symptoms which Della could not hide from her... a moist, faintly quivering lower lip, a secret pressing of her thighs tightly together whenever they stood still... decided that the time was ripe for her to commence the seduction.

"You realize of course, that our studio specializes in nude photography," she posed her body in a sexy stance. "Suggestive photographs... something that tells a story to the reader, and takes the place of endless words of description," she said relaxing herself again and deliberately standing very close to Della, looking deeply into her eyes. "I sure hope that you don't have any hidden inhibitions about showing off your body in front of the camera."

"Oh, no," Della replied quickly, her mind and body dazed by the aphrodisiac. "I – I'm sure I will be able to do it."

"Well dear," Ginny continued pushing herself even closer to Della, and driving the younger girl into a deeper passionate yearning, "It's important that we get these things straightened out at the beginning, constant re-shooting can be a very expensive waste of film footage. We've had the bad experience before of new models walking out right in the middle of everything... seems as though they were too shy about showing off their titties and cunts."

Della gulped back her surprise at the crude words, a becoming blush reddening her cheeks. "Are they?" she whispered softly, her voice a low, throaty whisper.

Ginny nodded, almost conspiratorially. "If you don't mind, Della, I'd like to examine you before Steve gets back. I'll save us both time... and it's necessary that I get myself familiar with your curves and your body in general... We must be sure that the lighting is set up properly for your test shots, you see..."

As she was speaking, Ginny drew Della towards the low-slung couch.

"Would you mind undressing and laying down here... on your tummy first of all?"

Half-entranced, Della slowly stripped down to her bra and panties, licked her lips and removed these items with mounting excitement.

"Do... do you want my stockings off too?"

Ginny nodded, her own eyes hot and misty as she wandered them over the girl's softly tanned limbs. The silken, triangular curl of hair at Della's crotch was just visible, though she was pressing her thighs as tightly together as possible. Della obediently removed her garter belt, then sat on the edge of the couch to peel her stockings down, giving Ginny a good view of her slightly-parted vaginal lips as she raised first one leg, then the other.

As she lowered herself head down onto the cushions, stretching her body at full-length on the couch, Ginny said softly, "You know, Della, you've got the most voluptuous figure I've seen in years. The way you move, it's really sexy... really exciting to watch." She moved closer to the trembling, outstretched girl, whispering, "Now I'm going to begin the examination, my dear. Please don't be offended by what I do, will you? It's in both our interests, I assure you... and strictly professional." She hesitated for a moment, then added, "Try to think of me as your doctor, and it might be easier for you to relax."

Della rested her cheek on her folded arms, closing her eyes languidly, presenting the slowly stooping Ginny with a magnificent view of her buttocks... firmly rounded, their texture white and smooth... and with a side view of her right breast, dipping into the cushion and half-squashed on the small bolster.

Ginny softly placed her hands on Della's shoulders then sat down on the edge of the couch. She began to massage and caress the taut muscles beneath the shoulder blades, her fingers rolling firmly into the rounded flesh, then moved down the girl's back, massaging slowly and with a thrillingly sensuous touch the wonderful silky-smoothness of Della's bare body.

Ginny's hands pressed at the girl's spine, then stole gradually over the raised buttocks, bending the cheeks first downwards, then apart... her face now so close to the tiny elastic ring of Della's anus that Ginny's breath whistled softly down on her girlish hemispheres.

Ginny continued to roll the yielding mounds from side to side, taking large handfuls of flesh between her fingers and releasing them, then gathering up another portion of the yielding skin and repeating the same manipulations. Della's buttocks began to glow an attractive pink under the exciting pressure... and Ginny's heart beat faster and faster as her eyes grew bright with desire. Her fingers parted the globular white mounds slightly apart, enough for her to get a good glimpse at the tiny, tight brown anus that kept appearing between them. Her hands moved down a little so that she could lift Della's buttocks higher towards her, giving her a clear view of the slightly inflamed opening of her vulva, now moist and open from her stimulating touch.

Shyly at first, then with mounting abandon, Della began to move her hips up and down in an effort to relieve the stimulus she was receiving. And when Ginny could see that the younger girl was ready for the next stage of her "inspection," she gently patted Della's buttocks and ordered her to turn over on her back.

Della obeyed, wriggling herself into position and afraid now to open her eyes, fearing the magical, sensuous spell might be broken. Sighing softly, she raised her arms above her head, making her breasts swell yearningly upwards, and lay beneath Ginny completely relaxed with her legs gently parted, her bare, flat tummy emphasizing the silky vulval mound of her luscious moist opening.

Ginny knelt by the couch, surveying the unadorned beauty that lay so helplessly before her.

"Now, my dear," she whispered. "It's necessary that I examine some of your most private parts... Try not to be embarrassed or offended. I must do this to discover exactly the size and shape of your body."

As she spoke in a low, throaty whisper, Ginny began to fondle at Della's hot naked breasts, her fingers pulling and twisting at the girl's nipples until they stood up high in a pointed peak, reaching full erection. Leaving one hand on the right breast, she caressed the other down to Della's crotch and slid three of her fingers down into the opening ridges of the girl's labia, forcing the moist slit to unfold slowly like a blooming hot house flower.

Feeling the slight wetness of Della's sex, Ginny decided to waste no more time and quickly brought her trembling lips to the rigid nipple, which her index finger and thumb were pulling away from the girl's breast... gently kissing it on the tip.

Della squirmed beneath her with open delight. "Could... Could you do that again?" Her voice sounded sexy and low, coming from far back in her throat and barely audible to Ginny.

Ginny smiled almost wickedly and slipped the nipple back into her mouth, sucking it deeply between her teeth, her tongue flicking over the inflamed bud and making Della's vaginal juices flow even more freely than before. The aphrodisiac she had dropped into the girl's drink was working even faster than she had expected, Ginny thought. Or perhaps Della didn't really need very much persuasion... maybe she had awakened this deep passion in the younger girl by her own physical attractiveness and expert manipulations. This thought appealed to her feminine ego, and she continued her lewd sucking until Della softly interrupted her.

"Wouldn't you like to take off your dress too, Ginny?" she asked shyly. "It's... it's so hot in here... You must be very uncomfortable."

"What a thoughtful girl you are, my darling!" she whispered. Then stood up and quickly unzipped her dress, stepping out of its brightly patterned folds and standing for a moment in front of Della, clad only in a tight pair of panties and a brief half-bra.

Della's eyes roamed deliriously over the sexy vision, stopping at Ginny's pubic mound and the swollen lips below it, lingering on the luscious sight of it, her own breath now coming in short, hard rasps.

Ginny started to unhook her bra. "I may as well take this off, if you've no objection. It is very warm in here, as you said... and, after all, we're both girls, aren't we? There aren't any secrets between us..."

While she was speaking, she released her breasts from their snug bondage. "Large, aren't they?" she giggled, weighing them in her hands and lifting them proudly toward her new friend. "It looks as if I could do with a little bit of examination myself!"

Ginny suddenly stopped giggling, her eyes narrowing into an expression as passionate as Della's, and covered the girl's body quickly with her own. She lowered herself firmly down onto Della so that the girls' breasts, tummies and thighs pressed tightly together. Almost immediately, Ginny felt Della's lips eagerly on hers and their mouths moved tenderly together in a long passionate kiss. Their soft, full feminine lips crushed hungrily together as their wet, trembling pink tongues mingled and explored the hot caverns of each other's mouths.

Della moaned, speaking into the closeness of Ginny's mouth, "Now it's my turn to feel you... I want to so much. Please let me!"

They broke for air and Della caressed Ginny's face with her cheek and then almost brazenly, reached down between Ginny's thighs to fondle the older girl's silken-haired cunt. Her fingers probed into the hot, narrow slit, feeling at the corners of the fleshy hole. Finally, two of them slid easily inwards, making Ginny squirm and groan lustfully in

her embrace.

Della thrust her fingers deeper and deeper into the pulsating cunt, while at the same time, her eager probing tongue poked itself into Ginny's ear and darted wetly around the tiny orifice. With hot excitement, Ginny swiftly lowered both her hands under Della's buttocks and began to finger both the puckered tightly pursed anus and the girl's tender burning cunt that lay a little further under the curve of her crotch. She dug furiously into both the tight narrow channels, causing Della to gasp with uncontrollable pleasure, as she began to work her fingers more rapidly in and out between her legs... steadily digging further, her fingers thrusting into her at a faster and faster pace.

Their mutual fondling continued with each of the women growing more and more frenzied until Ginny finally withdrew her fingers and took hold of Della's right vaginal lip. She started to squeeze the thick, moist flesh from top to bottom, pinching the fold and giving it the most thorough stimulation that Della had ever experienced.

With her last conscious action, Della kissed Ginny again, much more violently this time than before, and sucked on the girl's tongue with her full lips, making near hysterical moaning sounds at the back of her throat.

Suddenly, both girls gripped each other aggressively, rocking frantically together, Ginny and Della both realizing that they were about to reach their climax at the same time. Ginny's huge white breasts bounced and crushed down on Della's, her three fingers thrust harder than ever into the girl's cunt and darted in and out with a maddening rhythm, until they both shuddered and released their hot cum... spurting recklessly onto each other's fingers and down onto the soft cushions of the couch.

Della's body was exploding into a million tiny stars but she managed to keep her fingers tightly clasped down on Ginny's quivering buttocks, raising deep scratches on the flesh as she shook with the violence of her climax. Wanting to prolong it... wanting to go on and on so that she could keep this delicious feeling within her body forever.

Chapter 7

A few minutes before the two girls had worked up their hot passions to the great climatic peak, Steve had crept quietly into the studio, taking in the lewd scene with ice-cold anger in his eyes. But now when he saw Della watching him, Steve seemed to relax his forbidding countenance. He noticed that the new girl didn't appear to be very worried at his sudden appearance; in fact, she showed little loss of composure at all.

Ginny climbed to the floor and gave her brother a challenging stare, making no attempt to hide her nudity. Della rose from the couch and placed one arm across her breasts and the other over the soft hairy mound still throbbing between her thighs... more of a gesture of modesty than shame.

"Well, I see you two have got to know each other pretty fast," Steve commented wryly. He exchanged a knowing look at his sister and then relaxed his stance even more. "What do you think?" he asked his sister. "Is she suitable for our work?"

"Oh, yes!" Ginny responded eagerly. "There's no doubt about it." She placed her arm possessively around Della's shoulder, carelessly letting her hand rest on the upper swell of the girl's right breast.

Watching the stimulating scene, Steve felt his penis slowly rising uncomfortably within the tight confines of his pants. Della moved nearer to Ginny, feeling the older girl's hand now slipping further down her chest and encompassing the ripe globe of her breast, and stared back at Steve. Her eyes looked openly at the swell in his trousers where his cock was still stiffening... then she spoke to him for the first time, her voice still breathless from her sexual encounter with Ginny.

"I'm ready to begin posing right now if you want me to," she told him demurely. "What would you like me to do first?"

"Ginny will take you into the dressing room while I set up the equipment," he said, still amazed at the young girl's composure. He turned away from her then, busying himself by checking the cameras and lighting stands. Ginny took Della's hand and walked with her to the small room at the back. It contained nothing but a huge double closet and a separate, full-length mirror.

Ginny pulled the closet door open and revealed to Della a large selection of bras, panties and silk stockings, all hanging neatly in a variety of sizes and colours. She rummaged quickly through the stack of underclothes.

"Let me pick you out something special," she said, finally bringing out a black bra with a pair of almost transparent cups, a white garter belt, and the tiniest pair of pale blue bikini panties that Della had ever seen. They consisted of nothing more than a wispy vee of material at the crotch and black strings which fitted below the hips to hold the flimsy garment in place.

After Ginny had assisted Della into her costume, she led the girl back into the studio. Steve looked up from his camera and gave a low, breathless whistle, studying every line of Della's body, every curve and crevice of her form. He could feel his cock twitch nervously up against his tight crotch to another stiff erection, though he was able to keep his voice steady when he finally spoke again.

"OK. Della," he said. "If you'll just stand there against the backdrop with your legs slightly apart and your hands on your hips, I'll take a rear view of you." He looked through the viewfinder of his Polaroid camera and adjusted the focus. Then, walking over to Della, he lifted her head around so that she was looking pertly over her shoulder. Still not completely satisfied, he bent and lifted the lacy edge of her panties a little higher over her buttocks, letting her soft flesh there spill even more generously out of the briefs.

Steve moved back to the camera and pressed the button and then, waiting a minute, he pulled the finished print out of the back and scanned it briefly with a professional eye.

"Very nice," he commented. "Come over here and see, Ginny."

Ginny walked over to him and looked at the photo, raising her eyebrows in approval.

"You've really got a natural talent for posing, Della," Steve told her. He whispered secretly into his sister's ear for a few moments... but Della was unable to catch any of his remarks. When he had finished, she saw Ginny nod in agreement... and then Steve finally informed her that he wanted Ginny to film a special movie with him posing as an underwear salesman and Della as the young innocent customer.

Della agreed and within five minutes, they had arranged the dazzling spotlights over the "area of action" and Ginny was installed behind a 16 mm Bolex, trying out the zoom lens so that she could be certain not to miss any detail of the pair's intimate movements.

The camera started to whir, and Della began to play out her role perfectly, adopting just the right mixture of pretty demure artlessness that excited Steve and Ginny's jaded lust so strongly. For the role, Della had changed into another costume and looked sweetly pert in a schoolgirl's uniform of black and white, her short skirt nearly revealing the tops of her jet-black stockings.

Steve showed her a brassiere and she put her head coyly to one side, looking at it as if she couldn't quite make up her mind on a purchase. He spread his hands, indicating that she really ought to be measured before buying so important a garment... and Della nodded her head, turning around so that he could help her to unfasten her blouse.

Delicately, Steve unhooked her bra and placed it on the counter. He slipped both of his hands under her arms and closed his fingers around the bare breasts which the young girl was now offering him for measurement.

Ginny zoomed in for a close-up of her brother's hands as they massaged Della's round, full bosom, then zoomed out again to include the picture of the two of them... Della's eyes closing in pleasure as she received a prolonged and determined breast fondling.

When he had finished his sensuous massaging, Steve reached over and picked up a pair of lacy panties which lay on the counter and then offered them for the girl's inspection. Della put one finger pensively to her mouth then looked from him to the panties, and then back again. Pointing to the panties, she made it clear by a skilful piece of mimicking that she wanted Steve to try them on himself in order that she could judge the effect!

At first, Steve pretended to be completely shocked at this weird and indecent suggestion, but Della indicated plainly that unless he did as she requested she would leave the shop without buying anything. With a helpless shrug, he unzipped his trousers and lowered them to the floor. He stepped out of them, slid down the pants, and allowed the inquisitive girl a long view of his stiffening penis.

His rigid shaft stuck proudly in the air and Della, with girlish glee, urged him to draw on the tiny panties which he had offered her.

Obediently, he started to pull them up his legs and managed to get them as far as his thighs. Here, the tight, silky panties stoutly refused to be drawn over Steve's bulging penis. Try as he might, he was unable to stretch them so that they covered his fleshy manhood.

Della helpfully joined in the struggle, seizing Steve's cock and squashing it first this way and then the other, trying to jam it into the V-shaped base of the panties. She managed it at last, thrusting the hard, excited weapon within the confines of the flimsy material by holding his cock with one hand and pulling the waistband of the panties wide with the other. It surged violently outwards under its strange bondage, straining the silk to the breaking-point. With this task finally accomplished, Della forced her "salesman" to sit down while she delicately peeled off her own panties seductively down almost to her thighs, pausing when the elastic top clung just below her pubic region.

She moaned and covered the hairy treasure with her hand, massaging the mound and the outer lips while Steve watched with lust-crazed eyes. A few long moments of this torture lasted, and then the girl finally relented. She quickly tugged her pants right off her graceful limbs and stood posed sexily in front of him, dressed in nothing but her garter belt and black, nylon stockings!

Drawing Steve once more to his feet, Della hugged him firmly against her, squashing her bare tummy tightly against his penis, rubbing herself back and forth in slow rotations to get his cock as hot as possible... caressing her hard crotch into Steve's tightly-constrained cock. Then, taking his hands in hers, she moved them around her waist and laid them firmly on the plump cheeks of her buttocks.

Ginny crouched down and filmed in intimate close-up the sight of her brother's hands rubbing wildly over the globes which she herself had massaged into orgasm so recently. He pinched and pulled at her young, firm flesh, passing his fingers into the crack between the twin mounds of luscious softness and dipping their tips against the brown, damp anus which was now exposed so shamelessly for the camera's steady stare.

Della slid slowly to the floor in front of Steve as Ginny panned the camera round to get a side view of the passionate lovemaking. Kneeling in front of Steve, Della bit steadily into the elastic thread running around the tops of the panties which still imprisoned his bulging manhood. She held his hips to steady herself and began to tug the panties down with her sharp teeth, forcing them once more over his gigantic tool until it sprang free... quivering ecstatically along the whole of its length.

It stuck out just above Della's ready lips and, quickly pulling the panties down Steve's legs, she sucked the large, blood-filled head and three inches of his penis into her mouth, sucking long and hard at its juicy red thickness.

The two now began a fierce battle over Steve's climax. He wanted to delay his orgasm until he had fucked the hot opening between her thighs, while she wanted nothing more than to swallow his thick hot cum. She wanted to have his sperm wash like a hot, bubbling spring in her mouth and to feel between her teeth that final leap that she knew his cock would give before it shuddered helplessly and flooded her lips with its warm white liquid.

With amazing self-control Steve finally won the intense contest, forcing himself not to shoot off and tiring Della down with the rocking pulse of his beat. Della went limp as Steve's penis withdrew from her mouth, and he sank to the floor, pulling her wildly with him. She was still wearing her garter belt and black stockings, and as Steve rolled over the top of her, their practically naked bodies heaving together, Ginny's hands trembled in her lustful excitement. The sight of the girl's intimate garments roused her steadily and it was all she could do to hold the camera steady while it recorded the scene.

Della's pink, wet tongue pushed between Steve's teeth and licked quickly all round the inside of his mouth before joining his own tongue in a tingling, breathless French kiss. His hands had found her soft, quivering buttocks again and while he renewed his massaging of her luscious mounds, Della gradually slipped both her hands between their bodies and ran her fingertips up and down the man's throbbing penis, delighting as the round, hard skin jumped and twitched at her persuading touch.

They opened their eyes, staring at each other with unspeakable hunger. Then Della smiled sweetly into Steve's tense face and with deliberate slowness started to rub his penis firmly in her hands... rolling it round and at the same time levering it nearer and nearer to her eager, pulsating cunt, now gaping open between her parted thighs, waiting to be filled with his lengthy, rigid shaft.

Ginny quickly saw what she was doing, and moved around behind the lovers to lay on the floor and film between their legs just as Della started to bring his inflamed penis to the soft opening between her thighs. The tip of Steve's cock slowly parted the pubic hair and at last slid between the lips of Della's wide and willing pussy, guided safely to its destination by the girl's fondling fingers. They paused for a low suspenseful kiss at the very moment of its insertion, the camera grinding methodically away recording it all.

Then Della cried out, her voice throaty with longing and desire, her lips wet against Steve's neck.

"Give it to me again, darling! Give it to me now! Get it right up inside me, as high as you can! Please... please... Steve! Don't make me wait... ah, yes! Oh, yes, my baby! YES!"

He had gripped her shoulders, wriggled around to make sure that his cock was in exactly the right position, then lunged long and deep into Della's cunt. The girl raised her buttocks off the floor to receive as fully as possible the tight-fitting and relentlessly pushing weapon that surged up and up into her... until her lust-dilating inner muscles felt completely blocked by its huge thickness.

When he was inside her to his limit and could feel his pubic hairs and her mound of soft moist curls mingling together, Steve twisted his cock round in rhythmical jerks, making her moan with pleasure as his rubbery tool jiggled along the fleshy wet walls of her cunt.

By this time it was almost impossible for Ginny to obtain any more movie shots of them. Their bodies were too tightly squashed together. Instead, she left her position at the camera and lay on the floor, very close to the lewdly fucking couple, her fingers exploring the interesting recesses of her own quivering vagina.

Steve continued to heave his penis in and out of Della's giving loins, at first slowly... then with an ever-increasing speed, until his cock was fucking the girl at such a furious rate that Della's head spun and her senses reeled. He paused several times, fearful that he would reach his climax too quickly, but as soon as he had controlled the flow of his hot sperm, he returned to the attack with renewed vigour.

Ginny, whose jealousy had been aroused by the inactive part she was now playing, suddenly had an idea. With a cry of glee, she stood up and seized Della's twitching legs by the ankles; pulling firmly at them, yanking the stockinged limbs back and forth and rubbing the sole of Della's left foot against the hotness of her exposed burning cunt.

Steve quickly understood what his sister was doing. He stopped fucking the girl for a moment, raised himself as best he could from the floor by propping the weight of his body with his hands, and lay quite still with his cock imbedded to the hilt deep inside Della's hot, pulsating channel.

Ginny then started to pull the girl's legs backwards and forwards, in and out of Steve's straining penis. Della was a little frightened at first by this new development, but she quickly learned to relax and the two girls were soon engaged in a furious tug-of-war... with Della holding tightly to Steve's neck while Ginny pretended to try and pull her off.

This rough, pulling movement caused Della's hot mucous to jet thickly down her stocking-clad thighs and thoroughly lubricate Steve's already wet cock. Under the stimulus of the girl's climax, Steve got his hands up to her breasts again and rubbed his fingers intently across the red nipples, then slowly and firmly gripped each nipple between his thumb and forefinger and pulled them away from Della's breasts until they stood out... thick and unresisting.

At the same time, Della brought her hands down from his neck and began to fondle at Steve's nipples herself, wishing to share in the sharp mixture of pain and pleasure she was now receiving. She manipulated them in exactly the same way as he was fondling hers, pinching them mercilessly up to the limit they would stretch, then twisting the tiny naked balls round and round between her fingers...

Steve could no longer control himself as the young girl drove him closer and closer to orgasm by her unrelenting and passionate caresses. With a low moan, he let the long-delayed orgasm throb unrestrainedly through his shaking body... and then with a piercing cry, emptied deep into Della's straining cunt every ounce of thick white sperm that he could force out, thrusting his shaft forward in frantic spasms to rid himself gradually of the hot sticky liquid.

Della wrenched forward against his hard body, receiving his driving rod with wide-open thighs as he emitted the last of his searing juice deep within the confines of her womb, completely soaking her now deepened channel until it was wet and overflowing.

"Oh... fill me, fill me, darling," she groaned, not wanting the delicious sensations within her body to end. The hot walls of her jerking cunt sucked at the throbbing cock hungrily, until it gave one final spasmodic jerk, the last drop sucked from it.

Steve collapsed across her body, feeling her insides still gushing forth around his deflated limp prick. It seemed endless, until she too suddenly gave one last jerk and quivered to a limp stillness, her legs protruding lifelessly out on either side of his fatigued body. Her arms outstretched and relaxed, her belly filled to the bursting point with the mixture of their hot sticky-white cum.

Della was hardly able to keep her eyes open now as Steve slowly and reluctantly lifted his heavy weight from her with a deep sigh. All at once, the exertions of the morning seemed to pile up and overcome her. At the moment, all she wanted was somewhere nice and soft to lie her head and her aching body and drift pleasantly off to sleep.

"Poor darling," Ginny sighed. "You look so very tired. Come on, let me take you upstairs... there's a comfortable bed where you can rest and relax. Up we come!"

And she half-lifted the drowsy Della and helped her up the spiral stairway to the promised bedroom. Della, feeling drugged and completely satiated, was scarcely aware of the trip; she sank gratefully between the crisp sheets and was sound sleep almost before her pretty head had touched the pillow.

Chapter 8

Danny was worried and angry. He was anxious about Della and annoyed with himself because he hadn't taken a firmer stand with the girl over her visit to the studio. He realized that it really wasn't any of his business as to how the girl conducted her life. But that didn't stop him from worrying over her. He found after seeing her again that Della was much more to him than just another brief affair... maybe even more than he wanted to admit to himself right now.

He pulled his car into the circular driveway that led to Steve and Ginny's house, then paused to double check the address that he had copied from the phonebook. When he approached the house and noticed the blinds drawn at the upstairs window, Danny had guessed earlier that he might be too late to prevent Della from falling into Steve and Ginny's clutches.

The darkened window at two in the afternoon, together with his previous knowledge of the couple's well-known reputation, increased his anxiety over Della's safety. He opened the car door and stepped out, being careful not to slam it and draw their attention to his arrival, though he was certain they were probably already engaged in Della's seduction.

He entered the house carefully through an unlocked ground-floor window and quietly made his way up the winding staircase that led to the master bedroom, hoping against hope that he would not be too late to help the girl. He wasn't sure of exactly what his actions would finally be when he confronted the brother and sister. At the moment, his only thought was to somehow rescue the young girl and take her far away from Steve and Ginny and the rest of the wild people she had somehow gotten involved with in these last months.

When he got to the top of the stairs, he noticed that there were three doors on the second level and he wasn't sure which one was the master bedroom. Suddenly a small, muffled moan came from behind the middle door... he quietly made his way to it noticing that the door was slightly ajar...

* * *

Less than an hour before Danny's arrival, Della had awakened from a deep sleep to find Ginny standing by the dressing table drawer, her hand clutching a strong-looking rubber phallus with a determined look in her eyes. She stared in speechless wonderment as Steve helped her to don the artificial cock, slipping its thick straps between her crotch and knotting it tightly around her hips. The monstrous length bobbled in the air as Ginny came back to where Della was lying naked and gripped her new artificial growth proudly.

"Isn't it beautiful?" she asked the girl. "Doesn't it give you a thrill to see me wearing such a thing?" She smiled evilly down at the quivering girl beneath her, then added in a low whisper... "And in just a few moments, I'm going to push it right up into your tight little cunt."

Della trembled. "It's too big," she said in a small, frightened voice. It'll split me open,

Ginny… it won't go in!"

Ginny smiled at her. "It may surprise you to know that I've satisfied many younger girls just like yourself with this wonderful instrument." She touched the tip of the weapon and ran her fingers majestically along its thick, wicked-looking span.

Then Steve helped to hoist her onto the contraption, fitting her dildo carefully between Della's thighs. Her hands slipped beneath the girl's buttocks and, fondling her fingers into the divide, Ginny felt for Della's inflamed sex lips. They were already pulled apart by the position of her spread-eagled legs, and Ginny, fitting her thumbs firmly into the gash, easily stretched the flesh-folds to their widest opening.

She wriggled her hips until the huge phallus' pointed head moved into Della's outer lips, then skilfully transferred her fingers to it and began to push the hardened rubber shaft deeper and deeper into the girl's straining hot channel. Ginny surged forward, making the dildo penetrate to its hilt, ignoring the frantic cries which Della made, pleading and begging at first for the older girl to stop the torturous exercise. The pain which Della had suffered when the shaft was sunk the first two inches was almost unbearable; she writhed in exquisite agony, but was unable to prevent a sudden secretion of soft, slippery cum from oozing out of her cunt and lubricating Ginny's artificial cock.

Though she needed no encouragement, Ginny seemed to be spurred on by the milky fluid that Della had expelled. Some of it trickled onto her fingers and when she felt its juicy moistness, she redoubled her efforts... fucking harder and harder at the gradually enlarging hole beneath her.

The cord which attached her dildo to her loins was digging thrillingly into her own sex, and Ginny felt her own cunt begin to flow softly as she let her mind take on the fantasy that she was truly a man... that she did possess this vibrant penis... that it was made of flesh and blood! And now that it was bulging deeply within Della's vagina, Ginny's passion mounted to the point where she could no longer distinguish between her body and the girl's.

Steve, meanwhile, had lifted himself up onto the bed behind Della's head and was lowering his body down so that his stiffened cock rubbed against Della's mouth. Ginny made room for her brother, twisting herself sideways on top of the girl; her head and shoulders hanging over the side of the bed.

Steve moved his hands onto Della's quivering, white breasts and fondling almost angrily at the melons, crouched with his knees on either side of the girl's face. He rested his head on Ginny's contracting buttocks, his arms tucked beneath his body.

Almost beside herself now with horror and ecstasy at this bizarre method of coupling, Della... the crushing weight of Steve's loins almost suffocating her... opened her mouth to gasp air... and automatically began to work her lips against the soft cotton of his shorts in order to breathe. She could feel the man's prick straining beneath the thin material that was barely able to keep his hardening organ within its tightly stretched confines, and Della suddenly realized that her lips were deriving pleasure from grazing against the delicious pressure.

Perhaps it was the knowledge that she had been so humiliated by the couple, and had traveled so close to the insane limits of sexual pleasure under their tuition, that nothing mattered any more. She could now with her newfound freedom, obtain a sensual satisfaction from almost any source of stimulation.

Her mind began splitting off into two directions now: one yearning for complete domination from Steve, the other observing from a distance, her masochistic suffering, plunging her loins now in rhythm against the artificial cock with abandoned pleasure, as a series of white-hot climatic explosions, began to explode throughout her body.

She was still arching her cunt up into Ginny's dildo when the door crashed open and Danny Ritter hurtled into the room... a cry of disgust and anger wrenched from his lips as his eyes met the perverted and obscenely degrading scene before him. Faced with the lewd sight of Ginny and Steve huddled like parasites over Della's helpless and vulnerable nudity, he wanted to play the role of the avenging angel with every fibre of his being.

A wave of sickening nausea spread from his stomach into his mouth, leaving a vile taste on his tongue. Yet he stood before them transfixed, unable to take the first essential steps, completely entranced at first by the naked sensuality of the group before him.

The brother stood up and slowly removed the curious contraption from Ginny's luscious hips and advanced angrily towards him, only stopping when he was a few paces distant. Ginny's hand had gone to her mouth... the girl's body rolling off Della's until Danny could see the wet appendage that stuck out from her loins.

"What the hell do you think you're doing?" Steve demanded. "This is private property... Get out of here this instant! Go on!" he screamed. "Before I call the police!"

Danny stared at him, his violent rage suddenly crumpling before the ridiculous spectacle. Beneath his tight flimsy underwear, Steve's prick was straining fiercely upwards, and right now he looked more of a pitiful, than a menacing sight to him. Danny's shoulders shook a little; he was unable to suppress a muffled chuckle at the ludicrous vision.

Steve came a step nearer. His whole body had started to tremble with fury.

"Will you get out of here?" he yelled, his face terribly contorted. "Get out! Get out!"

Danny ignored him completely. He felt oddly detached from the whole situation... as if it was too farcical to be taken seriously. And yet... And yet something within him responded to the undercurrent of perverse sexuality that pervaded the room. He remained motionless, his eyes riveted to the sight of Della's still lewdly spread-eagled and perspiring body. A thought persisted in spinning round and round his mind – you don't really hate this kind of thing at all... you could just as easily be in Steve's place if you weren't so afraid of your secret desires!

Ginny had jumped off the bed and stepped quickly to her brother's side, holding Steve's arm tightly.

"Let me handle this," she told him quietly. Then she turned to Danny, "What are you doing here? What do you want from us?"

Before he could reply, Della's voice broke in. "He's a friend of mine, Ginny! Don't spoil everything for me, Danny… please don't! I'm perfectly all right… why don't you just go away and forget what you've seen here?"

Danny was dimly aware that his entire attitude, both towards Steve, Ginny and Della and towards his feelings about their setup was being quickly changed, coloured and mysteriously changed by forces he could only faintly recognize.

He heard his voice shatter the sudden hush that had fallen between them.

"I'll make a deal with you… Let me join in and I won't take any action against you! And you both know that I could do plenty to ruin your nice little house parties. I don't think I have to elaborate. A word dropped in a few ears…"

While he was speaking, Danny kept his eyes on Della. The girl had now relapsed into her state of sensual stupor, and she made no sign that she had understood the tenor of his voice; or even that she had heard him at all. Out of the corner of his eyes, he saw that Ginny had drawn Steve aside and was whispering urgently in her brother's ear. He waited, confident of their answer to his request. It was a relatively small thing he was asking; and they scarcely had a choice in the matter, he thought, keeping his mind cold and calculating, though a part of his brain was already trying to rationalize his decision.

If he participated in their orgy, he told himself, he might be able to show Della that their sickness was truly contagious, and that they would have to join forces to free themselves of the couple's influence. Beyond that, he tried to freeze his mind shut and was unwilling to probe farther into his consciousness. The far more profound, unconscious motivation which were operating to cause his abrupt decision would have to be thought over another time.

As Steve and Ginny turned back to face him, he realized that the palms of his hands were wet and nervous with anticipation, it was already far too late for him to change his mind now.

* * *

Della was lazily stretched out on the bed before them, her eyes closed as if they were too heavy for her to keep them open, and her legs spread wide apart, undulating her body up at them in complete abandonment. Danny hurriedly stripped to his underpants and his prick was growing hot and stiff as he gazed upon her stimulating movements. There was no longer any room in his heart for compassion. At the moment Della represented to him nothing more than an object on which he could vent his rising lust.

"I can see you're ready to begin," Ginny commented drily. Her eyes lifted slowly from Danny's growing bulge and stared into his face.

Ginny re-donned her huge, menacing dildo, and Danny couldn't help staring at it with open curiosity. She caressed the rubber instrument, noting his interest.

"Don't pretend you're disgusted," she said softly. "Not any more... You're really intrigued, aren't you? You're wondering what it's like to feel something this large inside of you..." She moved her body until the tip of the rubber shaft brushed against Danny's thigh. "Maybe I'll give you a nice surprise later on..."

Her sensuous words made his cock leap involuntarily inside his pants, his brain afire with sudden heat. Before Ginny could say any more, he pulled his shorts off, dragging them savagely down his legs.

"Very powerful!" Ginny whispered approvingly. She rubbed her dildo meaningfully back and forth until it touched the throbbing swollen knob at the tip of his penis. He tensed his body as he watched Steve wriggle himself beneath Della's back, almost completely covering his nudeness from their sight under the girl's body. She offered no resistance, and he began working his hands around her buttocks, stretching the soft pliant cheeks wide apart and then sliding downwards on the bed to manipulate his cock up between the hot, deeply creased valley.

Steve gripped his lengthened shaft with one hand, while trying to keep Della's buttocks spread apart with the other. Her tight elastic anus was already well lubricated by the wetness of her last orgasm and it required only a little patience and effort for Steve to work his penis well into the beautifully snug orifice.

His hands came around to the girl's hips and he began to thrust them downwards, at the same time urging his own loins up until he felt the entire length of his rigid tool slip slowly past her tight anal ring into the larger space of her rectum.

"Come and fuck me, Danny!" Della cried, suddenly coming to life as Steve's long, hard penis penetrated her anus, impaling her like so much meat on a skewer. "Look... I'm so helpless, I can't move an inch! You could do anything you wanted with me... I couldn't stop you!"

Danny, his throat dry, the saliva refusing to flow, moved to the bed, seeing from between Della's wide-open thighs Steve's hard, thick cock as it pulsed stiffly in and out of the girl's anus. The sensation of moving in slow motion through a dream suddenly left him. He flung himself down on top of Della's body, his mouth hungrily seeking hers, his hands reaching for her large pulsating breasts.

"I'm helpless!" she whispered against his lips. "So terribly helpless! Fuck me, darling... fuck me while I'm unable to stop you!"

He ran his hands from her tits to her shoulders, felt the flesh in rough and urgent caresses, thrust them back to her breasts again, then roamed his fingers all over the front of her body, pressing them finally into the inside of her thighs. His cock was already rubbing against Della's clitoris... pressing hard into her fully-distended vaginal slit, and he fumbled it down slowly until he could feel it sinking wonderfully into the girl's soft, wet pussy between her wide-spread legs.

He buried his hard shaft deeply inside her belly and he could feel every side of his instrument touch hard against her inner muscles, while at the same time Steve continued to pump up into her from behind. Together, the two men screwed into the young girl's yielding body, raging their pricks furiously in and out of her cunt and anus, sandwiching her between their bodies and fondling insatiably at her flesh.

The thought that had been growing steadily in Della's foggy mind for the last few minutes now burst into full flower; she was purely an instrument of pleasure for the male sex! She had no purpose in life other than to act as a captive slave for their lust! And this

fate seemed to her a truly satisfying one. It meant that she had relinquished her free will, abandoned her moral and physical freedom completely.

The excitement that this strange yet profound emotion generated within the girl was intense. Della gave herself up to it with the melting sensation of surrender coursing through her veins. She kept her cunt and anal muscles totally relaxed, letting Danny and Steve fuck her most private orifices and do with her whatever they wanted to do.

Seeing the three of them in such a thrilling and uninhibited coupling, Ginny felt her cunt juices beginning to flow again. She fingered her dildo, wondering how she was going to pry her way between them and have a portion of the girl for herself. Then she had a brilliant idea. Of course! There was no need for her to separate them at all, even if such a thing were possible!

Ginny then remembered her vague promise to Danny, and reached out for the large jar of Vaseline which lay on the dressing table, smearing the greasy ointment liberally over the length of her phallus. Then, moving as carefully and quietly as possible, the girl knelt between Danny's out-flung thighs. He was lying with his legs on top of Della's... his buttock muscles twitching wildly as he rammed his prick in and out of her cunt.

Ginny caressed the cheeks of his buttocks until she had opened the boy's behind, stretching it as fully apart as she could. With one hand gripping her dildo and the other stretching his left cheek apart, the girl adjusted her position so that the rubber head of her shaft was directed straight at the opening of his puckered anus.

Steadily, she began to insert the head of the huge, artificial cock into him, raking her fingernails firmly into the hollow when he tried to clench his muscles shut against it. He groaned and started to protest as Ginny eased the hard, thick rubber slightly into his anus. But his passion was too aroused to tear himself from the body of the girl writhing, lasciviously out of control between him and Steve. The delicious drag of her wet-walled pussy was far too exquisite for him to leave her for even one minute!

He groaned involuntarily as he felt the full thrust of the dildo digging into his anus, a staggering pain shooting through his intestines as the unfamiliar, much too thick intruder slipped into him all the way to its rubber hilt. His eyes misted and blurred, the hot tears filling them as he suffered the pain of having his anus almost ripped open by the tremendous phallus.

Slowly his inner muscles expanded giving room for the instrument to ease its way in and out of him in rhythmic movements and he realized through his heated passion that he was actually deriving a certain pleasure from its fucking into his wide-stretched anus.

The ultimate indignity of being fucked by a beautiful, naked young girl gradually ceased to possess any true meaning for him. The actual experience itself was so novel and beyond all the rules of normal sex patterns that he relaxed and began to regard it as something to be done and treated as nothing more than a bizarre and enjoyable experience.

The heavy weight of Ginny's ample breasts as they pushed into his back, just below the shoulders, was stimulating and exciting his senses to a higher peak. He could feel the girl's nipples ripe and stiff on his bare flesh, their round hardness rubbing as Ginny gripped him around the waist and writhed her body up and down. Her hands slipped lower until he could feel her fingers toying insistently with his prick as it fucked in and out of Della's cunt. Ginny fondled the rigid stem beautifully, tapping and caressing it until he was stimulated beyond all endurance.

The combination of Della's tight pussy, Ginny's perverted cramming of the dildo up his anus, and the itchy sensation of Steve's cock as it rubbed against his through the paper-thin sheath of Della's vagina, was suddenly too much for him.

The sounds of deep straining grunts and groans filled the hot stifling air of the room, mingling with the noise of sweat-soaked flesh smacking sharply against sweat-soaked flesh and the wet, viscous sound of his pile driving cock going in and out of Della's mucous-lined cunt. Danny began a sudden brutal ramming deep down inside her as he felt the hot, white cum building up inside his heated balls. He wildly shoved his tongue into her parted lips as he rammed his spewing cock all the way to the hilt in her soft unresisting cunt.

Her clitoris throbbed up against his shaft, its itchy, erotic pulsing on the boy's spurting organ sending Della into a delirious, swooning frenzy. Every atom of her body was seized by the new experience, shaken up and jolted into a state of excruciating ecstasy.

And now that Ginny felt the trio beneath her coursing through the final stages of their orgasms, she needed only to grip her dildo with one hand and draw its straps more tightly into her open cunt, the rough friction sending her entire body into a sharp climatic orgasm. Her cum started to soak the leather cord she loved so well, her open-lipped cunt spewing forth in a brilliant flash of orgasm she had never imagined could exist.

* * *

Afterwards, when his breath had returned to normal, Danny lay on the bed in a naked tangle of entwined limbs and flesh and began to wonder just what he was going to do about his relationship with Della.

For the moment, he felt too steeped in this den of evil to look at the problem objectively. If Della had been driven to the very brink of insanity by Steve and Ginny's manipulations, then he, too, was not so very far from the borderline. They had stirred impulses that he now wished with all his heart had remained dormant within his mind, locked safely away where they could do no harm in the depths of his unconscious.

He knew that he could never again enjoy a normal sexual experience after what he had just been through. He would always need the added stimulation of a third or fourth party to his lovemaking, and he would never be able to erase from his mind the picture of Della in the middle of it all: a helpless, sacrificial victim of their crude lusts.

He closed his eyes, and before his red-rimmed retina danced a succession of pornographic images... enticing, seductive, stimulating. Perhaps it was all a dream, a brief lapse into madness. When he reopened them the room would change into his own bedroom; Della, Ginny and Steve would all be gone.

The hope grew, and he held his breath, afraid to move, fearful of the least sound that would indicate the presence of his fellow orgiasts. He would count to five, then open his eyes. One... two... three... four...

The End

PUNISHMENT FOR CLAUDIA

Richard Steele

Prelude

Gestapo Headquarters,
Avenue Foch, Paris, 1943

Nineteen year-old Yvette Leblanc envied the confidence that seemed to emanate from the strong, shapely young woman who shared her cell. When the Gestapo had picked up Yvette that morning, she had feared the worst, for they had found her without the appropriate papers in an area where she had no right to be. Her cellmate, Milena, who had only the lightest of accents when she spoke French, told her that she came originally from Czechoslovakia and was being held by the Germans on similar charges. They had spent the day together, sitting side by side on the small cot with its thin mattress, whispering, confiding.

Towards the evening, a dim electric light was switched on, and Milena placed a protective arm around the young girl's slim shoulders.

"There's nothing to worry about, you'll see – we'll be out of here in a day or two."

Less certain of their fate, Yvette became tearful, and Milena hugged her fellow prisoner to her firm, generous bosom, covering her face with soothing little kisses. Then she kissed her mouth – at first with only the lightest pressure – but gradually becoming more insistent and finally slipping out her tongue and tracing a wet line between Yvette's lips. The French girl's eyes widened in wonder, then half-closed as she returned the compliment with grateful ardour, gliding her tongue over Milena's in a full, open-mouthed kiss.

"It's late. Let's take off our clothes and get into bed, *chérie*. It'll be more fun like that, more... cosy."

Colonel Stahler looked through the one-way window disguised as a mirror into the small cell where two young girls sat together on the bed. They were nearly naked now. The French girl was clad only in her cream-coloured knickers, her slim figure and small, pert breasts in contrast to her companion's voluptuous curves. There was no getting away from it – both the girls were pretty. Very pretty indeed. He sighed.

All part of the training, he thought to himself, bitterly. All perfectly justifiable in the name of the Third Reich and the glorious Fatherland. He shook his head. It seemed to be getting out of control. Training young, highborn German girls to behave in such a decadent and debauched way just to ensnare the enemy. lesbian entrapment! Is this what the secret service has come to? True, these were dark days that required desperate measures. All the same, he could remember when spying had more to do with low-profile, subtle gathering of intelligence, not the sort of sleazy tricks they were asking him to teach his agents now.

He stared through the pane of glass that separated him from the two girls who had taken off their last undergarments. Naked, they kissed and stroked and touched one another without inhibition. Milena took the initiative and Yvette soon reciprocated, writhing passionately under the sensuous caresses of her new friend. He had to admit, his latest girl was very good. Her hand was between the young Resistance girl's thighs, delving, probing, gently rubbing the wet slit of her sex. Yvette raised herself up on her elbows but Milena pushed her back down, spreading her thighs wide and ducking her head down between them. Her skilful tongue lapped at the tiny bud of Yvette's clitoris. Stahler felt himself getting hard. She had reduced the French prisoner to a whimpering, moaning wreck in almost no time at all. There was something almost predatory about her, he thought, and guiltily, he found it arousing.

Milena continued to pleasure the inexperienced French Resistance agent with her lips and tongue, her hands roaming all the while over her pert, responsive little breasts, squeezing the enlarged nipples so that they stood stiff and proud. Soon her whole body became rigid and shook with strong, orgasmic convulsions. Secretly, Milena smiled to herself. Now it would be easy.

Later that night, Yvette told her all that she knew about her local branch of the Resistance, under the foolish illusion that she was recruiting a new worker for the cause.

Early next morning, when Stahler entered the cell to collect 'Milena', both girls were dressed.

"You," he said, pointing at Yvette, "stay here. You, come with me."

Outside his girl relayed to him the names and addresses that Yvette had so thoughtfully supplied.

"What do you think we should do with her?" asked Stahler, jerking his head back at the cell.

"She's worthless," said the unscrupulous young spy in flawless, aristocratic, German. "You can take her into the yard and shoot her. Really – she is no longer of any use to us."

The older intelligence officer didn't know whether to be impressed or appalled. Such ruthlessness in one so young! He hunched his shoulders uneasily and shuddered. Fortunately for Yvette, others would decide her fate.

Chapter 1

"Claudia von Reichsapfel reporting for punishment, Sir!"

The words came out slowly and with obvious effort, and it was readily apparent that the attractive teenager who uttered them was having great difficulty retaining her composure.

Seated behind his oversize leather and mahogany desk, the Headmaster of St Mary's School for Girls did not at first look up from the report he was reading. The office of the chief administrative executive of the exclusive girl's school located in the north of England was quite austere and not calculated to ease the anxiety of the miscreants who were regularly required to report there for discipline. At the moment, the only relief came from a partially opened window, through which drifted a warm breeze that served as a reminder that the spring of 1939 had been one of the most pleasant in years.

"Mr. Blake..." The girl's words trailed off in despair. The comely eighteen-year-old knew that the wait was deliberate, and designed to increase her apprehension as well as humiliate her. Her hands clutched nervously behind her back, she could barely stand still. Her dark blue eyes constantly darted around the room, anxiously searching for that whippy, pencil-thin cane that she dreaded so much. For some reason which she did not comprehend, the hateful instrument was nowhere in sight. Normally, it was prominently on display.

At last, Don Blake set aside the report and looked up at the obviously troubled teenager who stood in front of him. A hasty glance satisfied him that she had complied with the academy rule that required all girls to report for punishment attired in their full school uniform. This consisted of white blouse, a discreet tartan tie, pleated black gymslip or pinafore held in at the waist by a red sash tied at the wearer's left, black stockings, and three-inch spike heel black patent leather pumps with straps from behind the ankle tied in a bow in front.

The schoolgirl uniform did not conceal the fact that Claudia possessed a highly promising figure, buxom and shapely. Her long blonde hair, tied in two pigtails, hung nearly to her waist in back, and the juvenile style required by school rules looked quite incongruous when compared with the obvious fullness of her ripe breasts, which pressed proudly outward against the top of her gymslip. Enhanced by her black stockings and elegant footwear, her shapely legs and highly arched feet looked absolutely stunning. Her gymslip was hemmed to end a full six inches above her knees, because the archaic and absurd school rules were designed to make the girls feel juvenile and this was supposedly accomplished by requiring them to wear styles associated with young girls.

But as Claudia and numerous other girls had discovered, the ridiculously short school skirts could create effects quite unintended by their sponsors. For, as the girls had learned, some to their embarrassment and others to their intense delight, the combination of short skirts, black stocking tops and milk white thighs was completely mesmerizing to the masculine eye. By flashing her white thighs, contrasting vividly with her black stocking tops and garter belt, a girl could usually get exactly what she wanted from the opposite sex.

"So we meet again, Claudia!" Mr. Blake finally spoke. The statement had its obvious implications, and their eyes met with understanding.

"Please, Don..." Claudia spoke hastily, using a form of address that no other girl in the school would have dared employ.

The Headmaster put up his hand in a manner that indicated that such familiarity was forbidden, at least at this stage of the proceedings. Her face hotly flushed, Claudia made no further attempt to speak and lowered her eyes demurely.

Don picked up the registration form that contained Claudia's vital statistics, and read parts of it aloud: "Claudia von Reichsapfel. Born 1921. Native of Hannover, Germany. Father, an importer currently working in London. Speaks English and French fluently."

With a shrug, he tossed the form back on his desk. "Let's face it, Claudia," he said quietly. "With the state of the world being what it is, you'll go back to Germany this summer and that will be the last we'll see of each other. So this will probably be the last time you will report to me for... punishment." He hesitated slightly before pronouncing the last word, as if it were not really adequate to describe what was to transpire between them.

"Please, Don, couldn't we just skip the punishment part of it?" Claudia spoke with obvious distress. "Let me... You know what I like to do for you!"

The Headmaster feigned amused indifference to the young girl's statement. "That's surprising," he remarked with the slightest tinge of sarcasm in his voice. "Particularly considering the offence for which you have been sent here!"

Claudia's face coloured visibly at the reference to her misdeed. Don reached into his desk drawer and pulled out a confidential and quite detailed report from one of the instructresses regarding a lesbian incident involving Claudia and another girl. The two of them had been caught in the ultimate lesbian embrace, which the Victorian minded authoress of the report had described in highly critical terms but with what might appear to be an unnecessary attention to detail.

"Their knickers were completely removed," Don read aloud from the report. "Their pinafores were rolled up above the waist. They were still wearing their garter belts and stockings. The two of them were simultaneously performing a contemptible act with their mouths and tongues, in a pose that they tell me is described as the 'French' position. Both of them were displaying a great deal of emotion."

Claudia wriggled with girlish shame as the details of her misconduct were read out.

"Claudia, I must say that I'm shocked to get this type of report about you, of all people," Don remarked as he set the report down.

"I'm not a lesbian," Claudia defended herself heatedly. "And you know it! It's just that... around here there aren't many boys, and a girl gets... gets itchy!"

"Yes, of course," Don replied dryly. "Your fellow miscreant has already been punished," he added. "Six of the best!"

His mind flashed back to the incident, which had occurred only an hour before. Attired in a uniform that exactly matched the one that Claudia was wearing, the hapless culprit had been obliged to bend over a straight chair until her rounded bottom was higher than the rest of her body. Don prepared her himself, slowly lifting the hem of her gymslip to reveal the enticing combination of black stocking tops, white thighs, black garter belt and lush feminine bottom encased in tightly stretched black knickers. He pulled the knickers down all the way to her ankles, catching a brief glimpse of her shockingly pink labia as the miserable girl attempted to hold her legs as closely together as possible, and allowing his fingers to brush momentarily against the bows of her high-heeled shoes.

The six cuts of the cane had been applied with deliberate slowness, the highly flexible cane cracking like a twig snapping each time it made contact with her tender feminine buttocks. Although the first application of the cane had produced a loud gasp, the stouthearted girl had managed to bear the correction in a relatively stoic manner. Tears were streaming down her eyes, however, when Don personally replaced her knickers for her and allowed her to depart.

"Not the cane!" Claudia pleaded, her

knees buckling slightly at the thought of that dreaded instrument.

"But for an offence of this type..." Don began.

"*Please!*" Claudia interrupted with great urgency. "Please! I'll do anything you like! You can degrade me any way you like! Please, but not the cane!" Her pretty face reflected the intense anxiety that she was experiencing.

Don slowly arose from behind his desk, and placed a straight wooden chair in the middle of the room. Her hands clasped prayerfully in front of her, Claudia watched the scene with growing alarm.

"Please, not the cane! Please! I can't stand it!" she implored, her voice occasionally cracking with emotion. "Please, I'll do anything! *Anything!*"

"Very well, Claudia," Don replied. "You may have a smacking instead of a cane, if you prefer. But in that case you must agree to accept some private, highly intimate punishment from me! Do you agree?"

"Yes!" the attractive eighteen-year-old answered almost too quickly. The sense of relief flowing through her body was quite apparent.

Don seated himself on the chair and motioned for her to approach him. Shamefaced and taking tiny, reluctant steps in her smart high-heeled pumps, Claudia advanced toward the Headmaster. Despite her eighteen years and mature, shapely figure, her demeanour suggested that of a very young girl about to receive a deserved spanking.

Taking her by the hand, Don gently but firmly pulled her face down across his lap. Nearly falling into position, Claudia lay with her palms on the floor to balance herself. Her gymslip rode up to reveal a generous amount of black stocking, and her knees were slightly bent. Knowing what was coming, she was scarlet with embarrassment.

Don reached down with both hands and, with great slowness, began raising the hem of her pleated black pinafore. Lush, tapering thighs, enhanced by black hosiery, came into view, followed by the heavier portions of her stockings. Then came milk white thighs, contrasting vividly with her black stockings and the black satin garter belt that held them up. The pinafore came up to the waist, slowly bringing into view formfitting black knickers that could barely contain her lovely and fully rounded buttocks.

With her stocking tops, bare thighs and black knickers on full display, Claudia was a picture of feminine embarrassment. Her face was a flaming scarlet and she kept her eyes tightly closed, as if that would blot out the shameful display she was making of herself.

Don paused for a moment to enjoy the breathtaking view, not missing a single detail as his eyes moved from the tips of her nicely shod feet to her blonde head. Both of them were aware of the erection that the display had already produced.

After a long pause, Don reached for the waistband of the young girl's lace-trimmed knickers. Claudia moaned and quivered with humiliation as she felt masculine hands committing the final indignity that would leave her totally bare and disgraced.

"Lift up a little, Claudia!" Don ordered her.

Haplessly, the attractive pupil lifted her hips an inch or so from his lap, and Don slowly pulled the knickers down. Claudia's breath-taking, perfect bottom flashed into view, a beautifully soft mixture of pink and white, and deliciously rounded. The pale contours were big – in a feminine sort of way – but far from being too big. Claudia trembled with humiliation and, as she did so, her pretty nates quivered like bowls of jelly. She remembered to hold her stockinged legs tightly together, for the moment at least, concealing her girlish treasure.

Don finished pulling the silken knickers down below the tops of her black stockings, and paused to enjoy an enthralled look at the lush and tender feminine buttocks that were just waiting to be disciplined. For a moment he thought about undoing her garters, but decided against it. The black garter belt and stockings perfectly framed her 'spank spot', and there was no reason to disturb such an intriguing picture. Claudia moaned and wriggled with girlish apprehension as Don clasped his left forearm and hand around her waist to hold her in position.

"You have lovely buttocks, Claudia!" he told her, knowing that the comment would embarrass rather than please her.

Don had no intention of rushing things. Slowly he raised his right hand and brought it down lightly upon her right buttock, leaving it in place right where it landed. Her youthful bottom felt velvety soft and resilient.

"Oooh!" Claudia's gasp reflected mortification rather than discomfort.

Don watched the pretty teenager shrivelling with embarrassment at the bare-on-bare contact. After a moment's pause, he raised his hand to observe the pretty pink spot that had suddenly appeared. Don applied the second slap to her right cheek, slightly lower down, and once again allowed his hand to remain in place for a moment afterward. The third smack landed slightly lower than the second. Don then repeated the procedure, this time making the smacks slightly more forceful.

"Oh! Oh!" Claudia gasped, her blonde

pigtails flying. "This is awful! Really, I'm too big for this!"

By this time the attractive pupil was a little breathless and her right buttock was a healthy shade of rose pink, which contrasted sharply with her still-unspanked and milky-white left cheek. After a moment's inspection, Don set about balancing up the colour scheme. Six carefully applied smacks to the left buttock and the task was completed. Claudia's lovely buttocks were a pretty pink all over, and the comely teenager was squirming with a mixture of embarrassment and discomfort.

After pausing a moment to admire his own handiwork, Don began the next series of slaps with a light slap just above the top of her right stocking. Claudia moaned and her right foot swung up momentarily. Don began working up her right thigh and bottom cheek with a light series of smacks, always allowing his hand to remain in place on the cringing feminine flesh beneath his palm. From there, he worked down the left side from her garter belt to the top of her stocking. By this time the entire area between her garter belt and stockings was a pretty shade of pink. He repeated the entire course again, working up, the right side and down the left.

"Please! Please!" Claudia pleaded. "Please stop! That's enough! Please don't humiliate me like this! Please, I'm eighteen!"

Once again Don's solid masculine palm traversed the course, working up one side and down the other. A distressed "Oh!" followed every smack, and her reddening buttocks began to squirm more and more over his lap despite her obvious efforts to control herself. Black patent leather pumps began swinging upward from time to time, and he knew there would soon come a time when she would no longer be able to hold those pretty legs together.

"Ouch! Oh, stop, please! Please!" Claudia pleaded, looking back anxiously over her shoulder. "Please, don't! It's so humiliating! Please, your bare hand on my... my bare... Please, it's too humiliating!"

Don paused once again to admire the scenery. From stocking tops to garter belt, Claudia's lush spank spot was a bright scarlet. She was wriggling miserably, her full buttocks continually flexing and puckering in a thoroughly provocative manner. Her pretty face was as red as her bottom, and her distress was all too apparent as she continually looked back over her shoulder. It was time for the bottom smacking to start in earnest.

Don raised his hand and brought it down forcefully on Claudia's buttocks, producing a loud smack as it landed squarely across the crevice.

"*Ouch!*" Claudia shrieked and suddenly

burst into girlish tears.

Smack! Smack! Don's hand began moving up one side and down the other, each smack crackling with a crisp report as it landed on defenceless feminine flesh.

"Ouch! Oh, no! Ow! Stop! Ouch! It hurts too much!" Claudia exclaimed, her voice reflecting her pain and shame. "Ow! Ouch! Oh, no! This is awful!" Shapely legs prettily attired in black stockings and high heels began swinging merrily back and forth as Don spread the stinging smacks throughout her already-smarting posterior, and the pretty teenager began wriggling furiously over his lap. As she reflexively began jerking her legs hard and wide, bright flashes of pink cunt lips could occasionally be seen along with an intriguing patch of fawn-coloured fleece.

"Oh, no! Stop! Ouch! It hurts too much!" Claudia begged, her voice nearly choking with tears. "Stop, please! I'm just burning up!"

Keeping her squirming, bucking body under full control, Don continued to apply the loud smacks in a lusty, energetic fashion. In his opinion there was nothing much more attractive than a shapely young woman, skirt up and knickers down, undergoing correction with her stockinged legs kicking wildly as her pretty bottom turned a bright scarlet. And Claudia proved the point once more for him. Shapely long legs in stockings and heels kicked frantically back and forth, and the entire combination of tear-stained face, glowing buttocks and swinging legs was exquisite.

"Oh, please, stop, I can't take it anymore!" the miserable girl sobbed between soprano shrieks of pain. "Stop, please! *Pleeeease!*"

At last, Don decided that his suffering victim had endured enough of that kind of discipline. As she lay crying hard across his lap, he finished removing her black knickers and tossed them on the floor. His hand slipped between her legs, discerning the heavy dew that was seeping between her labia and soaking her pubic hair. The lips of her warm teenage pussy felt deliciously soft and juicy, and he slipped a probing finger gently into the wet interior.

"You know what you have to do, don't you?" he asked quietly.

"Yes. Yes, sir!" Claudia managed to reply, trying to get her tears under control.

"Kneel in front of me and take it out of my pants yourself!" Don instructed.

Wiping the tears from her hotly flushed face with the sleeve of her white blouse, Claudia meekly slid into a kneeling position between Don's legs. Her pretty face clearly mirrored the distress caused by the spanking, but Don could also discern an underlying look of excitement about what was to come. She was quite breathless and her full young breasts heaved against the front of her school gymslip. Her expressive eyes narrowed intently as she focused them on the handsome curve in the schoolmaster's slacks.

"Go on," Don told her. "Take it out of my pants yourself!"

Her eyes flashed upward for a moment. "You don't enjoy sex unless you're humiliating a girl, do you?" she protested.

"You want to be humiliated, Claudia!" Don reminded her in an even tone of voice. "You want to be degraded. If it were otherwise, you wouldn't have let yourself get caught with your lesbian girlfriend!"

Claudia did not deny the accusation. Very shame-faced, the pretty eighteen-year-old began opening up Don's fly. Her small fingers worked slowly but showed no hesitation. Leaning back casually in his chair, Don watched closely. As Claudia pulled his open fly apart, his throbbing, bone-hard penis suddenly sprang out into full view. As she caught sight of his nine inches of rock-solid masculine meat, the comely teenager gulped audibly and involuntarily wriggled with girlish surrender.

"Go on, Claudia, you know what you have to do!" Don reminded her in a quiet voice.

Claudia extended her small right hand and encircled the hotly throbbing male member in a possessive grip. Her light, feminine grasp felt exquisitely pleasant, and Don caught his breath sharply. Licking her lips with her small pink tongue, Claudia slowly formed her pretty mouth into a wide oval. Leaning forward, she eased her pretty mouth down over the crown of his massive blood-distended cock. The full effect of the young girl's hot, wet mouth suddenly hit Don like a thunderbolt, and his entire body stiffened as if struck by a jolt of electricity.

"That's the way!" he told her in a deliberately controlled voice. "Perhaps a good meat and cream sandwich will help minimize those lesbian tendencies you've been displaying lately!"

Claudia held the velvety smooth glans of his stiffly erect penis in her mouth and sucked lightly on it, while at the same time her soft fingers played up and down the throbbing trunk of his elongated manhood. Don watched her intently.

There was no doubt that the young German girl was an expert fellatrice, and despite her protestations she thoroughly enjoyed having a rigid piece of man-meat jammed in her oral cavity. Her salivary glands were working overtime, bathing his pounding member with their warm fluids.

"Just take your time, young lady!" he told her. "There's no point in rushing things!"

Holding the pulsating cock in her hand, Claudia slowly withdrew her mouth from the head and began licking it with her warm pink tongue. Her makeup smeared by her tears and her face hotly flushed, the pretty teenager was obviously quite aroused. Eagerly she allowed the sleek head of his rigid shaft to explore her entire young face, brushing against her cheeks, forehead, blonde hair, chin, throat and even her closed eyes. Dripping with excitement, she could not refrain from running one hand under her pinafore to caress her thoroughly wet labia.

"Please, I want it in my cunt!" she begged. "Please, in my cunt! Please, put it in my cunt!" As she repeated her plea over and over again, she covered the stiff pulsating lance with hot, eager kisses. "Please, in my cunt! Please! Oh, *please!*"

"Put it back in your mouth!" Don ordered sternly, secretly enthralled by his pupil's coarse language.

Writhing about in the kneeling position before him, Claudia promptly surrendered. Once again forming her pretty mouth into a wide oval, she inserted his rigid maleness between her girlish pink lips and once again drenched it in a warm bath of saliva. Her enthusiasm and excitement were quite apparent as she began working the stiffly erect member deeper into her warm, wet mouth.

Don watched intently as more and more of his painfully throbbing cock disappeared beteen the pretty teenager's avid lips.

"Now, just keep it there and suck it!" he told her sternly.

Claudia offered no opposition. Kneeling obediently on her knees in front of him, the comely blonde began sucking his swollen organ in an eager fashion. Leaning back comfortably in his chair to thoroughly enjoy her efforts, Don watched her pretty blonde head bobbing up and down in his lap. Her cheeks were collapsed and he could hear the sucking noises produced by her mouth. The look of strain on her face from having so much cock jammed in her mouth made her look all the more feminine and appealing.

Her mouth continually filled with saliva and from time to time she was forced to pause and swallow it with an audible gulp. Thoroughly aroused, the shapely teenager continued fingering her wet pussy. From his position, Don could see a feminine finger eagerly exploring between the wet, parted lips of her cunt. Wriggling her luscious, well-spanked bottom, Claudia masturbated frantically as she sucked her Headmaster's massive prick.

Don remained motionless for as long as he could, but the tantalizing sensations produced by her busy mouth and tongue soon had their effect. Without really thinking about what he was doing, he began moving his pelvis with quick, jerky movements. That ticklish, highly pleasant sensation in his rigid maleness became more intense with each passing moment, and he knew that he would not be able to hold out much longer.

"Mmmmmm! *Mmmmmm!*" Claudia's faraway sounding moans were a mixture of discomfort and sexual arousal.

As his young pupil's mouth tormented him almost beyond endurance, Don's mind flashed back to the caning and spanking he had administered earlier. As usual, the images of red feminine bottoms, of howls and cries and pleas for mercy, of shapely stockinged legs swinging wildly back and forth, and of female private parts being unintentionally exposed, was a powerful aphrodisiac. In his mind, sex and pain and pain and sex were inextricably linked, so much so that one was not possible without the other.

"*Mmmmmm! Ahhhhhh!*" By this time, Claudia's moans had a frantic quality about them, suggesting a high degree of sexual arousal combined with the frustration of having her mouth rather than her steaming cunt filled with the desire-bloated flesh. Don could see her fingers working frantically between her legs, and noted that her fleecy pubic hair was glistening with feminine dew.

Tantalised to the point where he could think of nothing but the incredible sensation in his pounding cock, Don cupped his hands down over Claudia's blonde head and held her in a firm grip. Selfishly, and with no thought for his victim, he began forcefully moving her head up and down in his lap. Moaning and gurgling on her saliva, Claudia docilely submitted to the erotic torment that he was inflicting on her. Her wet fingers caressed her taut clitoris and served as a substitute penis for her vagina, making her twist and writhe her hips with coital movements.

Suddenly, Don could hold himself back no longer. Clamping his powerful hands even more tightly around Claudia's blonde head, he bolted almost to a standing position. Though prepared for the onslaught to follow, Claudia moaned with fear and anticipation. A hot load of thick, sticky semen jetted against the roof of her mouth, splashing the interior. Claudia instinctively attempted to snap her head back, but Don's hands forced her to remain in position. Another blast of thick sperm sprayed into her mouth, coating her tongue and trickling down her throat.

Claudia felt as if a warm fount of glutinous slime had been turned on in her mouth. Hot, cloying masculine lava sprayed forth in voluminous quantities, completely filling her teenage mouth. Gurgling and gulping on the virile, salty fluid, the handsome young blonde began swallowing it with loud gulps. Don could see her voluptuous body quaking as she experienced her own orgasm.

As Don settled back on his chair, Claudia obediently kept his cock in her mouth until it began to go soft. As she straightened up, Don discerned some residue of viscous white cum trickling down her cheek. Quickly catching it with her finger, she stuck her finger in her mouth to lick it up, as if she were simply starving for cum. With her pinafore still up over the tops of her black stockings, she made a delightful sex kitten.

"You *bastard!*" she spoke quietly but with conviction. "I hope you're satisfied!"

Chapter 2

Ordinarily he would have dismissed her at this point. However, there were other factors that entered into the picture. The school year was rapidly coming to an end, and that would mean the end of fun and games with his female pupils for the time being. Even more seriously, the political situation in Europe clearly indicated that war was just over the horizon, and Don knew that he would be in it. Like many young men in the

early nineteen-thirties, he had learned to fly simply as a hobby and had obtained a pilot's license although he had no aspirations as a commercial pilot. However, he knew that the Royal Air Force would be waiting for him the minute that the war broke out.

He watched pensively as Claudia slowly got to her feet. The attractive blonde picked up her knickers from the floor, and stuffed them into her small purse.

"Why don't you come over to my rooms this evening, Claudia?" he suggested.

She looked disdainfully at him. "Why?" she asked. "You got to spank me and you persuaded me to suck you off. That's all you *ever* want!"

Don ignored her hurt tone of voice. "I have a project that might even make a little money for you," he told her.

"What's that?" she asked, her eyes showing some interest.

"I have a photographic assignment from a detective magazine," he told her. "They want some pictures of a pretty young woman who's been tied up by a burglar."

Claudia's eyes flashed as if to inform him that she knew the story was pure fabrication on his part. "Fine," she told him. "I suppose you have some special way you want me to dress," she added, alluding to his fetishes.

"Thin white blouse," Don promptly

responded. "Black satin skirt, shoes and stockings just like you have on."

* * *

Claudia appeared at Headmaster's private quarters at the agreed time. The attractive young blonde was dressed precisely as he had specified. The outline of her frilly white slip and well-filled brassiere could be clearly discerned beneath her diaphanous, highly feminine white blouse. Her black satin skirt ended above the knees, revealing shapely legs attired in sheer black stockings. She wore the same elegant shoes that she had worn early in the day, their eye-catching bows quickly catching Don's interested gaze. She had undone her school pigtails, and was wearing her blonde hair loosely down her back, making her look older and more sophisticated than she had appeared earlier in the day.

"Thanks for coming," Don told her, leaning over to give her a greeting kiss on the lips.

"I'm surprised that you would consent to kiss the mouth that's usually considered only worthy enough to suck your big cock!" the attractive teenager replied sulkily as she quickly looked around at the ropes and photographic equipment that were spread around the room.

"My, aren't we in a bitchy mood this evening," Don remarked, looking her over carefully as he led her over to a plain, straight-backed chair which he had placed in the middle of the room.

"Is this a genuine photographic assignment?" Claudia asked. "Or is tying up girls just another of your hobbies?"

"What's the difference?" Don replied with a grin. "It'll just take a few minutes." He pushed her gently to a seated position on the chair and stepped back to look at her. "Your stockings are a little baggy," he told her. "Tighten them up."

Claudia looked slightly annoyed and hesitated for a moment. Her cheeks becoming prettily flushed, she slowly pulled back her black-satin skirt and white-lace-embroidered slip to reveal black stocking tops, white thighs, and black garter belt suspenders. Don watched with fascination as the attractive young girl proceeded to pull her sheer stockings up even more tautly, smoothing them wrinkle-free and once again anchoring them to her garter belt. Satisfied that she could not improve on the job, she yanked her skirt and slip down.

"Good," Don told her. "Now, I'm going to tie you to the chair. Put your hands together back of the chair with your wrists crossed."

Looking slightly worried, Claudia complied. Taking a length of clothesline rope,

Don quickly tied her wrists together behind her back. Suddenly feeling a little helpless, Claudia squirmed prettily in her chair.

Taking another length of rope, Don dropped to his knees beside her and began tying her slender ankles tightly together just above the bows of her high-heeled shoes. The white rope made a vivid contrast with her black hosiery. Next, taking another length of rope, he tied her legs together just above the knees. Her cheeks warmly flushed, Claudia watched the proceedings without comment.

"Now, let's get that skirt up!" he remarked to his quite helpless subject.

Grasping the hem of Claudia's skirt and slip, he pulled them up to leave black stocking tops, garter belt and a generous amount of bare white thigh on display. From the front, he could catch a glimpse of her pink knickers.

"Dirty bastard!" Claudia fumed, squirming unhappily in her chair, as she could do nothing to adjust her skirt.

Don picked up his camera and began shooting snaps of her at various angles.

"Do you have any film in there?" Claudia asked sarcastically.

Don pretended to ignore her. "I think a gag would make it look more realistic," he remarked.

Despite her protests, Claudia soon found her pretty mouth tightly packed with a folded white handkerchief. A light blue scarf was then passed over her mouth and tied tightly behind her neck to hold the handkerchief in place. Ignoring her almost constant attempts to communicate through the uncomfortable gag, Don proceeded to take more photographs of her.

Finally, he employed a black scarf to blindfold her completely. Her vision cut off completely and unable to communicate in an effective manner, Claudia had no choice but to squirm uncomfortably and helplessly in her chair with her black-satin skirt well above the tops of her stockings. Thoroughly stimulated by the provocative display of helpless feminine pulchritude, Don dawdled with the camera and took shots of her from every angle he could think of.

"There, I think that's enough shots," he remarked at last.

Setting the camera aside, he walked over to his helpless victim. Standing behind her, he moved quite close to her, making her aware of his erection as the front of his slacks brushed against her blonde hair. Looking downward at the well-filled cups of her brassiere pressing outward against her diaphanous blouse, he reached down with both hands and grasped her resilient breasts firmly.

"Mmmmmm!" Claudia could do nothing but moan and squirm anxiously in her seat.

After amusing himself for a few moments by handling her helpless body in an intimate fashion, Don removed the young girl's blindfold. Their eyes met and he could see the mixture of fear and excitement in them.

"Perhaps you want something in that mouth instead of that gag?" he tormented her. "Perhaps the real thing? Gags are really phallic substitutes, you know." He removed the gag.

"Bastard!" Claudia spat out. "Why can't you just do something that's normal for once?"

Still standing behind her, Don ran his hands over the front of her blouse once again. "Okay," he told her. "I want you to do something that's perfectly normal. Take off your clothes for me, as slowly and seductively as you can! What could be more normal than that?" His hands continued to fondle her breasts as he spoke.

"And what do I get out of it?" Claudia asked defiantly.

"Some hot, hard meat between your legs!" Don replied in a deliberately quiet voice. "If you got enough of that, perhaps you wouldn't have to be punished for performing contemptible acts with other girls."

"All right," Claudia agreed. "Please untie me. It's uncomfortable."

He quickly untied her and put away the photographic equipment and props. Seating himself in a comfortable chair, he leaned back to thoroughly enjoy the strip tease that Claudia had promised him. Her face prettily flushed, the comely blonde stood in the middle of the room fully attired in her transparent white blouse, black-satin blouse, black stockings and smart high-heeled footwear. In his racing imagination, Don was already progressively stripping away the various layers of clothing that covered her lush young body.

Looking confident but girlishly embarrassed, Claudia reached behind her back and began unbuttoning her blouse. The movements thrust her breasts forward into even greater prominence, and Don watched the performance intently so as not to miss a single detail. With her blouse unbuttoned, Claudia removed it with deliberate slowness and slowly hung it over the back of the chair where she had posed.

Her white brassiere and frilly white slip made a vivid contrast with her black skirt, while her soft pink and white bare shoulders and arms looked delightfully feminine and appealing. Although his fingers were clasped together meditatively in front, Don was already beginning to squirm at the thought that that lush young female was actually going to take off all of her clothes right in front of his very eyes.

After posing in front of him at various

angles, Claudia reached to her side and unsnapped her black skirt. She pulled the tight garment slowly from her rounded hips and stepped out of it gracefully, giving him a flash of stocking top and bare thigh as she did so. She hung the skirt over the back of the chair and posed in front of him in her slip. The highly embroidered, clinging garment emphasized the lush fullness of her vibrant young body, and through it Don could clearly discern the outline of her brassiere, knickers and stockings.

"How am I doing?" she asked, confident as to what the answer would be. She twirled in front of him, allowing him to view her seductive body from different directions. Although her face was hotly flushed, it was apparent that she was thoroughly enjoying the opportunity of flaunting her young luscious body before the older man.

"All right so far!" Don replied. Although he wouldn't admit it, his young pupil had him almost ready to climb the wall.

Reaching down with both hands, Claudia grabbed the frilly hem of her white slip and began pulling it upward ever so slowly. Don watched entranced as stockinged legs, bare white thighs, black garter belt suspenders, pink satin knickers, more smooth white flesh and her well-filled brassiere all came into view, one after the other. Claudia pulled the slip up over her head, slightly untidying her immaculately combed blonde hair, and removed it.

The slip joined her skirt and blouse over the back of the chair, and the attractive young blonde stood in front of him attired only in her white brassiere, black garter belt, pink knickers, black stockings and smart high-heeled shoes with their elegant bows. Don's roaming eyes eagerly inspected her from head to foot, noting every detail. The form-fitting brassiere moulded her full young breasts into two steep points, while the filmy pink knickers left the outline of her fluffy triangle clearly on view. Above the tops of her tightly suspendered stockings her luscious milk-white thighs shimmered with erotic invitation.

Squirming in his seat, Don could hardly resist the temptation to seize her and ravish her on the spot. Totally enthralled, he watched with fascination as Claudia seated herself on the chair and crossed first one leg and then the other as she removed her high-heeled shoes. She performed the act with the skill of a burlesque performer.

Minus her shoes, Claudia extended her shapely legs together in front of her and unhooked her right stocking. Don could feel his blood racing hotly as she slowly and delicately rolled the stocking downward, black hose departing from milk-white flesh. Her bare, tapering thigh, perfectly rounded knee, svelte but curvaceous calf, trim ankle and dainty bare foot slowly came into full view.

Aware of the almost-hypnotic effect that she was having on him, Claudia removed her left stocking in an even slower, more seductive fashion. Rolling the filmy garment downward in a neat roll, she slowly slipped it from her foot and hung it over the back of the chair. Attired only in her brassiere, garter belt and knickers, the buxom young blonde smiled provocatively at her older admirer.

"Well? Do you like what you see?" she asked, deliberately stalling to tantalise him all the more.

"I think you know what the answer to that is," Don replied, trying to conceal his impatience.

Although she kept her eyes averted, Claudia could feel him staring intently as she reached behind her back to unsnap her brassiere. Slowly pulling the straps from her bare white shoulders, she hesitated for a moment before pulling the cups away from her voluptuous breasts. The lusciously plump, rose-tipped mounds tumbled seductively from the cups of her brassiere, and jounced invitingly in front of Don's eyes. Making no attempt to cover herself, the pretty young girl smiled teasingly at him.

Standing up, she hooked her fingers into

the waistband of her knickers, and then paused for what seemed like an eternity to Don. She began lowering the delicate garment with an almost maddening slowness, only gradually bringing her fluffy triangle of light brown hair into full view. With the knickers below her hips, she let them slither down her shapely legs until they formed a small ring at her ankles. Slowly she stepped out of them, giving Don a flash of her coral-lipped cunt as she lifted first one leg and then the other.

Removing her black garter belt, she stood completely nude in front of him. Don's eyes eagerly drank in her entire body as she slowly turned in front of him, allowing him to inspect her gorgeous young body from every angle. Noting that her cute bottom was still a bright pink from the spanking that he had administered earlier, Claudia's headmaster displayed a handsome curve in the front of his slacks as he slowly and deliberately got to his feet.

"Now it's your turn to do a strip tease for me!" Claudia remarked with an amused little laugh.

Without wasting a single motion, Don quickly peeled off every stitch of clothing. As he stood erect after discarding his underpants, Claudia grabbed his iron-hard penis in a tight grip and held it firmly.

"Remember what you promised!" the

pretty teenager told him.

With his pupil's soft hand encircling his rigidly erect shaft, the two of them quickly retired to the bedroom. Without bothering to pull down the covers, they jumped on the bed together, their bare bodies slapping against one another. The collision of bare flesh sent shivers racing through their respectived frames. Don pressed his mouth tightly against hers and in a moment their tongues were in contact.

Claudia squirmed with girlish delight and ran her soft, smooth hands over Don's hard masculine body. As their stabbing tongues explored each other's mouths, Don's fingers squeezed and moulded and massaged the pretty teenager's full breasts until they were standing taut with desire. Claudia flung one bare leg around his legs and nestled against him sexily. One small hand reached excitedly for his stiffly erect prick.

"Please! I want it inside me! Yes! In my cunt!" the excited teenager begged. "Please, put it in my pussy! Please, I'm just dying to have it inside me!"

With no desire to rush things despite his pupil's eagerness, Don lowered his face to her rose-tipped bosoms. He began kissing them firmly all over, extending his tongue and flicking against the two pink nipples in a manner that left Claudia gasping for breath. Arching her back in kittenish fashion, the lovely young blonde held his face down against the almost rubbery firmness of her fleshy peaks as though she never wanted him to stop.

"Oh, that's the way! Keep doing it! I need it so bad! You don't know how much I need it!" she exclaimed in a highly agitated voice. Her small hand yanked and pulled on his stiff member, holding it in a firm grip.

As his mouth and tongue continued to caress her delightful breasts, Don's hands roamed over her velvety smooth body. His fingers gently caressed and moulded her lovely buttocks, which he had spanked so firmly earlier in the day, and could tell from her reaction that she was still quite sensitive from her earlier punishment. From there, his hand moved to her shimmering, soft thighs, the same thighs that had tantalised him so much when her skirt came up over her black stockings.

From there his hand began exploring the pretty nest between her legs. The comely young teenager was already deliciously creamy, and responded to his manly touch with purely instinctive thrusts of her pelvis and hips. He separated the pink inner lips and, working his fingers into the slippery opening, began teasing her tiny passion-distended button and vaginal orifice.

"Fuck me, please! Oh please, Don, please put it in my cunt!" Claudia pleaded, her voice almost distraught. "Just do it! Fuck me! I want it so *badly!*"

His hand caressing her smooth inner thighs and vaginal crevice, Don began to slowly move his face down over her smooth hairless belly. Still holding his maddeningly pulsating cock in a possessive grip, Claudia squirmed with anticipation as she realised what he intended to do. Her shapely legs were wide open and her knees were drawn upward, leaving her girlish charms lewdly exposed. A glistening film of feminine dew completely covered the entire area, and the bright pink groove stood out vividly in the nest of fluffy hair.

Using the fingertips of both hands, Don gently separated the plump, downy outer lips of Claudia's sex. The two fleshy flaps opened with an audible squishing sound, and Don slowly began spreading them apart as far as he could. The lush expanse of bright inner lips flesh that opened up in front of his very eyes was truly a lascivious sight to behold. Peering intently into the opening, it was as if he could see all of her yearning sexuality awaiting him. Without further ado, Don buried his face against her warm, wet cunt meat with his tongue extended.

"Ooohhh!" Claudia exclaimed at the

electrifying contact. Wriggling girlishly, she allowed her smooth bare legs to drape down over Don's back and eagerly ran her hands through his hair to encourage him.

His nose buried deep in the pink furrow, Don began running his tongue up and down inside her slippery inner lips with quick stabs. A gush of female juices covered his face and seeped into his voracious mouth, and he could feel her squirming prettily in response to his caresses. Vaginal dew began to bubble up spontaneously, leaving the entire area drenched with the musky perfume of well-lubricated sex. Her pelvic muscles jerked spasmodically every few seconds, and her laboured breathing quickly became quite audible.

"Fuck me, please! Fuck me!" the young German aristocrat begged, yet again. Biting her lip to keep from crying out, the shapely young girl found herself in a torment of sexual arousal. Her entire body tingled with erotic sensations, and the hot, itching fire in her pussy was threatening to engulf her entire body. Her eyes were glazed and her breasts were rising and falling rapidly as she gasped for air.

Pausing from time to time to nibble on the plump young pussy lips, Don continued to run his tongue up and down the length of her split. Teased almost beyond endurance by the intimate flicks of his writhing tongue, Claudia squirmed and tossed on the bed, furiously biting on her lip to keep from crying out. Each time that his warmly wet tongue came into contact with her ultra-sensitive little button, her entire body jerked convulsively and her thighs coiled tightly around his head.

"Fuck me! Give it to me! *Fick mich! Fick mich!*" Claudia chanted mantra-like, lapsing into her native German. "*Fick mich! Oh ja, bitte! Geb's mir!*"

As his tongue thoroughly explored her wet vaginal channel, Don's mind flashed back to the disciplinary scenes earlier in the day. The caning that he had administered to Claudia's lesbian girlfriend was still vivid in his mind, and he could still see those lush buttocks lined with six angry red stripes. And with equal vividness he could recall Claudia squirming frantically and kicking her stocking-clad legs merrily back and forth as he repeatedly applied his bare hand to her reddening bottom.

"*Fick mich!* Fuck me with your great cock!" Claudia begged, her voice signalling a rising hysteria. "*Fick mich mit deinen grossen Schwanz! Oh, ja, bitte - fick mich!*"

Don suddenly drew back, using the back of his hand to wipe the excess feminine dew from his face. "I ought to *fick dich*, all right!" he told her. "I really ought to jam it down your throat!"

"*Nein! Nein!*" Claudia screamed. "*Fick mich! Fick mich!*"

In full command, Don stretched out on top of her. "I'm going to give you... the fucking of your life!" he told her in a breathless but determined voice.

Grabbing his rigidly stiff cock to guide it inside her, Claudia emitted an almost-savage cry of delight as it began dilating her vaginal canal. Don could feel the young girl's wet, clinging meat encircling his stiff member in a warm embrace, and both of them caught their breath at the thrill of masculine and feminine meat suddenly coming into direct contact. She was delightfully tight.

"Oh, wonderful! *Wonderful!*" Claudia exclaimed, hugging him with all four limbs and pulling him down until his bare chest was directly into contact with her hard, swollen nipples. "Oh, it feels so good in my cunt! Doesn't it feel good? Do you like my cunt? Does my cunt feel good for you?"

"Shut up!" Don told her. "And start throwing your ass around like you did when I was spanking you!"

Her smooth arms and legs coiled tightly around Don's hard masculine body, Claudia eagerly awaited the attack. She was not to be disappointed. Don was a dominant male in a highly aggressive mood, and he was determined to ride her like a stallion breaking in a young filly. His entire weight pressing down masterfully on top of her writhing young body, he thrust back and forth with powerful, punishing strokes that left her quite breathless. Her cunt was incredibly juicy and he could feel her girl juice constantly lubricating his achingly throbbing cock, making it as slick as grease.

"*Fick mich! Fick mich!*" Claudia begged, yet again lapsing back into her native German. "Fuck me... harder! My cunt needs it so bad! *Harder!*"

Their sexual organs fitted together like two beautifully oiled pieces of machinery. Claudia was moving her hips around under him as though they had ball bearings in them, and he could feel the walls of her juicy young cunt sucking at him, as if trying to grab his cock and pull it deep inside her young body. Her small hands worked down his back and wound up clutching at his hips, her fingernails digging in like spurs.

"Harder! *Harder!*" Claudia screamed chokingly, breathing almost too hard to get the words out. "Make me cum! Make me CUM! *Harder!*"

Faster and faster the two of them ground against one another. The blonde schoolgirl behaved like a young tigress under him, clawing and scratching and squirming and throwing her hips around in every direction conceivable. Still, Don totally dominated her lithe, bucking young body. Claudia felt all but helpless under his powerful masculine thrusts, and her response was largely an instinctive form of self-defence. At times, the forward thrusts of his massive prick were almost brutal, and the relatively inexperienced young girl wondered if she could really stand it much longer. She had never dreamed that sex could be such a savagely raw, primitive experience. But she had no time for thoughts such as these as her crisis suddenly hit her with the force of a tropical storm, taking her unawares.

"Oh, I'm cumming! *I'm cumming!*" she managed to gasp as she felt the initial waves of the climax of raw, sexual pleasure crash over her entire body, overloading her senses, blowing her sexual wiring.

The young girl threw her hips upward as Don slammed forward with all his might. His aching cock plunged into her wanton cunt right up to the hilt and burst like a cannon. As the hot masculine lava poured into her lust-convulsing cunt in voluminous spurts, Claudia shook like a palm tree in a typhoon. Her entire body trembled uncontrollably and, hugging Don tightly with all four limbs, she emitted one half-strangled cry of joyous delight after another. Don could feel the intense convulsions deep in her vagina massaging his prick as if trying to drain it dry of every last drop of his thick sperm. Her climax was much more intense than either of them could have imagined, and Claudia found herself crying and trembling with a raw, purely physical intoxication that she had never experienced before.

For the next several minutes, the two of them lay together with their organs united while they struggled to catch their breath.

"That was some fuck, Mr. Blake," Claudia told him when he had at last dismounted. "Perhaps normal sex like that would be good for both of us."

Don shrugged. "You'll be going back to Germany in a few days," he reminded her. "And I doubt if we'll see each other again."

His battered cock slipped out of her tight, narrow sheath with an obscene little noise followed by a cascade of thick, pearly semen.

They returned to the living room and Don watched as the young blonde snapped on her black garter belt and sat down to replace her stockings. Although his physical desire for the moment at least was spent, he still watched with fascination as she carefully smoothed the sheer black stockings up her white legs and fastened them to her garter belt.

"I think we will see each other again," she told him, her eyes bright. "I think we're destined to see more of each other."

"No," Don replied quite quickly, attributing her lack of sophistication about the state of the world to her youth. But as he watched her carefully adjusting her stockings, he began to have second thoughts. Perhaps she was right, and the two of them *were* destined to meet somewhere again.

Chapter 3

Four years later

"Since we're going to be working together on this case, Mr. Blake, perhaps you wouldn't mind telling me about yourself," said the beautiful young American girl sitting across from him. Her bright pink lips were very full and sensuous, and her dark eyes sparkled with teasing promise. Her name was Anne Carfax.

Prickteaser! That was the first word that occurred to Don as he studied the features of the young girl who had been assigned to work with him in the puzzling wartime venture. But there was no doubt that she was a very appealing young woman. Beneath her thin white blouse he could clearly discern a well-filled white brassiere that came to two sharp tips, and from the way she carried herself he could tell that she was proud of her full figure. The restaurant table concealed the lower half of her body, but he had previously noted her beautifully rounded hips and full, shapely legs.

"There's really not much to tell," Don replied quietly, his voice giving no indication that he was aware of the understatement he was making. "Since I was a pilot, I went into the RAF the minute the war started. I was assigned to a fighter pilot base designed to protect London and the south of England."

The girl was listening quietly, her eyes beaming with admiration that girls often displayed for fighter pilots. Don had seen that look often back in England. He remembered his last sexual conquest before leaving for the States. For some reason he could no longer recall the girl's name. She was a member of the Women's Auxiliary Air Force, and the two of them had been trapped in a sudden and completely unexpected air raid.

They embraced suddenly, impulsively, instinctively, their mouths and tongues meeting. There was no time for them to remove their uniforms. Don's hand slid up under her thick WAAF skirt, over her cobwebby black stockings and toward the elastic of her directoire knickers. He slipped his finger under the elastic and up to the top of her stockings. The touch of her warm bare thighs sent quivers up and down his spine, and her small hands began working on the buttons to release his uncomfortably stiff manhood from his fly.

Moving up her velvety thighs, Don's fingers soon found the deliciously warm cascade of feminine juices. As his fingers separated her plump labia and explored the wet interior, her small hand closed tightly around his pulsating, blood-filled penis. The girl hastily removed her knickers, and with her uniform skirt up to the waist, lay back with her hairy mound framed by the black garter belt and stockings she wore. Don quickly mounted her and plunged his painfully throbbing cock into her welcoming cunt. The spontaneity of it all and the danger of the air raid more than made up for the lack of foreplay, and the two of them climaxed together in a joyous celebration of life – while they still had it.

The memory was still vivid of how she had tenderly wiped him off afterwards with her silken knickers.

"To stay alive in the Battle of Britain," Don continued his narrative, "you had to be either lucky or good, or a little bit of both. I was very lucky. After America had decided to come into the war, US Intelligence did some research, put two and two together, and came up with this operation. The Bureau immediately drafted me as one of their secret boys, liaising with our own British intelligence service, and here I am."

He left unsaid what his dinner companion already knew. His former pupil, Claudia von Reichsapfel, was alleged to be a Nazi spy operating in wartime Washington, D.C., and according to the briefing that Don had received she had apparently successfully compromised a high U.S. official. Don's mission was to find her and, if possible, use her as an unwilling double agent to transmit false information to the enemy. The mission was complicated by various factors, one of which was that Claudia had apparently undergone an operation to disguise her identity. Another factor, which he didn't like to think about, was the possibility that she would recognize him first and then take steps to eliminate him.

"And how do you propose to go about this operation?" Anne asked, taking a cautious look around to see that no one was listening. "I was told that you have some special qualifications for the job, but apart from that I'm completely in the dark."

"I don't think we should talk here," Don told her. "Perhaps there's some place we could be alone."

Anne's eyes lit up with promise. "We could go to my apartment," she told him. "It's within walking distance."

Outside the restaurant, Don was keenly

aware of the sharp click of her high heels on the sidewalk. She was wearing black patent leather spike heels and pointed toes and, despite the hosiery shortage, sheer dark brown nylons. He had noted earlier that her stocking seams were perfectly vertical, and emphasized the swelling curvaceousness of her full calves.

Her apartment proved to be small but comfortable, and well furnished – for a working girl. Anne smiled at him as she switched on the lights. "Housing conditions being what they are, I'm lucky to have my own place," she told him.

"Nice. Very nice," Don observed quietly, taking a quick look around.

"Sit down and I'll bring you a brandy," she suggested.

Don seated himself in a comfortable chair, and watched her luscious bottom jiggling under her navy blue skirt as she disappeared from the room. She returned in a moment with the drinks, and placed them on a small coffee table in front of him. Picking up his drink, Don pretended not to notice as she seated herself across from him and crossed her shapely legs with a flash of nylon.

"Now tell me what you're planning," she told him. "And what part I'm supposed to play in it."

"There are seven girls sharing an

apartment," he told her, naming a location a few blocks away. "All of the intelligence people are sure that Claudia is one of those girls, but they don't know which one. Now I'm told that there's room for one more girl in that apartment, and that's where you come in. We can arrange to have you meet one of the girls and sign on as an additional roommate. So, what kind of a cover story do you have?"

Sipping lightly on her cognac, Anne was leaning back comfortably and slowly swinging her free leg back and forth. Her blue skirt had started to ride up, and Don could catch a glimpse of the darker portions of her stockings.

Suspecting that she was deliberately teasing him, Don tried hard not to notice. But the irregular sex life imposed upon him by the wartime conditions left him continually horny and susceptible to feminine charms, and he could already feel the initial stirrings of a potential erection.

"I came here in 1938 when my uncle was elected to Congress," Anne told him. "I was his secretary."

From the way she hesitated before pronouncing the final word, Don wondered if mistress might not have been a more appropriate description of her duties.

"He was defeated when he ran for

re-election a couple of years later and went back home," she continued. "However, I stayed and took a position with the Bureau." A sudden flicker of a smile crossed her face as she spoke, as if she had only that instant become aware of the stimulating effect she was having on her English visitor.

"Well, you'll have to work out some kind of a story," Don told her, not bothering with the details. "Make them think you're a new girl in town or something."

"Okay, But how do I go about finding out which one is Claudia, assuming she's there?" she asked. "Why can't you just pick her out yourself?"

Don shook his head. "No, they've shown me pictures of all the girls and I can't pick her out."

"Then why did they bring you all the way over here?" Anne asked. "It seems to me that she'll recognize you first and put some strychnine in your tea."

"There's always that danger," Don agreed. "But I was sent here because I could recognize things about Claudia that others couldn't." He spoke slowly, obviously trying to speak in the most discreet fashion possible. "She's obviously had plastic surgery, but there are other areas of her body that..."

"So it's *that* way, is it?" Anne interrupted with a smirk as she suddenly grasped the true nature of the relationship between the headmaster and his former pupil.

"Yes," Don readily admitted. "And I know what things get her going, what things excite her sexually. For example, she has certain lesbian tendencies that can get the best of her under certain circumstances."

Anne's cheeks suddenly flushed a bright crimson. "You don't think that I'm a..." she fumed.

"You may have to pretend," he told her. "But Claudia has an even bigger hang-up. Nothing turns her on like a good hot spanking!"

For a moment Anne looked at him in an uncomprehending manner, as if she were waiting for him to finish the punch line of a joke. "So what?" she finally asked. "You just can't go around spanking girls..."

"I have a plan," Don told her quietly. "One that I think will work."

"Let me get another round of drinks and then you can tell me about it," Anne told him, giving him a tantalising glimpse of white thigh as she uncrossed her legs to get up.

Don watched her leave the room, noting from the way that her provocative bottom jounced under her skirt that she was obviously wearing a garter belt rather than a girdle to hold up her stockings. By this time he found himself with a firm erection that was becoming difficult to conceal. Anne returned with another round of drinks and, seating herself, crossed her legs with almost no attempt to control her skirt. Her stockings ended a little more than halfway up her thighs, revealing carnation-white flesh that contrasted vividly with the black suspenders of her garter belt. The stocking bands were wide, about a quarter of the length of her entire thigh, with two distinct shades melding into each other.

"All right, tell me your plan!" she told him, giving him a candid downward glance that indirectly informed him that she was now well aware of his large erection.

Swinging her leather-clad foot back and forth in a thoroughly distracting fashion, Anne listened first with disbelief and then with almost unconcealed amusement as Don outlined his plan to her. "It'll never work," she laughed when he had finished. "These are grown women. In their twenties. They wouldn't agree to something that wild."

"Yes, they will," Don confidently told her. "If necessary, we can tip off some of the girls so that they can pretend to go along with it."

"Well, we can try it at least," agreed Anne.

The business portion of their meeting having obviously ended, there was a brief silence as each waited for the other to make the next move.

"I don't suppose you've time for a little, ah, *cultural* activity after all that serious espionage stuff?" Don asked her. "After all, we allies are meant to be co-operating fully with one another..."

"Well, maybe I just might have, at that!" Anne replied, flashing a dazzlingly seductive smile at him.

Don quickly moved to a seated position beside her on the couch, his bulging erection now perfectly obvious. Anne slipped her slender arms around his neck and pulled his face down to hers in a long, lingering kiss. Her full, sensuous lips tasted sweet and were yieldingly receptive; gradually she opened them so that their tongues could meet. With a quick, darting movement, she skimmed the warm tip of her tongue around the inside of his mouth.

"You're a very attractive young woman Miss Carfax," Don told her, his hand brushing against her sheer nylons as he began pulling up her navy blue skirt. She made no attempt to stop him and in a moment her skirt was up over the darker bands of her stockings, revealing white thighs and garter belt suspenders.

"How do you like these nylons?" Anne asked, extending her legs together so that he could view their entire length. "They're really hard to get."

"Well, why don't you leave them on while I fuck you? I'd like that," Don suggested with a smile.

"Okay!" she agreed, her amused laugh indicating that she had no objection to either of these proposals, or even Don's crudely direct vocabulary. "But you'll have to take off all your clothes!"

"Fair enough!" Don smiled in agreement.

As his pretty hostess sat watching with her skirt pulled up over the tops of her stockings, he quickly began peeling off all of his clothing. After removing everything else, he stood facing her as he removed first his slacks and then his shorts. As he straightened up after discarding his shorts, Anne's eyes widened and flashed with undisguised pleasure at the sight of his nine-inch, blood-engorged and rigidly hard cock.

"Mmmmmm, that's enough to make any girl's mouth water!" she exclaimed softly, impulsively leaning forward and planting a moist, warm kiss right on the sleek crown. Grasping the elongated trunk with one hand, she quickly skimmed her warm pink tongue over the entire head. "You don't know how hard it is to find a good prick these days, honey!" she told him, punctuating her remarks with hot, eager kisses down the base of his aching masculine shaft. "Here in Washington there's a real manpower shortage."

More than a little amused by her total capitulation before his rigidly upright, pounding manhood, Don took in a deep breath and held it as her pretty mouth worked its magic on him.

"I love it! I just *love* it!" Anne went on, turning her head from one side to the other so that the smooth head could brush against her soft, feminine cheeks. "So hard and so *big*!"

Without further ado, the comely young brunette began disrobing. His steeply erect spear quivering with virile anticipation, Don watched as she quickly kicked off her shoes and began unbuttoning her blouse. Her pretty face was quite flushed with an appealing mixture of embarrassment and excitement.

The blouse quickly came off to reveal a tightly packed white brassiere that stood out vividly against her pink, blushing flesh. Standing up, she unfastened her blue skirt and quickly stepped out of it, revealing feminine curves outlined in trim white knickers and full, shapely, stocking-clad legs. Attired only in her matching white knickers and brassiere, black garter belt and dark-brown stockings, she paused for a moment to allow him to inspect her the superbly feminine symmetry of her body. A teasing smile on her hotly flushed face, she kept her eyes riveted on Don's almost vertical, hotly pulsating phallus.

Don watched intently as she reached behind her back to unsnap her brassiere. Slowly, she pulled the straps from her shoulders and permitted her full ripe breasts to spill from the cones of the brassiere. The two rosy tips, slightly uptilted, stood out vividly against milk-white flesh as the two mounds quivered with their newfound freedom.

"Good Lord!" Don muttered to himself hoarsely, a remark precipitated by the fact that he had suspected that there must have been at least some padding in her brassiere.

Anne hooked her slim fingers into the waistband of her white knickers and began peeling them downward. Don could feel his blood-swollen cock aching with erotic tension as the triangular tuft of luxuriantly brown hair, filmy with feminine dew, came into view. The heavy growth of soft brown pubic hair permitted only a teasing display of her pinkish, sensuously full, outer labia as she stepped out of her knickers.

Now completely nude except apart from her black garter belt and tautly suspendered, dark brown stockings, Anne stood in front of Don with her arms opened. Her voluptuous body was a lush mixture of feminine curves and contrasts, her narrow, almost tiny, waist emphasizing the lush fullness of her breasts and hips.

"Still want me to leave my stockings on?" she asked with a teasing smile.

"Oh, yes," Don replied tersely. "Come here."

Anne stepped forward and their bare bodies melted against one another in a warm embrace. Her soft hands around the back of his neck, the vibrantly warm and obviously highly sexed young woman eagerly pulled his head down to her upturned face. Her mouth was open and their tongues quickly met, flicking and stabbing against one another with little darting movements. Don's perpendicular, rock-hard prick was pressed tightly against her smooth tummy, while her voluptuous, satiny breasts were crushed against his broad, hairy chest.

As their tongues skimmed the insides of one another's mouths, Anne sighed eagerly and submissively in his arms. One small hand slowly came down the side of his masculine body and came to rest on his pulsating, blood-inflated manhood. Her slim fingers worked down to his scrotum, gently cupped his heavy, sperm-laden balls for a moment, and then slowly journeyed upward in a provocatively teasing manner, ending with a firm squeeze. The squeeze became progressively more tight and demanding. It was all too apparent that the gorgeous young brunette was simply starved for cock!

At the same time, Don's hands slowly moved down her warm, smooth back, massaging the tender flesh and pulling her even closer to him. Moving downward, his hands firmly cupped her satiny smooth, girlishly plump buttocks in a firm grip, squeezing and kneading the soft, resilient flesh. How he would love to spank that delightfully feminine bottom of hers! And perhaps he would get that chance, he told himself. Slowly, he slipped his right middle finger into the moist crevice of her buttocks, and traced a course downward to the small, tan-coloured hole. Anne quivered and moaned with a mixture of pleasure and discomfort as he gently insinuated his finger into the narrow channel. Her warm, feminine body wriggled convulsively and pressed even closer to him.

"Let's go into the bedroom," Don told her, momentarily breaking the tight embrace in which they had been locked.

In Anne's small bedroom, Don quickly stretched out in a supine position on the bed. When she saw him in that position, she knew at once what he wanted her to do. Her eyes fastened on his turgid, rock-hard bone and pinkish, swollen sac of his testicles, the pretty brunette stretched out at right angles to his body. Brushing her hair back so that it would not fall down over her eyes, she reached out and grabbed his hot, hard man-meat in a tight

grip. Her pink tongue moistening her full lips, she leaned forward and kissed the sleek cock head hungrily right on the blunt opening.

"Such a beautiful cock!" she murmured quietly but with obvious agitation. "I want to kiss it and suck it and love it! Oh, let me suck it! I want to get it all the way into my mouth! And then I want it in my... *cunt*," she moaned, deliberately enunciating the same crude word for her sex that Don had used earlier on.

The lascivious words were accompanied by excited, emotional kisses up and down the full length of Don's hot, pulsating hardness. Her stockinged legs were open and he could see the telltale juices oozing like clear honey from her thick, sensuously swollen pussy lips. Like a heavy dew, drops of moisture had bespeckled the thick brown bush that partially camouflaged the rosy groove of her labia, a clear indication to Don of the steaming heat that was beginning to build up in that centre of feminine desire.

"Oh, I just love the taste of it!" she exclaimed. "So virile and masculine! I want to eat it so badly!"

Eagerly but gently, she cupped his swollen, sensitive balls in one palm and leaned down to lick them with her warm, pink tongue. The voluptuous brunette's tongue washed them all over, even opening her mouth and sucking each individually inside her mouth in a teasingly playful but highly provocative fashion. As Don watched closely, she continued caressing him in this manner until his entire scrotum was coated with her warm, sticky saliva.

"That's the way, sweetheart!" Don told her. There was nothing like a talented fellatrice to remind him of how much he had been missing lately. Even at this early stage of the game, his hot, rigid shaft was aching painfully for release and his pelvic muscles were automatically moving back and forth with quick, somewhat jerky movements.

Next, Anne began to move her eager mouth up the rigid, almost frantically sensitive underside of his vertical penis, nibbling and kissing the tense organ in an avid, adoring fashion. Although her brunette hair, which had become slightly disarranged, was partially obscuring his view, Don could clearly discern the blissful expression on her brightly flushed face. As she worked her way up to the mushroom-shaped, mauve-hued glans, she discerned a trickle of clear lubricating liquid trailing down from its small opening. With a quick stab of her warm pink tongue, she lapped up the transparent fluid and Don could see that she thoroughly enjoyed that exotic taste in her mouth. Forming her full pink lips into a pretty oval, she slipped them down over the tip of the massive head and started sucking him into her mouth.

"Oh, wow, yes, like that honey!" Don told her. "Now let's see how much of my cock you can get into your mouth!"

He watched as more and more of his pounding masculine tool began disappearing between her voracious lips, and could feel her tongue busily at work with tantalizing flicks and stabs. Her eyes were closed and she had an expression of dreamy contentment on her face despite the obvious strain of having such a large penis in her mouth. Every nerve in his frantically throbbing prick was twitching spasmodically, causing him to groan with pleasure and from time to time arch his back up off the bed.

"That's the way to make it grow, girl!" he told her, his hoarse tone of voice reflecting his pleasure.

With several inches of rock-hard, masculine meat jammed into her oral cavity, Anne paused to let herself get used to it. Her salivary glands were doing double duty, constantly bathing his pulsating virile organ with their warm, soothing juices and also forcing her to swallow quite audibly from time to time. Her voluptuous body, its pink white flesh contrasting vividly with her black garter belt and dark stockings, was constantly in motion with cat-like, sensuous, coiling movements that were thoroughly provocative to watch.

"Go ahead and suck it for me, girl!" Don spoke in a semi-whisper, watching her closely and immensely enjoying the visual as well as tactile pleasures of having a warm, wet feminine mouth surrounding his almost-painfully aching cock.

He watched her lips pulling out into saliva-slick pink ridges as she began moving her beautiful mouth back and forth on his pulsing manhood. Each time she tried to get just a little more of that thick pole of meat into her mouth, she invariably succeeded although the effort of working it in so deeply was now becoming apparent. Occasionally she would gag as the blunt head of his phallus touched the back of her throat.

"Oh, wow!" Don exclaimed, watching her lush breasts jouncing seductively as she swayed back and forth. "That's getting it in deep, girl! Really deep!"

"Mmmm! *Unnnhhh!*" Anne moaned from time to time, the purely animal noises revealing sheer sexual pleasure and total involvement.

The sucking movements became progressively faster and the penetration correspondingly deeper. To his amazement, Don could now feel the oversize crown of his penis sliding from the roof of her wet mouth deep into her throat. Good god, she's swallowed me up completely, he thought to himself! Looking downward, he could see her ovalled lips brushing against his dark pubic hairs, and could hear her gurgle as she swallowed a large accumulation of saliva. "That's beautiful, Annie, beautiful!" he told her, reaching down to run his hand through her dark, lustrous hair. "I didn't think it was possible for a gal to get nine inches of cock in her mouth!"

With the thick column of virile meat penetrating so deep into her throat, Anne lay almost motionless for a few moments. Don could feel and observe her pink lips nibbling on the base of his pounding shaft, and could feel her slippery tongue busily at work with little snake-like movements. She was having some problem breathing, and he could feel her hot breath against his aching balls as she exhaled.

Without discernibly moving her head, she began sucking once again. Don could clearly hear the gurgling sound of feminine saliva being drawn inward, and could see that her pretty cheeks were fully drawn in. With those innate sexual talents, what a match-up she would make with that little bitch, Claudia! Don could easily envision the two of them with their lush bodies tangled in a hot, wet sixty-nine, their pretty faces drenched with the juices of one another's pussies!

"Right, my dear, I think it's time for the main course!" he told her brusquely, pushing her head back with one hand.

His throbbing saliva-coated penis slid from her mouth with a lewd plop, and she hastily brushed some excess saliva from her lips with the back of her hand. Breathless and hotly flushed with excitement, the comely brunette quickly crawled up beside him and stretched out in a supine position, her arms and stockinged legs opened invitingly. Her rose-tipped breasts rose and fell rapidly, and she continually arched her back in a feline manner.

"Fuck me, Don! Fuck me!" she begged as he grabbed one large, resilient breast in his hand and squeezed it hard. "Please! Please! Don't make me wait!"

Don leaned forward to press his face against her voluptuous breasts. "Is cock really that hard to get around here?" he asked, a little surprised that a girl so attractive could be so horny.

"Yes!" Anne admitted. "Especially when you're as... as oversexed as I am!"

Don buried his face against her melon-like breasts, and rapidly began kissing and tonguing them all over. Roaming all over them with his eager mouth, he at the same time kneaded and massaged her two heavy bosoms with his hands in a firm and sometimes almost rough manner.

"Ouch! Oh! *Ow!*" Anne cried out, although it was quite apparent that she found the vigorous massage quite stimulating. "Please, not quite so rough!" she pleaded in a breathless voice.

Despite her protests, however, Anne's sexual involvement quickly reached a new plateau of excitement. The ruddy nipples of her ripe, voluptuous breasts became hard and incredibly sensitive, and her entire body writhed with the pre-coital movements of a young woman who was simply starving for cock meat. Her stockinged legs were upraised and thrown wide open at the knees, leaving her pink cunt lips and sopping wet bush lasciviously on display.

"Fuck me now? Please? *Please!* I need it so bad!" she begged. "Do it now!" Her small hand clawed excitedly at his throbbing, saliva-slick member as she spoke. "I must have it... oh God, I'm just *dying* for it!"

"Really need it that bad, huh?" Don tormented her, smiling, his hand grasping one nylon-clad knee and moving slowly but firmly up to her bare thigh and then to the wet opening of her sex.

Anne squirmed girlishly and gasped as his fingers separated the thick, juicy lips of her vulva and explored the soaking interior.

A cascade of wet feminine syrup inundated his fingers as he slid two fingers past her tensely humming clitoris and into her vagina. Impaled on the two probing fingers, the highly aroused brunette twisted and writhed with sexual torment. Clutching and grabbing frantically at his pounding, brick-hard prick, she began breathing in a loud, deeply passionate manner.

"Fuck me! Oh yes, FUCK ME!" she screamed softly in a distraught, almost tearful fashion. "*Please fuck me, I want your cock inside me – NOW!*"

Don rolled over and mounted her between her outstretched stockinged legs, manoeuvring so that his bulging blood-filled cock was directly aligned with her dripping, steaming hot pussy. Anne's hand slipped under his hard masculine body, grabbing the thick stiff muscle to escort it inside her. Her velvety soft, squirming body felt delightfully feminine and submissive under him, and he could feel her stockings brushing his bare flesh as she excitedly hooked her legs around him. The immense glans of his penis fitted between the slippery outer folds, and Don drove forward with a forceful thrust that penetrated her vagina like a hot knife shoved into butter.

"Oooooohhhhh!" Anne cried out exultantly as she felt the rigid, thick organ dilating and completely filling her tight pink tunnel.

Don thrust forward as hard as he could, uniting their sexual organs completely in an almost brutal thrust. Resting on his knees and elbows upon her recumbent body, Don could feel her delightfully wet vaginal walls clinging tightly to his throbbing, rock-hard shaft. Her lush smooth feminine body was hot and tense, and he could feel her twisting with instinctively sensuous movements as the rigid blood-filled cock penetrated to her very nether depths. Feminine juices, as if bubbling from some magic inner fountain, bathed and lubricated his massive pleasure tool with their pungent fluids, leaving it as slick as grease.

"Fuck me! Oh, fuck me *hard!*" Anne begged. "Your cock feels *huge*... so goddammed good between my legs!" Her voice was almost distraught, and he could see that her eyes were widely dilated with pure lust.

Timing himself carefully to obtain the maximum gratification for both of them, Don begin thrusting back and forth astride her magnificent body, driving his aching prick deep into her tightly stretched cunt. Her smooth arms and stockinged legs wrapped tightly around his naked, thrusting body, Anne began moving her hips around under him with expert movements. She was breathing quite heavily and he could feel her steeply erect breasts tormenting his bare chest as she continually arched her back and twisted around under him with feline movements.

"Harder! *Oh yes, harder!* Fuck my pussy!" she pleaded breathlessly between loud gasps. "I don't care if it hurts – just *do* it!"

Don progressively increased the tempo and she could feel his heavy, bloated balls slapping against her with each forward thrust. His pelvis was pressed down hard against hers, and each surging stroke titillated her highly charged clitoris with an almost-electric jolt of raw, physical pleasure. Her own expert thrusts threw her gorgeous buttocks up at him, working his wildly pounding prong even deeper into her wetly clinging little pussy as if furiously milking it for its magic juices. Their bodies felt fused together in a wild maelstrom of tantalizing physical sensations.

"Oooooohhhhh! Oooooohhhhh!" Anne gasped. "Just keep fucking me like this! Don't ever stop! It feels so *gooood!*"

Thoroughly lubricated by her bubbly feminine juices, Don's blood-distended, painfully aching prick slid back and forth inside her hotly clinging vagina at a progressively faster rate. Flinching and gasping each time the bone-hard shaft penetrated to her cervix, Anne squirmed wildly and clutched frantically at his wildly surging body. Her nylon-clad legs coiled upward and she began kicking at his hips with her heels, forcing him to plunge even deeper into her hotly burning, totally vulnerable pussy.

"That's the way, girl!" Don told her. "Go for broke! Let yourself go completely!" What a sexpot, he told himself. How I'd love to have her and Claudia in bed with me for a session of three-way sex!

"Ow! Ooooohhhh, harder! *Harder!*" Anne cried out, sheer sexual pleasure mixed with a tinge of masochistic pain as the thick hard rod drove relentlessly back in her twisting, frantic cunt. "*Nnggghh!* Harder! Ohhh, make it hurt!" she pleaded. "Ouch! Oh! Ooooohhhh!"

As the dizzy pace threatened to get completely out of control, Don found himself ramming back and forth with powerful, punishing strokes that thrust his painfully aching cock in to the hilt. Anne gasped and shuddered with an intense mixture of pleasure and pain each time he slammed his weight downward against her, and responded to each thrust by throwing her hips upward to maximize the penetration. The juices bubbled from her blisteringly hot cunt and seemed to glue their lewdly welded bodies even tighter together.

"Oooooohhhhh! Oh! Ohh!" Anne tried to speak but was too breathless to get the words out. "I'm cum..."

"Let yourself go! Let go!" Don exclaimed

although he was almost as breathless as she.

The incredibly ticklish, intense sensations in his throbbing, nearly bursting penis began to overwhelm him, and Don pumped and thrust with wild lunges that threw his entire weight down against his partner's voluptuous body. Despite the pounding she was absorbing, Anne kept throwing her ass upward in response to his almost-brutal thrusts. He could feel her vaginal walls squeezing the length of his cock with reflexive spasms, while at the same time her heels continued to beat a frantic tattoo on his upturned buttocks.

"Ooooоohhhhh!" Anne screamed as her initial orgasmic release began to convulse her entire body.

Realizing that the two of them were about to explode together, Don thrust forward as hard as he could and pinned her wildly squirming body under him as his bloated balls suddenly began emptying themselves with spasmodic spurts. Anne emitted a shrill, almost hysterical cry of sheer sexual ecstasy as she suddenly felt the steaming semen spewing deep into her twitching vagina.

"*Oooooh hhhh, fuuuuuuuck!*" the overwrought young woman screamed, her long fingernails pressing almost painfully deep into Don's bare back as she hugged him fiercely to her. Her violent orgasmic convulsions lifted them both high off the bed, and he could feel her vaginal walls frantically squeezing his bursting cock in an iron-grip, as if trying to suck out every last driblet of cum.

Totally breathless, the two of them collapsed on the bed afterwards in a tangle of arms and legs. Don was in no hurry to disengage, and could feel the young woman's delicious young body still quivering and shivering with pleasure as they lay with their organs soaking together.

"That was beautiful!" she told him, her voice filled with gratitude. "When I took this assignment, no one warned me that I was going to get such a stud."

As Don's limp penis oozed out of her dripping cunt, Anne quickly grabbed it and spread the excess cum over her fingers. With a teasing smile on her face, she began licking her fingers one by one in a manner that left no doubt that she thoroughly relished the virile, salty taste of cum. "Mmmm, is that delicious!" she told him, smacking her lips with satisfaction.

"Yeah, that's right," he told her. "Let's live it up tonight because we may not get the chance when we get started on this operation."

"Okay," Anne agreed. "Do you still want me to keep my stockings on?" she asked with a teasing smile.

"I think you know the answer to that!" he replied with a wry laugh.

Chapter 4

"Mr. Blake, how would you like to be in charge of disciplining eight young women?" As might be expected, the highly unusual question was asked with a blush and nervous giggle.

When Don heard that particular question addressed to him from one of the two young women seated across from him, he knew that the unusual plan he and Anne had worked out was starting to pay dividends. In accordance with his instructions, Anne had arranged to move into the apartment shared by the seven other girls. Don himself had taken a apartment one floor above them in the same building, where he had spent the last few days discreetly keeping an eye on the girls in the hope that he might detect some sign of Claudia.

"That's a highly unusual proposal, I must say," he replied, pretending to be surprised.

As he spoke he avoided looking directly at Anne, who was blushing and looking nearly as flustered as her companion. Instead, he looked directly at the other girl, a platinum-blonde whose name was Belinda Danvers. She appeared to be in her late-twenties, and her form-fitting sweater and slacks revealed a promising figure that merited attention. According to Anne, Belinda was more or less the ringleader among the girls, and he was therefore not surprised by her presence.

"Well, when eight girls share an apartment, or 'flat' as I think you call them in Britain, things can get to be a real mess," Belinda explained. "Chores don't get done, clothes get borrowed without permission, phone messages get lost, and so on. And there's the manpower shortage, which means that there is open competition for any eligible male who shows up."

Unseen by Belinda, Don winked knowingly at Anne as he listened to the expected recitation. Seated across from him, Anne had crossed her pretty legs to display an amount of nylon apparently calculated to remind him of their liaison a few evenings ago.

"So, last night we all held a council of war," Belinda continued. "We laid down some rules and agreed that violators were to be punished by spankings." A pretty blush spread over her face as she finished the sentence.

The other two exchanged knowing glances. Don, of course, knew that it had been Anne who had suggested the spanking plan. Young Claudia Von Reichsapfel might dye her hair and have plastic surgery on her face, but there was no way that she was going to change the lush contours in that beautiful ass of hers! Don had devised the spanking scheme for the express purpose of identifying Claudia, but there was no doubt that he was going to have a great deal of enjoyment in carrying it out. And, after the war, it would be quite amusing to tell the story of the eight young American gals who got their bums tanned for Old Glory!

"A rather novel idea, I must say," Don interjected, smiling at his blushing visitor. "And I gather you want me to administer the discipline!" He spoke in a deliberately low-keyed fashion.

"Well, if you don't mind," Belinda replied.

Don's eyebrows came up at that innocent remark. Apparently his attractive guest did not grasp the true nature of spanking, and what it was really all about. Well, she'd learn!

"You see, we wanted an outsider to do the job," Belinda went on. "No girl would dish out a really effective spanking because she'd be too afraid of retaliation."

"I understand," Don told her. "By sheer coincidence, it so happens that I have some unique qualifications for that sort of thing.

He proceeded to tell them in some detail of his duties as headmaster of an English girls' school before the war. Anne, who had only a sketchy idea of his background, sat as wide-eyed and attentive as her companion as he told them of the strict discipline administered to the pupils, even those in their late teens. Obviously unfamiliar with such practices, they listened with fascination as he told them about the standard practice of requiring girls to bend over while their uniform skirts were raised, their knickers lowered, and six or more cuts of the cane applied to their completely bare buttocks. From the way both young women squirmed in their seats, Don could see that both of them could just feel one of those whippy canes being applied to their unclad posteriors.

"Well, I suppose a cane would be too severe for your tender American bottoms," he remarked with an amused laugh.

"Yes!" squeaked both girls in unison, for once prepared to let this slur on American womanhood's bravery go unchallenged.

Don shrugged to indicate that it wasn't all that important. "I can just use my hand, of course," he told them. "That can be quite effective, too."

"Yes, I'm sure it can!" Belinda rather breathlessly agreed. It was clear that she was quite intrigued to be talking to a man who had experience in disciplining the opposite sex.

"However, I do think there should be some sort of ritual," Don explained. "Otherwise, the atmosphere would be too much like a birthday party spanking, and the girl wouldn't think of it as punishment."

"That makes sense," Anne supported him. The attractive brunette had once more allowed her skirt to ride up to give him a full glimpse of the two wide bands at the top of her stockings and a fleeting glimpse of bare white thigh.

"Well, what do you mean?" Belinda asked, obviously curious.

"Well, for example," said Don, pretending to improvise, although he had thought it all through beforehand, "a schoolgirl-type uniform, something to give the impression that she's a big girl being treated like a little girl. White blouse, short pleated black gymslip, but worn with nylons and high heels. Pigtails, perhaps."

"Nylons are hard to get these days," Belinda objected.

"We can manage," Anne said.

"And perhaps the victim should stand in the corner before and after the spanking," Don added. "However, we can work out all those details. Now, perhaps, you two would like to join me in a drink."

"I can't. I have to run," Belinda told him.

"I'd be happy to!" Anne replied, flashing him a knowing smile and swinging one pretty leg back and forth as she spoke.

When Belinda had departed, Don poured them each a drink and once again sat down across from his attractive visitor.

"Well, do any of the girls resemble your little Nazi girlfriend?" Anne asked.

"There are only two of them who could be her," Don said. "The others are wrong for one reason or another."

"That's funny," Anne told him. "I thought you'd say all seven of them resembled her, just so you could spank all seven of them."

Don laughed. "I'll admit that that fiendish thought had occurred to me," he admitted. "And I'll wager that I wind up spanking all eight of you, anyway!"

Anne gave a derisive snort, as though the idea were totally preposterous. "That's absurd," she told him.

"But you don't understand how much girls like to see other girls punished," he explained. "Once one or two of them have gotten it, they'll want a couple of more to get it and so on. It'll be contagious!"

From the look on her face, he could tell that she agreed he had a point. "Alright, but you'd better not try spank me, buster!" she told him archly.

"Since you're the one who suggested the spanking idea to the girls in the first place, I'm sure there's no way on earth we'll be able to save that priceless bottom of yours!" Don told her with a laugh.

"Well just don't enjoy it too much!" replied Anne.

"Now, tell me what you've found out," asked Don. "Any clues, suggestions, or hints? Anything?"

Anne hesitated for a moment, obviously embarrassed to bring up whatever was on her mind. "You said Claudia had lesbian tendencies," she remarked, her eyes lowered.

"Well, well," Don exclaimed, registering surprise. "OK, go ahead and tell me about it."

"One of the girls is a lesbian," Anne told him, looking quite shamefaced as she spoke. "She and I had, er... um... a... session together!"

"Which one?" Don asked, leaning forward with obvious interest.

"Jean Wright," Anne said. "Is she one of your suspects?"

"Yes," Don replied. "Well, go ahead and tell me about it."

Anne looked quite embarrassed. "Please, let's spare the details," she demurred.

"No, I have to know," Don insisted. "Some little clue that you might not think important might make all the difference."

With considerable embarrassment, Anne began recounting her story.

"It was late..." she began.

The apartment that the eight girls were sharing had been partitioned off into two main rooms. The rear room served as a dormitory where all the girls slept on various divan or camp beds. The front room served as a combination living and dining room. Unable to sleep one evening, Anne had gotten up from her bed and gone into the front room for a cigarette. It was a warm evening, and she was wearing light summer pyjamas, through which the outline of her full figure was easily discernible.

Thinking that all of the other girls were asleep, she was visibly startled when she heard the sound of a key turning in the front door. Before she could react, however, the door opened and in popped Jean.

"Hi!" Jean exclaimed, flashing a smile at her new roommate. She spoke in a semi-whisper to avoid disturbing the other girls.

"Where have you been?" Anne asked with some surprise, also speaking in a low voice. "It must be two o'clock."

"Looking for some action," Jean replied, sitting down beside her on the couch. "Can I have a cigarette? I hate to bum one when you have to stand in line all day for a pack, but I really need one."

"Okay," Anne replied, handing her a cigarette. As she did so, she discreetly looked over her attractive roommate. Jean was a full-figured young woman who appeared to be in her early twenties. She had jet-black hair with darkly expressive blue eyes that seemed constantly in motion, as if she were searching for something. She had seated herself quite carelessly, allowing her dark skirt to ride up over the tops of her tightly suspendered dark brown stockings. “And how was the night life tonight?” Anne asked.

“Rotten,” Jean spoke with a discouraged sigh. “I got picked up by some overworked young lawyer who works for OPA, but he couldn’t keep it up despite my valiant efforts.” As she spoke, she kept darting glances at her roommate, as if trying to discern what reaction she might provoke. “Honestly, sometimes I think men are a complete waste of time!”

It might have been just an idle remark, but Anne could sense an invitation in Jean’s eyes as she spoke. It was a distinctly uncomfortable moment for Anne. She had never had the slightest lesbian contact in her life, and had always considered the idea of sex between girls as almost repugnant. Moreover, she didn’t have the foggiest idea of how to proceed, although she knew that it was her duty to do so.

“Those are very nice stockings, Jean,” she remarked. “I envy you. I’m down to my last pair.”

“They are nice. Look at them!” Jean

replied, pulling her skirt back well over her stocking tops and extending her shapely legs in a straight line to give Anne a complete view of her attractive, nylon-clad legs. "Here, feel them and see how sheer they are!"

Anne could feel her heart pounding rapidly as she accepted the invitation. Running her hand over the darker band at the top of Jean's right stocking, she allowed her fingers to brush against the young woman's smooth, warm bare thigh. It was immediately evident that the intimate contact was thrillingly disconcerting to her young roommate. A pretty flush appeared immediately on Jean's face and she squirmed girlishly in her seat.

"Perhaps I'd better get undressed out here where I won't wake the other girls," Jean said, her eyes directed at her roommate in a searching manner. "Do you mind?"

"Not at all!" Anne replied, although she could not refrain from gulping noticeably.

Crossing first one pretty leg and then the other to unfasten and then remove her elegant high-heeled sandals, Jean unsnapped her nylons from her black garter belt. She rolled them down and removed them with infinite care to avoid causing any runs in them. As the black hose departed to reveal milk-white flesh, Anne told herself that she must not look. She had already observed enough to conclude that Jean possessed strong lesbian tendencies, and that was all she really needed to know.

Minus her shoes and stockings, Jean quickly unbuttoned her blouse and removed it to reveal feminine curves outlined in a white brassiere and light, highly embroidered slip. Standing up, she undid her skirt and quickly stepped out of it to reveal the full length of her attractive slip.

"Really, it's a rotten shame," she mused, "I wear all these nice undies and my date can't even get his erector set working!"

As she began pulling the slip off over her head, Anne kept telling herself that she must not watch. But, try as she might, she could not avoid gazing intently as the slip came off to reveal Jean's lush young body attired only in bra, white knickers and garter belt. From her vantage point, she could clearly see the fleecy triangle under the wispy knickers, and could feel her blood beginning to race. Her face felt hot and she could not refrain from squirming in her seat.

"What's the matter, Annie?" Jean asked in an apparently innocent voice as she reached behind her back to unsnap her bra. "You look as if you were uncomfortable or something."

"It's nothing," Anne managed to reply, although her voice betrayed her underlying turmoil.

Jean casually removed her brassiere and

made no attempt to conceal her full, ripe breasts. Although she kept telling herself not to do so, Anne could not tear her eyes away from those two fleshy, jouncing mounds with their saucy pink tips. She was a little dismayed and considerably disturbed at the stimulating effect that another girl's body was having on her.

As if she were deliberately flaunting her most intimate parts in front of her, Jean quickly stripped down her knickers and tossed them aside. Anne's heart skipped a beat as she caught sight of the swollen pink valley nestled in the fluffy triangle of light-brown hair. As Jean removed her garter belt, she seemed quite aware that her attractive roommate was gazing at her in a highly intent fashion.

"Look at me, Annie!" Jean spoke quietly but confidently. "Look at me and then tell me you're not interested!!"

Anne gulped and found herself swallowing quite hard. Her face was a pretty crimson as she gazed at her roommate's inviting breasts and soft pubic curls. "Please, Jean," Anne heard herself protesting in an embarrassed voice. "I wouldn't have the vaguest idea what to do with another girl!"

Jean smiled quietly at her and motioned for her to stand up. "Don't worry! I'll show you!" she promised.

Feeling as if forces beyond her control were propelling her, Anne stood up. The two of them embraced and Jean kissed her firmly on the mouth. Anne felt the buttons of her pyjamas being undone by delicate fingers, and then suddenly she could feel Jean's full breasts brushing up against her own ripe mounds. The sudden experience of nipple meeting nipple sent electric shivers racing through her body, and she felt herself excitedly returning Jean's kiss. Their mouths opened and feminine tongues coiled around one another in a deep lesbian kiss. Anne sighed ardently and could feel ice-cold chills racing up and down her back.

"The other girls will hear us!" Anne warned her in an urgent whisper.

"No, they won't. They're all asleep," Jean replied, pushing her back toward the couch.

Jean was taking charge of the proceedings, and Anne was content to allow her to do so. Gently pushed backward by her companion, Anne stretched out supine on the couch. Jean knelt on the floor at her side and quickly removed her pyjama pants for her. Blushing deeply, Anne felt pleasantly light headed and giddy with her worshipful feminine partner kneeling before her, her expressive eyes drinking in everything.

"You have such beautiful breasts, Annie!" Jean told her in an admiring voice. The shapely young woman quickly leaned forward and kissed one pink nipple lightly, allowing her lips to linger for a moment.

"Ooooohhhh!" Anne panted, her voice reflecting a mixture of pleasure and surprise. Given her first taste of lesbian pleasure, the voluptuous young woman caught her breath and arched her back sharply.

Licking her full, ripe lips with obvious anticipation, Jean leaned forward and began to kiss the two full, highly sensitive mounds again. Extending her warm pink tongue, the comely young woman alternated between the two upright, twitching nipples with gentle flicks, while at the same time her small hands gently moulded and caressed the two fleshy domes. Her face deeply flushed and biting her lip to keep from crying out, Anne writhed and twisted with growing arousal as the intimate caresses left her magnificent breasts taut with sexual tension. Try as she might, she could not deny that girl-love had its special pleasures.

"You know, I've never done anything like this before!" Anne admitted to her attractive partner in a voice that was hoarse with excitement.

"I want to suck your pussy for you!" Jean told her, continually nibbling at her companion's large breasts even as she spoke. "Honestly, there's nothing like having another girl eat your pussy for you! You'll just love it!"

Taking one rose-coloured nipple into her mouth and gently sucking on it, Jean slowly allowed one hand to slide down the velvety smooth flesh and in to the dense thicket of Anne's fluffy pubic hair. Neither was surprised to find that the area was already deliciously creamy. Anne trembled with agitation and quickly sucked in her breath as Jean's fingers lightly caressed the pink lips of her sex with a gentle, exploratory stroke.

"Spread your legs open a little, honey," Jean suggested in a quiet voice.

By this time, Anne knew that she lacked the willpower to resist. Breathing in short, excited gasps, she opened her smooth, tapering thighs in anticipation of the lesbian pleasures to come. Her pink tongue constantly skimming her pretty lips in an expectant manner, Jean extended both hands and used her fingers to pry the two pink petals open. As she unveiled the lush rose-pink girl flesh, Jean quickly buried her head between Anne's wantonly outspread thighs.

"Ooooooohhhhh!" Anne gasped as she suddenly felt Jean's probing little tongue directly in contact with her ultra-sensitive, hotly throbbing clitoris. Her entire body quivered spasmodically and her thighs coiled tightly around Jean's head, locking them in a soft but firm vice. A gush of hot feminine dew erupted from her heated pussy, bathing Jean's face in its pungent female aroma. Smacking her lips with obvious delight, Jean began running her tongue up and down inside the pink crease, tasting the delicious girl flesh and drinking in the feminine juices that soaked her ever-probing tongue.

"Oooooohhhhh, it feels so *beautiful!*" Anne purred, lewdly fondling her own steeply erect breasts as she spoke. Her lust-swollen little clitoris was sending its hotly tingling messages racing through her entire body, and she was unconsciously thrusting her pelvis back and forth with reflexive movements. "So good! So very good!" she murmured. In some ways she felt as if she were dreaming, that it really wasn't her. She couldn't be doing something like this with another girl.

"Let me kneel between your legs," Jean told her, moving from the floor to a kneeling position between her attractive companion's smooth, shapely legs. "Slip your legs down over my back!" she instructed. "That's the way!"

In a moment, Anne's bare legs were dangling down her lesbian friend's smooth back. Using her fingertips once again, Jean carefully pried open the two outer folds to expose the lush pink, well-lubricated interior. The steaming, pungent heat that suffused Anne's pussy blew against her pretty face as she leaned forward, her tongue coiled in readiness for the lesbian invasion.

"Now, I'm going to give you a cum like you've never had before!" she promised her wriggling, breathless partner. "You're just going to love it!"

With her warm pink tongue extended as far as possible, Jean began licking and nibbling the wet girl flesh in an expert manner. Although Anne kept telling herself that she shouldn't permit herself to be so thrilled by another girl's unnatural caresses, she gasped and arched her back in kittenish fashion as Jean's feminine tongue teased and caressed her intensely quivering, desire-swollen clitoris with teasing, thrilling swipes. A hot, deliciously burning sensation originating in her tormented little button spread through her pussy, and from there radiated warm waves throughout her body. She was dismayed by the intensity of her own arousal. She had never dreamed that another girl could raise her to such a fever pitch of arousal!

"Ooooohhhh! Oh, it's wonderful! So good! So very, very..." Anne heard herself murmuring between excited gasps of pure physical joy. "Don't ever stop! I need it so bad!"

Sliding her hands palm upwards under Anne's satiny feminine hips, Jean worked her probing tongue as far as she could into the

steaming hot, slippery wet cavern and flicked it around in a serpentine manner. Anne's deliciously warm girl's honey was flowing in generous quantities, bathing her eager young partner's face and filling her mouth with slurping noises that were quite audible. Lifting Anne's hips a few inches from the couch, Jean hastily ran her tongue down to the other hole and twirled it around Anne's brown rosette for a brief moment.

"*Aaaaahhhh!*" Anne gasped with surprise and delight, and quickly bit her lip to keep from crying out. "Oh, my goodness!" She could hardly believe the lewd wickedness of her young companion! She kept telling herself that she should stop right then and there, that she shouldn't permit herself to enjoy such perverted activities, but the sheer physical sensations were quite overwhelming and she was a helpless prisoner of her own highly erotic personality.

Jean worked her way back upward to the fragrant juicy slit, and plunged her darting, stabbing tongue in once again. Anne's hips jerked up frantically at the sudden resumption of the lesbian assault, her back arching steeply off the couch for a moment. Her warm tongue swimming in the swirling rapids of Anne's overheated cunt, Jean quickly found the pink, lust-swollen bud and began concentrating on it. Anne shuddered violently at the incredibly thrilling contact, and began jerking her pelvis back and forth in a manner that made clear that her emotions ware rapidly going out of control.

"*Ooooohhhh! Ooooohhhh! Oh, don't stop! Ohh!*" Anne gasped in a distraught voice. "Ooohhh! Oh, I'm... Ooooohhhh!"

Her eager face plastered against the sopping wet underbrush, Jean constantly teased the maddeningly erect little button with her experienced tongue. Completely carried away with sexual arousal, Anne clawed at Jean's head in an apparent attempt to push her face deeper into her burning hot pussy. She could feel an intense orgasm coming on, approaching with the force of a tornado. The fever-pitch intensity of her sexual arousal produced muffled sobs of delight and despair, and she could feel her entire body on the verge of an explosion.

"*Oooooohhhhh!*" Anne wailed with sexual anguish as a violent, mind-blowing climax suddenly engulfed her entire body. Convulsive shudders racked her body and her shapely legs jerked upwards spasmodically, as if pulled on strings. I'm in heaven, she told herself! Wave after wave of raw, almost savage erotic spasms assaulted her quivering body, and left her limp and totally breathless.

Her new lover kept her face nuzzled against Anne's sopping-wet, ravished sex until her convulsions began to subside.

"Oh, that was wonderful!" Anne exclaimed, her eyes bright with tears of excitement.

Her face glistening with feminine juices, Jean slowly withdrew her face from the wet, pink furrow. "Didn't you just love it?" she asked, a pretty flush of excitement on her face.

"Yes! Yes!" Anne admitted. "I suppose..." she found it difficult to put into words what she knew she had to say next. "I suppose you want me to... reciprocate?"

"Sure, of course!" Jean seemed a little surprised that her friend found it necessary to state the obvious.

The two of them quickly traded places, and Anne watched as Jean stretched out supine with her legs wide apart to reveal her pink vulval slit in all its feminine glory. I'm not a lesbian, I'm just pretending to be a lesbian, Anne tried to tell herself. But as she found herself staring at the luscious coralline groove that was obviously brimming with the most delicious sweet nectar, she could not deny that she was hungry for the lesbian banquet that awaited her.

"Hurry up, honey, my pussy's just dying for some girl love!" Jean told her, squirming prettily on the couch and watching her companion with intense expectation.

As Anne moved into a kneeling position

between her smooth bare legs, Jean pulled her knees back until they were nearly in contact with her full breasts. Anne gulped quite hard and felt her face becoming hotly crimson as she found herself only inches away from the lasciviously displayed girlish charms, the plump pink furrow standing out vividly in the pretty nest of light brown hair. Glittering moisture adorned most of the area and, somewhat to her shock and dismay, Anne could feel her own mouth watering expectantly.

"Go on, Annie!" Jean pleaded. "Eat me! Eat me, please! Don't make me wait any longer!"

With some further hesitation, Anne extended her fingers and slowly, somewhat squeamishly, separated the plump, pink folds. The lovely girl flesh and the musky feminine aroma emanating from it assaulted all of her senses, and she found herself studying the lewd display with a fascination she could not really explain. Jean squirmed girlishly as feminine fingers opened up her treasure trove, and she hooked one leg gently over Anne's back.

"Suck me, Annie! Please! Suck my pussy!" she begged, repeating herself over and over again. "Suck me! Suck my pussy! Suck it for me!"

Anne hesitated for a long moment,

gathering up courage to perform the act that she had so long considered so disgustingly perverted. Finally, she extended her moist pink tongue, and slowly buried her blushing face in Jean's eagerly waiting pussy. A hot gush of feminine cream greeted her and for a moment she felt as if she had dived into a warm, wet pool.

"Oh, that's the way!" she heard Jean exclaim. "Eat me, honey! Eat it!"

Her mouth and cheeks bathed in warm cunt juice, Anne began exploring the moist interior of Jean's juicy, fragrant slit with her long, twisting tongue. To her dismay, the taste was indescribably delicious, sweet and honey-like, and she found herself impulsively sucking it in with noisy, eager slurps. Jean's pelvis began jerking back and forth instinctively, and Anne became strangely excited to hear the young girl's ecstatic gasps and moans as she submitted to the lesbian caresses.

"Don't stop, honey!" Jean encouraged her. "It's wonderful! Oh, it feels so good! So good! So very... very... *mmmmmm...*"

Tormented by her female lover's flicking and stabbing tongue, Jean writhed and twisted on the couch with sensuous, erotic movements of her entire body. Despite her total lack of experience, Anne seemed able, perhaps instinctively, to tease and tickle the tiny, desire-swollen clitoris and the dilated vaginal orifice with little flicks that sent sparks of electricity racing through the other girl's body. Jean's soft thighs coiled tightly around her lowered head with a constrictor-like squeeze that left her imprisoned, and Anne could tell that her attractive roommate was rapidly approaching the same level of savage sexual bliss she herself had enjoyed earlier.

Swimming in rivers of feminine juice, Anne concentrated all of her efforts on the swollen tingling bud, tonguing and sucking simultaneously. Jean's pelvic movements rapidly accelerated, and Anne could bear her lusty grunts as she began breathing quite heavily. Before long her pelvis was jerking uncontrollably against Anne's face and a steady stream of girl honey was gushing from her gaping vaginal orifice.

"*Ooooooohhhhh! I'mmmm cummm-iiiiinnnnngggggg!*" Jean cried out rapturously, a fist balled into her mouth in an attempt to stifle her passion, her entire body heaving with sexual lust. "*Oooooooohhhhhh!!*"

A ball of fire seemed to explode in Jean's steaming hot pussy, and spasms of pure sexual bliss convulsed her voluptuous young body. Trapped between her shuddering partner's tightly coiled thighs, Anne sucked lovingly on her female lover's delicious cum. The delicious, sweet taste filled her mouth while her nostrils were overwhelmed by its spicy, thrilling scent and, blotting out of her mind the depravity of what she was doing, she relished every drop of it.

At last, Anne withdrew her face from the opening of her ravished cunt, and stretched out beside her naked girlfriend on the couch. Their arms entwined, the two of them exchanged a moist, affectionate kiss and the tongues that had driven each other frantic with sexual lust met once again.

"Wasn't it beautiful?" Jean asked, her eyes smiling brightly at her female lover.

"Oh, *yes!*" Anne admitted, kissing her once again.

Without really thinking about what they were doing, the two of them slowly drifted into a sixty-nine position on the couch. In a few moments, their faces were snuggling against each other's soft, bushy pussies.

* * *

Don listened to Anne's narration with absorbed interest. There was no doubt that Jean's behaviour was highly reminiscent of the youthful Claudia that he remembered back in England. Long before Anne was finished with her story, he found himself with a powerful erection that demanded satisfaction. During the intense lovemaking that followed, Anne seemed to be striving determinedly to prove that she was really a normal woman and had not become addicted to the Sapphic pleasures that she had just experienced. Afterwards, they lay quietly in each other's arms trying to catch their breath.

When he began recovering from his post-coital stupor, Don tried to collect his thoughts. In addition to Jean, there was only one other girl who fitted Claudia's description. Her name was Betty Anderson, and apart from her jet-black hair she could easily have been a double for Claudia. The slight facial differences could have been caused by surgery. They had met once and Don thought that he detected a flicker of recognition in her eyes, although he realised that he could easily be mistaken about that.

"Thinking about business?" Anne asked.

"Right," Don replied.

"Don't you think Jean's our girl?" she asked.

"Could be," he said.

"Who else?" Anne asked curiously.

"Betty Anderson," he told her.

The answer provoked an amused laugh from Anne.

"What's so funny about that?" Don asked curiously.

"She hardly fits your lesbian profile," she

told him. "Betty's the biggest manstealer in the whole group."

"Good," Don replied. "Let her try to steal somebody's date, and then have the girls sentence her to a spanking for that. Let's see what effect that has on her."

Anne smiled knowingly at him. "I bet I know what effect it will have on you!" she told him, her eyes bright with amusement.

Chapter 5

Don was waiting for the telephone call when it came. He recognized the voice of Belinda Gibson before she identified herself.

"Mr. Blake," she told him. "We have a flirty little manstealer who needs to be taught a lesson!"

"I understand," he replied. "When?"

"Give us about an hour," Belinda told him.

"Remember the details we discussed," Don reminded her.

"Yes, but I'm afraid our victim is putting up quite a little fuss about it," she said.

"Just tell her that that will make the punishment all the more severe," Don said quietly, hanging up the phone.

One hour to the minute later, Don knocked on the front door of the girls' apartment.

Even before the door was opened, he could hear animated conversation from inside. In a moment, the door swung open.

"Hello," Belinda told him, flashing a bright smile at him. "Do we ever have need of your expert services!"

All eight roommates were present as Don stepped inside the apartment. An attitude of underlying anticipation and excitement was readily discernible amidst a general hubbub of giggles, snickers, girlish titters, catty remarks and general merriment. The carnival atmosphere was exactly what Don had expected, because he knew from experience that females were invariably stimulated, sometimes even sexually aroused, by the idea of a fellow female undergoing correction.

"Look what we have over here!" Belinda told him, pointing to one corner of the room.

Don whistled softly as he looked over to the corner. Blushing furiously and obviously simply dripping with embarrassment, Betty Anderson was standing in the corner with her face to the wall like a naughty but overgrown child. She was costumed perfectly for Don's purposes – white blouse, pleated black pinafore, black stockings and spike heeled black patent leather pumps with straps from behind the ankle tied in a large bow in front. The gymslip was hemmed to end a few inches higher than the prevailing fashion, which added a juvenile but eye-catching dimension to the outfit. To add to the juvenile effect, her jet-black hair was done in two long pigtails and tied with large pink ribbons. "Seems like our little tart is waiting for her medicine!" one of the girls cattily informed Don. Others joined in with similar remarks. Obviously, everyone except the victim was looking forward to the occasion.

"Girls, please!" Betty protested, blushingly looking back over her shoulder in an effort to decrease the merciless hazing.

"Perfect costuming," Don commented quietly to Belinda as he gazed intently at his intended victim.

The scene brought back many vivid memories of England before the war; Don's eyes drank in every detail of Betty's appealing figure as he looked her over from head to toe. He noted the swelling curves of her ripe buttocks beneath the pleated gymslip, the narrowness of her waist, the full curves of her nylon-clad thighs, her slender ankles and her dainty feet steeply arched in the attractive black high-heel sandals. And he also noted the exquisite look of embarrassment and shame on her pretty, hotly blushing face. There was always something vividly erotic about the look of humiliation on a young woman's face when undergoing correction.

"Well – what are we waiting for?" one of the girls yelled. Others joined in the clamour.

Looking around, Don discovered a plain, sturdy chair and pulled it into the middle of the room. As he seated himself on it, Belinda clapped her hands to silence the other girls.

"Come and get it, Betty!" Belinda called out.

Betty gulped hard and her pretty knees buckled noticeably as she turned around to find Don seated and flanked by her expectantly grinning roommates. "Please, girls, this has gone far enough!" she burst out impulsively. "Please, I've learned my lesson. I'll never do it again!"

"Go on, you little slut, take your medicine!" one of the girls told her in a distinctly hostile tone of voice. Others joined in with words to similar effect.

"Please, girls, be reasonable!" Betty continued in a despairing tone. "Please, be reasonable! I'm too old to be spanked. For chrissakes, I'm twenty-four years old!"

The latter entreaty merely produced a few snickers from the assembled girls. It was obvious that Betty had no sympathizers among them.

"Come on, Betty, you're just getting a spanking!" Belinda told her. "You're not going to the electric chair."

Betty's eyes darted hastily around the room in the hopes of finding at least someone who would take pity on her. But the girls were implacable. "Go on, Betty, you had it coming – now take your medicine like a good little girl!" they told her.

Watching the wretched young woman miserably trying to beg off, Don remained quiet for a few moments. "Come here, Betty!" he said with quiet authority, spreading his legs slightly apart and patting one knee with his open hand. The room went silent.

Betty swallowed quite hard and it was evident that she was fighting back tears of shame and humiliation. Her pretty face a flaming crimson, she reluctantly teetered towards Don with legs that plainly threatened to buckle at any moment. Her hands were clasped anxiously behind her back, an unintentionally childish mannerism that seemed really quite appropriate for the occasion. Inspecting her lush young figure in the appealing punishment uniform, Don kept telling himself not to rush things and that it would be much more enjoyable if he took his time.

"Please! Please, don't spank me too hard!" Betty pleaded when at last she stood in front of him. The distressed young woman wriggled rather naughtily in anticipation of the punishment to come.

The remark drew a few giggles from the other girls, who had formed themselves into a semi-circle in front of the chair. All of them had pleased, expectant looks on their faces, and some were blushing almost as much as Betty.

"Over my knee, Betty!" Don told her, grasping her by the wrist and propelling her forward.

"Oh, it's so embarrassing!" Betty protested, but made no effort to resist as he pulled her face down over his lap. "Please, girls, don't let him do this to me!"

Don paused to cast an admiring glance at his trembling, protesting victim. Blushing as red as a beet and trying to keep her face averted as much as possible, she was obviously struggling to retain her self-control. With her long black pigtails streaming down to the floor and her short black pinafore riding up to reveal shapely legs and thighs encased in sheer black nylon, she couldn't have made a more appealing picture.

Her comely, well-proportioned buttocks were sticking up higher than the rest of her body, her black gymslip drawn tightly over them.

"Oh, no, this awful!" Betty pleaded. "Please, let me go! Girls, please! Please!"

Don grabbed her right hand and held it firmly in the small of her back. With her left hand blocked out by his body, there was no way in which the hapless young woman could defend herself. Although she was trying very hard to hold still, Betty could not help squirming anxiously about on his lap. The next step was obvious and Don reminded himself to do it very slowly. As the other girls stood around giggling, smirking and tittering at Betty's expense, Don reached for the hem of her short black gymslip.

"*Eeek!*" Betty screamed with horror and flopped around on his lap like a fish out of water. "*No!* Don't you *dare!* Never! Don't you *dare!*" From the way that some of the other girls screamed and clasped their hands over their mouths, it seemed apparent to Don that they had simply assumed that the spanking would consist only of some swats across the skirt-covered bottom. But hearing objections only from Betty, he saw no reason not to proceed with his original plan.

"No! Don't! Don't you *dare!*" Betty screamed again furiously. "Girls, don't let him! Don't..."

Taking his time, Don slowly gathered the pinafore back, revealing lovely tapering thighs encased in sheer black nylon. Trying to prolong the ceremony as much as he could, he pulled the skirt further back to the heavier webbing of her stockings where he could see the snaps of her black garter belt and a glimpse of white thigh. The assembled girls were all watching intently, and it was apparent that most of them were quite delighted with Betty's ordeal.

"Girls, for heaven's sakes, this is shameful!" Betty protested, casting a quick shamefaced look back over her shoulder to appeal to them. "Please, this is awful!"

Slowly Don worked the skirt up over the tops of her black stockings. Her ivory white thighs, plump and tapering, made an almost breathtaking contrast with her black hosiery. Gathering her gymslip up inside out, Don occasionally permitted his hand to brush against the silken smooth flesh of her bare thighs. He could feel her shrivelling and could sense that she was too ashamed to struggle.

"Please! Please! Don't go any further! Please!" Betty pleaded in growing desperation. "Girls, make him stop!"

It was obvious that she would get no help from her roommates. Don slowly pulled the gymslip back to expose her panty-clad buttocks. She was attired in an obviously expensive pair of pink silk knickers, trimmed at the legs with white lace. The wispy garment could barely confine her girlishly plump and widely rounded buttocks, and the lower portions of her pretty nates were in fact visible. Beneath the tightly stretched material, Don could see the exciting muscles in her comely lovely rippling and tensing in anticipation of the chastisement to come.

"Pull my skirt down!" Betty demanded. "This is awful! You have no right to do this!"

The highly distressed young woman continued to plead and protest to everyone present as Don paused to take a panoramic view of all the scenery on display. It was an unforgettable sight, delightfully feminine and rotund buttocks encased in pink, lace-trimmed knickers, smooth and plump bare white thighs, full shapely legs in sheer black nylons and the toes of pretty black sandals touching the floor. Snickers, titters and giggles from the onlookers only served to make the ordeal worse for the blushing and miserable young woman.

"Now, girls, I trust I have the authority to remove the final barrier to a truly effective spanking!!" Don spoke in a deceptively quiet voice.

"Yes!" Anne quickly replied. "Yes! Yes!" other girls joined in with eager voices. It was unanimous.

"Oh, no!" Betty screamed, trying to struggle but only managing to wave her stockinged legs quite prettily. "No! No! I simply couldn't stand it! Please, this is too humiliating!"

Her face was a deep shade of scarlet as she haplessly glanced back over her shoulder, and

Don resisted the temptation to tell her that her bottom would soon be as red as her face. Instead, he confined his attentions to the task of getting those fragile knickers down out of the way. The baring of that attractive young Washington secretary proved much more exciting than Don, or any of the attentive onlookers, would have imagined.

While poor Betty screamed and struggled to preserve her modesty, Don rolled the pink knickers down as if he were unwrapping a Christmas present. Everyone stared as girlishly wide and beautifully rounded buttocks, as smooth as satin and a delicious pink white in colouration, came into view. The two lush globes quivered lasciviously as Don slowly pulled her knickers down below the expanded tops of her black stockings.

"Oh, this is horrible! Simply awful! Please!" Betty was nearly beside herself with anger and humiliation. Glancing back over her shoulder to confirm how obscenely she was exposed, the distraught young woman shut her eyes as if to block out the sight and hastily turned her head away.

Once again Don paused to admire the scenery. Apparently expecting the spanking to begin at any moment, Betty could not refrain from flexing and puckering her lovely buttocks in a manner that was almost outrageously provocative. Although the other girls had been tittering and smirking, they were now quietly staring at those naughty, quivering mounds that were soon going to have to take their spanks from a masculine palm.

Don was tempted to begin with a real hard smack that would sound like a revolver shot as it cracked against her pretty rear, but he decided against that. Instead, the spanking would start lightly and slowly, letting the heat build up gradually. Like some artist, he was going to paint Betty's gorgeous posterior and upper thighs a flaming red, and he was going to apply the paint very slowly and spread it around very evenly. When he got through with the job, Betty's charming hindquarters were going to resemble a couple of overripe tomatoes!

Don inspected the quivering target area carefully and raised his right hand in the air. The other girls were watching intently, some of them biting their lips. He could feel Betty's entire body tensing in anticipation of that first spank.

Slap!

Don applied the first spank lightly and quite low, just above the top of her right stocking.

"Ooohhh!" Betty gasped, more from horror at having a masculine hand in contact with her precious posterior than from discomfort.

Some of the other girls also gasped, and it was obvious that they were thinking about what it would be like to be in that position.

Don left his hand resting in place right where it landed, discreetly allowing his fingers to probe the silken flesh. Betty puckered with embarrassment and instinctively tried to squirm away from the man's hand. Raising his hand and pausing for a moment to admire the light pink spot, Don administered a second light slap slightly above the first.

"Oooh!" Betty once again jerked her hips as his hand came into contact with her pretty posterior. "This is awful! Please! I'm a grown woman I… I…"

"Take your medicine, you little manstealer!" one of the girls spoke out, and it was readily apparent that she was echoing the sentiments of the others.

"You just wait till you have to take it bare!" Betty retorted hotly.

Slap!

The third light spank landed at the very base of her right buttock, and Don's exploring hand pressed downward against the almost-unbelievably resilient feminine flesh.

"Ow!" Betty protested. "Don't, please! Please!"

Smack!

The next crisp spank landed squarely upon the surface of her right bottom cheek.

The vulnerable target felt velvety smooth and springy-soft beneath Don's palm, and he could feel the hapless young woman shrivelling with humiliation at the intimate contact. The other girls were all watching intently, and Don could see some of them squirming as if vicariously undergoing the experience themselves.

Slap!

Switching to the left buttock, Don applied the next spank lightly and quite high on her rotund posterior.

"Ooohhh!" Betty gasped, unintentionally pumping her lush bottom provocatively as Don's masculine palm pressed down firmly against the softly yielding flesh.

Taking his time about it, Don slowly worked down her left buttock and thigh to the top of her stocking. Each spank produced a gasp and a pretty wiggle from his attractive victim, who was obviously having considerable difficulty retaining her self-control. By this time, her comely spanking surfaces were a light shade of pink all over and were obviously ready for the second instalment.

"Please, this is too humiliating!" Betty implored, twisting around miserably on his lap. "Please, girls! Make him let me go!"

"This has only been the warm up!" Don informed her. "I think your bottom is ready for a real spanking now!"

"No, please!" Betty sounded thoroughly alarmed. She looked back over her shoulder and twisted about in his lap in a frantic effort to reason with him. "Please! I couldn't take it! Please! Oh, *please!*"

The fingers of her right hand clawed back in an effort to provide some protection to her exposed posterior, and Don could feel her entire body cringing in anticipation of the coming punishment. He could see the deep fear in her eyes as she desperately tried to talk him out of it. Pressing down firmly against the small of her back with his left hand, he raised his right hand high above his shoulder.

WHACK!

Don's hand cracked squarely across the crevice of her lush bottom with a resounding smack, momentarily flattening the resilient flesh beneath his palm.

"*Oww!!*" Betty shrieked, her pretty stockinged legs jerking backwards with a flash of black nylon. Her full, womanly hips jerked spasmodically and she instinctively struggled to free herself from his grip. "That hurts! Stop! Don't!"

The other girls gasped and some of them shuddered at the crisp sound of a man's hard hand landing squarely upon a bare, voluptuous feminine bottom. Don pressed his hand down firmly against the soft, quivering target to emphasize his control over her. Looking back over her shoulder with a look of total distress on her pretty face, she squirmed with mortification as Don's fingertips explored her charming orbs.

"Please, make him stop! That hurts something awful!" she pleaded with her roommates. "Please, you don't realise..."

Splat!

Don's flattened palm cracked smartly against her right cheek, once again compressing the flesh and inspiring her shapely, nylon-clad legs to swing backwards reflexively. Several of her roommates gasped at the ear-splitting crack of firm masculine flesh landing on soft, resilient feminine flesh.

"Owwww!" Betty shrilled in a high soprano voice, haplessly trying to twist out of range of Don's punitive hand. "Please, you're hurting me! Stop! I can't stand it!"

Splat!

Don applied a noisy spank to her left bottom cheek, flattening the pretty mound and this time allowing the tips of his fingers to explore the crevice that separated the two lush globes.

"Oww!" Betty yelped, and high-heeled sandals momentarily pointed toward the ceiling. "Please! You have no idea how much it hurts!"

Warm, salty tears were beginning to

course down the young woman's cheeks, spoiling her makeup. Her distress and shame were clearly mirrored on her hotly flushed face, and she constantly twisted about in an unsuccessful effort to alleviate her discomfort. Shapely legs outlined in black nylons and garter belt were waving back and forth with her feet rarely touching the floor, and she was beginning to have difficulty holding them together.

Splat! Smack!

Beginning just above the top of her right stocking, Don began applying another series of spanks to her comely posterior. Some of the on-looking girls were biting their nails rather feverishly as the extent of Betty's suffering and shame began to register on them, while others were smirking with unconcealed delight that the little bitch was getting her just desserts. And there were others that Don was almost positive would have dearly loved to trade places with the squirming, red-bottomed victim.

"Look how red her bottom is getting!!" one of the girls exclaimed in a voice that mixed wonder with excitement. Others joined in. Most spoke in a low, confidential tone of voice but poor Betty could still hear most of what was said, and words like "red" and "hot" predominated.

"Ouch! Oh, no! This is awful!" Crying quite

hard, Betty sounded thoroughly distraught as Don's solid hand began spanking down against her unprotected and girlishly tender bottom with dreadful regularity. "Ouch! Oh, no! Please! That's enough! I can't stand it anymore! Please, girls, I'll never do it again! Never!"

"That'll teach her!" someone remarked vengefully.

"Gee, I didn't know a girl's bottom could get that red!" another onlooker added.

As her curvaceous bottom and upper thighs turned a bright, feverish shade of scarlet under Don's broad palm, Betty miserably wiggled like a snake and kicked her shapely, stocking-clad legs back and forth in an undignified but highly appealing dance of shame and pain. In her growing distress, she could no longer preserve her modesty and her pretty legs were jerking hard and wide, frequently revealing her bright pink cunt lips and the dark, fleecy hair surrounding them.

"Oh, my!" more than one girl gasped as the watching girls realised how much Betty was exposing herself. Nearly all of them blushed prettily at the sight of another girl's pudenda so lewdly displayed, and while some of them reacted with great embarrassment, others showed almost total fascination. Although he really didn't know, Don was quite sure that more than one pair of knickers was quietly being soaked by feminine juices.

Splat! Smack!

Don continued applying his open hand to her ever-reddening spank spot, carefully distributing the firm applications to keep the colour scheme even. Betty's rosy and frantically twitching bottom, her anguished tear-stained face, her wildly swinging, nylon-clad legs, and indecently displayed deep pink groove all combined to provide him with a great deal of sadomasochistic gratification. He hadn't felt so exhilarated since his days as headmaster back in England before the war.

"Ouch! Oh, no! Stop! I beg you!" Betty pleaded almost hysterically as Don unmercifully continued building up the raging bonfire in her attractive backside. "That's enough! Please! *Oh, pleeeeeeease!* I can't take it anymore!"

Don paused to rest his arm for a moment and to inspect the results. By this time, Betty's delightfully curvaceous feminine bottom and upper thighs were a brilliant shade of scarlet all over and were obviously burning with a deep, penetrating heat. Sobbing quite hard now and swinging her legs back and forth in a totally abandoned manner that afforded a wanton display of bright pink pussy lips, the miserable young woman thrashed about wildly in a futile effort to get some relief for her thoroughly scalded buttocks.

"Look how red she is!" one of the girls remarked in a low but audible voice. Others exchanged similar comments that the suffering young secretary couldn't help overhearing.

"Please, no more!" Betty begged although she was almost too breathless to get the words out. "Please! I'm simply burning up! Girls, I promise I'll never do it again!"

Taking a quick look around the room, Don could see that Betty's roommates were almost hypnotized by the sight of frantically squirming, bright red feminine buttocks and exposed girlish charms. Several of them were positively squirming with what was obviously erotic stimulation.

"One more spank and then it's over to the corner with you, young lady!" Don announced.

Whack!

The final spank, the hardest of them all, cracked like a pistol shot as it crashed against Betty's flaming spank spot.

"*Arrrghhh!*" Betty screamed, her head snapping back and her sandaled feet flying upward.

Don promptly lifted the sobbing young woman to her feet and forcefully marched her back to the corner where she had been standing when he first entered.

"Hold your skirt up!" he demanded. "Otherwise, you'll get some more of this!"

he added, smacking her burning rear to show what he meant.

Sobbing heavily and obviously willing to do anything to save her blistered bottom from further torment, Betty haplessly grabbed the hem of her gymslip with both hands and held it up above the waist. Her knickers forming a small ring around her ankles, she stood sobbing and sniffling with her beautiful, bright red buttocks on full view for everyone to see. Framed by her black garter belt and stockings, her scarlet spank spot glowed like a brilliant sunset.

To complete her disgrace, all of her roommates applauded appreciatively as Don stepped back and collapsed into a comfortable seat where he could observe his miserable victim.

"That was beautiful!" one girl told him. "That little trollop deserved to get spanked clear down to her stockings!"

"Oh, but I'd hate to get spanked bare!" he heard another girl say as the various roommates excitedly began discussing the session. No one left the room and there were frequent glances over at the bare-bottomed culprit snivelling in the corner.

"Bet you could use a drink after that," Belinda told him, handing him one as she spoke.

"Thanks," Don replied, leaning back

to enjoy his drink and the sight of Betty standing disgraced in the corner. He listened carefully to the comments of the other girls, and could tell that they were quite intrigued by the system of roommate regulation that he had just demonstrated for them. "There's one souvenir of the occasion I would like," he spoke quietly to Belinda, whispering his request in her ear.

"Sure!" she replied, a broad grin on her face. She immediately got to her feet and walked over to her Betty. "Come on, Betty, step out of those knickers!" she told the hapless girl. "Your Master would like a souvenir."

Amid amused giggles and comments from the watching girls, Betty managed to step out of her pink knickers. Belinda picked them up and handed them to Don as if he'd won a prize. Pocketing the wispy garment, be dawdled over his drink for the next quarter hour. When he finally left, Betty was still standing bare-bottomed and humiliated in the corner.

Chapter 6

When Don returned to his apartment, he was rather confident that one of the girls would soon be trailing after him. The spanking session had contained so many sexual undertones that it seemed inevitable. As a result, he was not surprised when he heard a knock on the door. Feeling relaxed and in a rather pleasant frame of mind, he opened the door.

"You *bastard!* You son-of-a-bitch! I ought to call the police!"

She spat the words out in a furious tone of voice. It was Betty, blushing and enraged!

"How dare you do such a thing to me?" she hissed. "That spanking was just supposed to be some kind of gag. You weren't supposed to..."

Don smiled at the display of spirit. "Come in, Betty," he told her, standing aside.

The furious young woman lunged at him, and it was only at the last minute that he saw the gleaming scissors in her hand. He grabbed her wrists, deflecting the blow as she nearly fell against him. The scissors nicked his shirt and clattered noisily to the floor. Don kept his hold on her wrist and she struggled to get away.

"Let me *go!*" she demanded. "Let me go! You fiend!"

"Why, you little hellcat!" Don spoke with a trace of amusement in his voice. Holding her wrist and dragging her inside the flat, Don kicked the scissors aside and shut the door.

"Let me out of here!" Betty demanded, still struggling to get free.

Don released her wrist and she backed up, breathless and glancing warily about. She was still wearing the outfit in which she had been spanked, and Don noted that the black gymslip was a little creased from being held above her waist for so long. He could feel a powerful erection beginning to form as he recalled that event and gazed at the outraged but inviting young woman in front of him.

"Come on, let me out of here!" Betty once again demanded. "Let me go!" Perhaps without realizing what she was doing, she reached behind her back with both hands and gingerly rubbed her bottom, which was apparently still stinging from the punishment that Don had inflicted upon it.

"There's nothing cuter than a well-spanked gal rubbing her bottom!" Don told her.

"You bastard! I ought to go to the police!" she told him angrily. "You didn't have any right to completely bare me like that!" Her face flushed a pretty scarlet as she spoke.

"Oh, come off it!" Don told her, advancing a step toward her. By this time, his developing erection had formed a promising curve in the front of his slacks, and it would only be a moment before she noticed it. "You liked it!" he told her. "It got you all hot and bothered, and that's why you're here!"

"Are you kidding?" Betty flashed an angry glance at him. "Why, I... I never heard of such a thing!"

Without saying anything, Don took another step forward. Suddenly Betty noticed the threatening bulge in the front of his slacks! Her eyes widened with a mixture of horror and fascination, and she suddenly clasped a hand over her mouth.

"Hey, you're not..." she spoke in a hoarse voice. "Oh, for heaven's sakes! Please! Let me go!" As she spoke, she began backing up with slow, tiny steps, like a cornered animal looking for an escape. "I didn't come here to..."

"Sure you did!" Don replied, advancing toward her in a confident manner.

"There are laws against rape, you know!" Betty reminded him, continuing to back up.

"Rape?" Don told her. "You came here of your own free will. No court would ever convict me." A confident gleam in his eye, he watched as she unknowingly backed through an opened door that led to his bedroom.

"Let me out of here!" Betty pleaded, gasping when she was in the bedroom.

Don stepped forward quickly and grabbed her wrists. The terrified, distressed look on her face made her all the more appealing, and Don could feel his hot, hard penis pounding with lustful urgency.

"That spanking was just the warm up!" he told her. "Now you're going to get some real punishment!!"

"Please, you're hurting me!" Betty protested, her voice mirroring her distress. She made something of an effort to struggle, but it was readily apparent to both of them that he was much the stronger and could handle her at will.

"Don't fight and you won't get hurt!" Don replied, keeping a firm grip on her wrists and pushing her toward the bed.

"Let me go!" Betty protested, quickly becoming quite breathless. "Let me go!"

"No point fighting it!" Don told her. "You know you want it! That's why you came here! That spanking has got your little box all steamed up, and you're just dying for it!"

"No! No! No!" Betty protested, almost in tears. "I'll scream!"

"Then I'll have to gag you!" he warned her.

Still holding her wrists, he forced her

down on the bed on her back and used his weight to control her body under him.

"Let me go! Let me go, please!" Betty pleaded in a voice that sounded increasingly desperate.

Don held her down until he felt her heaving, breathless body go limp under him. Her face hotly flushed, she stared up at him like a trapped animal. She had undone her pigtails and her black hair had become quite dishevelled in the struggle. Her gymslip was well up over her knees, providing an appealing display of shapely legs and trim feet attired in sheer black stockings and fancy high-heeled sandals.

"Now, don't fight and you won't get hurt!" Don told her, releasing her wrists and preparing to disrobe.

Breathing hard and continually looking around as if seeking an escape route, Betty watched as Don hastily removed his clothes. As he stripped off his shorts to reveal the full dimensions of his huge, desire-bloated penis, Betty gasped hard and stared at it with a mixture of awe and enthralment. He could see her eyes drinking in the entire length of his throbbing muscle and his scrotum with its two heavy, swollen balls, dangling below.

"You beast!" she exclaimed, her young body shuddering. "You can't make..."

At the last second, the attractive young

secretary decided to make a fight of it. Catching him by surprise, she suddenly came up off the bed and lashed out at him with both arms and feet. With strained gasps, the two of them started struggling. When he recovered from his initial surprise, Don's greater strength began asserting itself. He forced her back to a supine position on the bed, and in the struggle her black sleeveless dress came up nearly to the waist. She had not bothered to replace the knickers she had forfeited earlier, and Don caught sight of the luscious pink lips of her cunt in the black vee at the fork of her legs.

"Go ahead and fight all you like!" Don told her, finding the struggle quite exhilarating.

"No! No, please let me go!" Betty pleaded, almost in tears.

Her efforts were obviously tiring her and her struggles began to subside.

"Stop fighting it, girlie!" Don told her. "You know you want that big cock in you!"

"No, please! Oh, this is awful!" she begged in a desperate voice. "Please, don't rape me!"

"Rape? Who's talking about rape? You'll be begging to have that big sausage inside you soon!" Don laughed.

Satisfied that he had her under control, Don stood up and gazed down appraisingly at her lush young girl's body. Flushed and breathing quite hard, she made no attempt to pull her gymslip below her waist. Her black garter belt and matching stockings contrasted vividly with the white flesh that surrounded the fleecy triangle of pubic hair; the dark curls partially obscured her glittering little jewel of a pussy. His thick, rigid manhood pounding with increasingly urgent desire, Don licked his lips with expectation. He could see that her gorgeous buttocks were still a glowing scarlet from the thorough spanking that he had administered.

"Please don't do this to me!" Betty pleaded, looking up at him with troubled eyes.

"You're going to be asking me very sweetly for it by the time I'm through with you!" Don promised. "Now take off your clothes!"

Watching him apprehensively, Betty complied. Off came her black schoolgirl's dress and white blouse, and the voluptuous young secretary lay in front of him attired only in steeply pointed white brassiere, black garter belt, tautly suspendered black stockings and elegant black sandals with their neatly tied bows standing out against her trim ankles.

"That, too!" he told her, pointing to the brassiere.

Blushing with girlish embarrassment, Betty unhooked the garment and slowly removed it. Don's eyes narrowed appreciatively as he gazed at her stiff-nippled young breasts. The two big, saucy mounds jounced with their newly acquired freedom, and Betty ineffectually tried to use one arm to cover them up.

"Please don't hurt me!" she pleaded, her pretty lower lip quivering.

Don quickly produced a couple of lengths of white clothesline rope from the bureau, and dropped down on the bed beside her.

"Don't tie me up!" Betty exclaimed in sudden alarm. "Please! Please!"

She started to struggle again but only in a token manner. Don quickly looped one of the ropes around her right wrist and lashed it to the bedpost.

"Please!" Betty pleaded. "Don't!"

"Shut up!" Don told her. "I can't trust anyone who comes in here and attacks me with a pair of scissors."

Wrapping the second length of rope around her left wrist, he quickly lashed that wrist to the opposite bedpost. Her arms spread-eagled to the two bedposts, Betty could do nothing but squirm helpless on the bed. She yanked at the two ropes that held her prisoner, but they were obviously quite firm.

"What are you going to do to me?" she asked, her voice filled with an apprehension tinged by lust.

Don stood at the foot of the bed and gazed down at her lush young body attired only in garter belt, black stockings and spike-heeled sandals. Although she tried to hold her legs tightly together, there was no way that she could avoid wantonly displaying her brightly glistening pink pussy. Despite, or perhaps because of, the ordeals that she had just endured, there was a heady feminine aroma of burgeoning sexual arousal in the air. Her face hot from embarrassment, she could not refrain from staring at Don's rigidly erect, blood-inflated penis and the two heavy testicles dangling beneath it.

"Oh, please, this is terrible!" Betty pleaded, tears trickling down her cheeks. "I'm completely helpless! Please, you can't do this to me! Have you no shame?"

"Nonsense!" Don replied. "You know you like your sex rough! That's why you're here!"

Clasping the spike heels of her pretty sandals in his hands, he began pulling her ankles apart to expose her all the more. Betty did not attempt to resist but turned her head aside with revulsion as she realised only too well how lewdly she was exposed. She wanted to kick at him, but felt weak and afraid. Don's eyes began at her narrow ankles and slowly moved up her fully curved calves rippling beneath her sheer nylons, past her delicately rounded knees to her quivering, beautifully tapering smooth thighs. The two wide bands, one slightly lighter than the

other, at the top of her stockings emphasized the marble whiteness of the flesh above them. His lustful gaze travelled up her silky inner thighs to where he could see the desire-swollen, rosy outer labia of her cunt, puffy and slick with juices in a thicket of jet-black pubic curls.

"Oh, please!" Betty pleaded, her voice sounding very low and faraway. "Please, I'm so helpless and ashamed. First, you spank me and humiliate me in front of all those awful girls! And now you tie me up and abuse me!"

"Maybe if you had something really big in your mouth, you couldn't talk so much!" Don told her in a sardonic voice.

Don wanted his mouth to travel that same route his eyes had just taken, and stretched out on the bed at her feet. Leisurely, he kissed the bow of each pretty sandal and then the cobwebby nylon just above it. He then began kissing her nylon-clad, fully curvaceous calves, gradually working his way upward. At the same time his hands gently caressed her shapely legs from toe to thigh, massaging and enjoying every lush curve.

"Oh, how can you treat me this way?" Betty whimpered, her voice filled with self-pity.

"You have beautiful legs, sweetheart!" he told her, ignoring her protests.

Moving upward, Don kissed each

delicately rounded knee, letting his lips linger against the tightly stretched nylon. His hands roamed high up her shimmering thighs, his fingers digging into the warm quivering flesh. Pushing her legs further apart, he began moving his face up from her knees along her inner thighs, thoroughly enjoying the feel of cobwebby nylon against his face.

"How can you torment me like this?" Betty protested, squirming and writhing against the bonds that held her in place. But her repeated pleas were beginning to lack conviction as now they contained the unmistakeable accents of sexual arousal.

"You love it! You know you do!" Don told her, his lips reaching the heavier bands of her sheer black stockings.

The pretty young secretary watched helplessly as her masculine assailant began kissing the incredibly smooth flesh of her inner thigh just above the tops of her tightly drawn stockings. Goose bumps formed on her legs and her entire body stiffened with erotic pleasure. Without being forced to do so, she was holding her beautiful legs wide open for him.

"Please, untie me!" she begged. "Please, it's so unnatural! Please, it's just awful to have to lie here while you torment me and do things to me!"

Taking his time and savouring the musky

aroma of feminine arousal that wafted into his nostrils, Don worked his way up the trembling young woman's lush inner thighs. Stroking the full length of her thighs with his hands, he began deftly exploring her flowering little pussy. The initial light, tentative strokes produced moans of excitement and embarrassment, and ripe pungent juices suddenly began trickling over his fingers.

"Please, don't hurt me! Please! I'm scared!" Betty pleaded in tones that more than ever lacked conviction, squirming with a combination of embarrassment and unwanted erotic arousal. She watched with growing dismay as Don continued moving his face upward in the direction of her pink, hotly dripping vulva. "Oh *no!* You're not going to... ?"

Lightly fingering the slippery, plump pussy lips, Don slowly opened them up. Her back arched sharply, Betty bit her lip and wriggled with helpless vulnerability as he spread the two pink juicy petals open.

"What a beautiful cunt you have!" he told her, whispering the message into the widely dilated, pink cavern.

"Oh, how can you talk like..." Betty protested, looking hotly embarrassed.

Without further ado, Don buried his face in the wet and gaping gash with his tongue extended its full length.

"Ohh!" Betty almost screamed at the lewd assault on her feminine treasure. Her entire body shuddered convulsively and she arched her back even more sharply as Don's sturdy masculine tongue sliced into the juicy playground and flicked her quivering little button. Somewhere inside her a dam broke, flooding the entire area with warm, wet feminine dew.

"That's the way, girl! Don't fight it!" Don told her, nibbling on her plump outer lips as he spoke. "I'm going to have you begging for it!"

"No! No, please!" Betty pleaded softly. "It's awful to be tied up like this! Please, it's so humiliating! Please, it's degrading to have to lie here while you do anything to me you want!"

Don's tongue began moving up and down inside the wet pink furrow in a ticklish and thoroughly tormenting manner. He could feel her vibrant young body beginning to respond, slowly surrendering to sexual bliss despite her apparently conscious opposition to it all. As she squirmed girlishly on the bed, her stockinged legs brushed against his hard masculine body in a teasing manner.

"Stop, please! Oh, stop, please!" she begged, making one last effort to ward off the raw physical pleasures to which she was about to succumb.

"Relax and enjoy it!" Don told her. "You're going to get eaten until you just beg to have cock in there instead of my tongue!"

"Oh, how can you talk like that?" Betty spoke with obvious distress. "How can you do this to me?"

Don did not reply but instead resumed tonguing her lush pink interior, his darting tongue brushing past her nervously palpitating clitoris and roaming into her juicy vaginal orifice. He could sense that all thoughts of resistance were beginning to melt under the spell of the magical erotic sensations that were flowing through her body. One low and faraway sounding moan followed another, and her pelvis began those instinctive coital thrusts that betrayed her own inner feelings.

"Please! Please, for the last time!" Betty pleaded, fighting back tears.

"You love it!" Don told her. "You're as wet and dewy as any schoolgirl with a crush!"

Once again his tongue ranged deep into the wet juicy groove, touching off electric sparks as it flicked her quivering clitoris. Sucking in her feminine juices with loud slurping noises, he flicked and stabbed at her magic button from various angles. He could feel the tiny bud responding to his lustful caresses, and it wasn't long before the highly sensitive membrane was taut and quivering with sexual desire. A river of feminine juices flowed against his face as the young woman finally gave way to the overpowering sexual sensations.

"Oh, please, I can't stand it any longer!" she impulsively exclaimed. "Go ahead! Go ahead! Please, you're driving me crazy! My cunt's on fire!"

Don savoured his moment of triumph by lightly skimming his tongue over her choice inner meat, and then chewing and nibbling for a few moments on the succulent outer lips. The delicious feminine aroma assailed his nostrils and signalled her eager readiness. Her stocking-clad legs were open and drawn up at the knee, and he could feel the rippling muscles in her inner thighs quivering with feminine surrender.

"Fuck me! Fuck me!" Betty pleaded, her voice urgent with desire. "Fuck me! I can't stand it any longer! I just have to have a cock in there!"

Don finally drew back to a kneeling position between her outstretched legs, his red-crested penis rigidly to attention and his heavily dangling balls swinging freely. Betty stared at the primitive-looking masculine organs with deep sensuous desire written all over her hotly flushed face. Her pelvis was twisting back and forth, revealing the damply matted hair surrounding her hot, wet cunny.

"Fuck me! Please! I need it so bad!" she

begged. "Go on! You wanted me to beg, so I'm begging!"

"Well, beg some more!" Don told her, relishing his control over the shapely young secretary.

As he spoke, he spread his knees and began crawling up over her. His purpose was quite obvious and Betty uttered a cry of despair.

"No! No! Please! In my cunt!" she begged, tears filling her eyes. "Please, in my cunt! Not my..."

He moved forward over the helpless young woman's body until she was staring upward at his enormous masculine shaft. As he lowered himself over her, Don caught his breath sharply as he suddenly felt his hotly throbbing penis pressing against her warm face while his balls brushed against her throat. Given no choice Betty began kissing his turgid, desire-bloated cock, moving from the sleek, purplish head to his scrotum with moist, sensuous kisses. Beneath him she felt very small and feminine, and he could sense the innate submissiveness in her helpless young body.

"Please put it in my cunt!" she begged in a low, pleading voice. "Please! Please. Oh, please put it in my cunt!"

"Put it in your mouth first!" Don told her in a commanding voice.

"All right! All right!" she replied, surrendering without a whimper.

Her wrists helplessly spread-eagled to the bedposts, the pretty young secretary lay back on the pillow with her eyes closed and her pretty mouth open submissively. His weight resting lightly on her, Don began moving about on top of her so that her entire face would come into contact with the bulbous head and sensitive underside of his throbbing prick. The sleek crown of his rigid shaft explored her eyes, her cheeks, her forehead, her hair, her chin and smooth throat. Dripping with female arousal, Betty squirmed and gasped as he prepared her for the insertion to follow.

"In my cunt..." she whispered dreamily.

Once more Don explored her velvety smooth face with his hotly throbbing cock, this time concentrating on her eyes. Tormented by the massive masculine organ and eager to get on with the proceedings, Betty squirmed about under him with delightfully feminine wriggles. Once more she began kissing the sleek underside of his hard, twitching prick, working from base to tip and concentrating on the wildly throbbing vein that coursed in bas-relief along the lower side. Completing the tour, she once again lay back on the pillow with her pretty mouth wide open and expectant.

Don's turgid brick-hard maleness quickly found the warm, moist and inviting target. Feeling the full, sensuous lips encircling the mushroom-shaped crown, he paused for a moment to savour the deliciously warm, wet sensations that suddenly engulfed him. Her little tongue instantly went to work. Don thrust it in a little further, gradually letting her get accustomed to having the large slab of meat in her mouth.

"Mmmmmm!" Betty's groan was a blend of pleasure and mild discomfort.

After another brief pause, Don shoved it in another inch and waited. In no time, his wildly pulsating joystick was soaking wet from her saliva, and he began sliding it back and forth just between her teeth with slow but firm thrusts. Under him he could feel her soft, highly aroused young body squirming and writhing with sexual passion, and he could distinctly hear the slurping sounds as she obediently sucked on his madly throbbing penis.

Pacing himself carefully, he thrust his thick member in a little further. This time he could feel it scraping against the roof of her mouth. Betty shuddered and seemed to be trying to say something, although her well-bloated mouth made the words incomprehensible. Don drew back momentarily and then pushed it forward again. This time the husky shaft went far into her mouth, nearly to her throat, and he could hear her gulping and gurgling submissively.

"That's the way, girlie!" he told her. "You really want that big thing in your little box, don't you?"

"*Mmmmmm!*" Betty's muffled response was highly affirmative.

Don suddenly drew back, his glistening penis exiting from her pretty mouth with a loud plop.

"FUCK ME! FUCK ME!" Betty shouted out, breathless and squirming. "PLEASE! PLEASE! FUCK ME! PLEASE! COME ON, I'VE DONE EVERYTHING YOU WANTED!"

With a confident smile on his face, Don drew back until he was in a kneeling position between her outstretched legs. Beneath him he could see her pelvis simply twitching with anxious expectation. Lowering himself on her helpless body he manoeuvred to align the crown of his rigidly pounding penis with her sopping wet, musky pink slit. The bulb-shaped head cut through the juicy outer lips and slid past the lust-swollen, twitching clitoris into her wet vaginal canal. His rigid sabre of flesh pierced the narrow pink tunnel with a virile, powerful thrust that lifted Betty's hips right off the bed.

"*OOOOOHHHH!*" Betty squealed as she

suddenly found herself impaled on the thick shaft. Her vibrant young body responded to the assault with a violent shudder of pure erotic excitement, and shapely, stockinged legs coiled tightly around the backs of Don's bare legs.

As his hotly throbbing penis firmly plugged into the young woman's deliciously wet, tight vagina, Don rested on top of her in commanding fashion. "How do you like having all that meat in you, girl?" he asked with a confident smile.

"I love it!" Betty admitted, breathless and squirming beneath him. "Even if you do spank me and tie me up and torment me something awful, I still love it! Fuck me! I need cock so bad I could just die!"

Don began pumping back and forth on top of her bound body in a relaxed fashion. His strong, masculine body seemed to overpower her small, yielding form, and she felt delightfully feminine and dependent under him. She began writhing and twisting her hips around in a highly sensuous manner, and he recalled how she had thrown them about during the spanking he had administered earlier. Even at this early stage of the proceedings, her hotly eager, wet cunt was sucking and eagerly pulling on his aching meat, trying to get all of it inside her.

"Oh, that's beautiful!" Betty gasped. "Oh,

am I ever hot! I can't believe my cunt could get this hot!"

His heavily hanging balls slapping against her smooth feminine flesh, Don gradually speeded up the cadence. He was keeping his pelvis down tightly against hers, and she kept struggling to force herself upwards in response to each surging stroke. He could feel her tiny but lust-crazed clitoris scraping eagerly against his slick, aching cock as it rode back and forth inside her. Her wet, clinging little pussy continually sucked him with beautiful little milking movements, and their madly throbbing organs became locked in a fierce struggle.

"Oh, it feels so gooood! So gooood!" Betty exclaimed. "Your big cock feels so good! Harder! Fuck me, harder! *Harder!*"

Don's long, iron-hard prick swept back and forth with long lunges, the thick crown drawing back almost to the vaginal orifice and then plunging in all the way to the cervix. Hot feminine foam bubbled up in voluminous quantities, bathing his pounding muscle with their soothing oils. As the hot, raging fire in her loins spread through her body, her buttocks tossed and writhed in a progressively more and more frantic fashion. Despite the weight he was throwing down on her, she was able to meet him thrust for thrust, humping her cute and recently spanked posterior high off the bed.

"Harder! Harder!" she begged breathlessly. Her voice was hoarse with lewd desires. "Harder! Please! Fuck me till I die!"

This little hellcat can really fuck, Don thought to himself. No wonder her roommates wanted her spanked. He began pumping with rapid, punishing strokes that sent his weight slamming down against her helpless but wildly tossing body. Her swollen cunt lips kept trying to suck him all the way inside her, and he could feel her rapidly twitching little clitoris slapping wildly at his surging cock. Her stockinged legs were coiled about in a tight embrace, the spike heels of her sandals scraping against his bare legs.

"Ooooohhhh! Ooooohhhh!" Betty moaned mindlessly. Completely carried away by the lustful pleasures that she was experiencing, the attractive young secretary was totally lost in sexual bliss. "Harder! Harder!" she begged, breathing almost too hard to make herself understood.

Sensing that his distraught young partner was rapidly careening toward a wild, mind-blowing orgasm, Don abandoned all efforts at self-control. Fucking with almost savage strokes that sent his madly throbbing, burning penis deep into her lush channel with each forward thrust, he continually slammed his entire weight down against her frantically twitching body. The final, almost brutal, thrust sent scalding jets of his thick male sperm into her vagina with explosive force.

"Oh, my! Oooooohhhhh!" Tormented beyond endurance by the sexual punishment her beautiful young body had absorbed, Betty surrendered to an intense orgasm. Convulsed with passionate spasms that originated in her lust-swollen clitoris and vagina, the young woman climaxed with ecstatic cries of joy. The deep vaginal contractions caught Don's exploding penis in a tight vice, pulling him far inside her boiling cunt and milking his thick, hot semen in a hungry, demanding fashion. "*Ohh!* Oooooohhhhh! *Ooooohhhh! Whaaat a fuck!*" she moaned as her convulsions began to subside.

Breathlessly, the two of them rested on the bed with their hot bodies still lewdly glued together. Don made no attempt to untie her wrists and, for some reason, Betty neglected to ask him to do so.

"You know," she told him with a bright smile. "I never realised that a spanking could lead to hot bed sex like this."

"You ought to thank those horny sorority sisters of yours for setting you up," Don told her, kissing her lightly on the lips.

The two of them lay quietly for several minutes, and Don found himself drifting into a pleasant nap. Suddenly Betty's young body stiffened with fear.

"Don, Don!" she whispered urgently at him. "There's someone in the living room!"

Chapter 7

With a crash, Anne burst through the opened bedroom door, a drawn gun in her hand.

"Eeek!" Betty screamed, her stockinged legs flailing as she futilely tried to break loose from the bonds that held her to the bed.

"Annie!" Don cried out, embarrassed at having been caught in the compromising position but, seeing the way in which Anne was waving her gun around, was feeling more concerned for his and Betty's safety.

"What's going on here?" Anne demanded, looking around warily.

"It's okay, Annie. It's okay," Don reassured her. "Now put that gun away before someone gets hurt."

When Anne realised that Don was completely nude and that Betty, clad only in her garter belt, stockings and shoes, was helplessly tied to the bed, she relaxed and put the gun back in her handbag. "Sorry," she told Don. "When I realised that she had sneaked out of the apartment and probably..." she paused, not wanting to say too much in front of Betty. "Well, I thought she might be someone else... and then I heard what sounded like a struggle up here..."

"Okay, okay," Don told her, beginning to see the humour in the situation although he realised that Betty might start asking some questions that wouldn't be easy to answer. "It's not what you thought at all," he continued. "It's just that Betty felt that her spanking was insufficient punishment for all of her misdeeds, and came up here for some additional discipline!" He flashed her a conspiratorial smile as he spoke.

"So I see!" Anne replied, glancing at Betty's spread-eagled and partly clad body. She tried very hard not to notice the drooling pink gash of her cunt lips that nestled in the forest of jet-black hair, and her face became hotly flushed as memories of her recent lesbian experience suddenly flooded her consciousness.

"Will someone please tell me what's going on around here?" Betty demanded, yanking helplessly at the bonds that held her wrists to the bedposts.

"It's okay, honey," Don told her. "Annie is an old girlfriend of mine who has fits of jealousy now and then."

"But I don't understand..." Betty persisted.

"Don't ask too many questions," Don told her. "Sometime I'll explain the whole thing to you."

"Can you at least untie me?" Betty asked, a distinct note of irritation in her voice.

Instead of replying, Don got to his feet and took Anne's handbag from her. Stepping behind her he placed his hands on her shoulders and leaned forward to allow his face to brush against her wavy brunette hair. The attractive young woman tensed, made a little uncomfortable by the situation and wondering what was going to happen next. Don quickly discerned that she was doing her best to avoid looking at Betty's lush young body, and could easily guess the thoughts that were running through her head.

"Now you're going to apologize, aren't you?" he asked in a deliberately quiet voice.

"Am I?" Anne asked, darting a highly embarrassed glance back over her shoulder.

"Yes," Don replied. "To both of us!!" He spoke in a quiet but deliberately salacious tone of voice that left absolutely no doubt what he meant.

Anne gulped heavily but did not reply.

"Will someone please untie me?" Betty demanded. "This is embarrassing." The pretty young woman squirmed haplessly on the bed as she spoke.

Using his hands on her shoulders to propel her forward, Don escorted Anne over to the bed. She moved unwillingly but made no attempt to resist.

"What's going on here?" Betty asked insistently. Unable to preserve her modesty in any way, the attractive young secretary blushed scarlet as the two of them looked at her.

"Now you are going to apologize to both of us, aren't you?" Don asked quietly.

"Y-yes!" Anne replied with a gulp.

Still not comprehending what they meant, Betty looked inquisitively from one to the other. "Will someone please tell me what's going on around here?" she asked. "She comes bursting in here with a gun and..."

"It was all a mistake," Don assured her. "And she's going to apologize to you for it!"

As he spoke, Don began undoing the buttons that ran down the back of Anne's blouse. Her pretty face a bright scarlet and her eyes averted, the attractive brunette stood quietly in front of him. The blouse came off, revealing smooth feminine shoulders and a prettily embroidered white slip worn over a trim white brassiere.

"You mean she's…" Betty voice expressed dismay as she began to catch on.

"That's right!" Don replied.

It was Betty's turn to gulp, and the cute young secretary squirmed girlishly on the bed. "Well, gee, I never..." she mused. From the way her face lit up, it was quite apparent that the idea intrigued her.

Don's hands moved to the side fastener of Anne's dark skirt. Undoing it, he pulled it down over her round, buxom hips and allowed it to slide down her legs to the floor. Standing there in her flimsy slip with the outline of her brassiere, knickers and dark brown stockings clearly visible, Anne stepped out of her skirt and kicked it aside. Running his hands downward from her shoulders, Don cupped them momentarily around her well-filled brassiere and then ran them downward, exploring the narrow contours of her waist and full, womanly curves of her hips. From there he ran his hands down her full, tapering thighs until his fingers reached the embroidered hem of her light slip.

Anne stood blushing prettily as he slowly pulled the slip up over the top of her head, revealing her shapely, stockinged legs, shimmering white thighs contrasting vividly with her black garter belt suspenders, almost transparent white knickers, smooth, gently curving tummy, steeply pointed brassiere and soft feminine shoulders. Her hair became slightly dischevelled as he extricated her from the slip.

"Are you thinking about what you're going to be doing for us?" Don asked, his hands cupped over her shoulders.

"Y-yes!" Anne admitted. Despite her

embarrassment, she couldn't avoid looking at Betty's lewdly displayed body stretched out on the bed.

"I don't know..." Betty sounded a little dubious.

"Oh, don't worry, Annie is an expert when it comes to pussy-sucking!" Don remarked caustically as he unsnapped the clasp of her brassiere. "You've had plenty of experience, haven't you?" he teased.

"Well... y-yes... some!" Anne admitted hesitantly.

Betty's eyes widened slightly at that admission. Squirming prettily on the bed, she watched as Annie' brassiere fell away to expose her large, lush breasts. Still standing behind her, Don slid his hands around under her arms and cupped them firmly over the two resilient, pink tipped mounds, moulding them into even more compact globes. He could feel her sensitive nipples hardening at the masculine contact.

"Now, let's get these little things off!" he suggested, running his hands downward and catching them in the elastic waistband of her knickers. He removed the small garment with maddening slowness, working it off her hips to reveal the dark delta of her pubic bush at the fork of her legs and then dropped to one knee to finish the job. To ease the task, he slipped off her high-heeled shoes for her. "There!" he announced as he pulled the knickers from her feet.

Naked except for her black garter belt and dark brown stockings, Anne stood blushing in front of them with her lush naked body revealed in all its glory. Don moved over to an easy chair and seated himself casually with his bare legs well apart.

"Come here, Miss Carfax, and let's show Betty what an expert cocksucker you are!" Don told her, an evil smile on his face.

Anne swallowed hard as she walked over to him. "Please, it's so embarrassing to do something like that in front of someone else!" she protested, a slight shudder of distaste going through her body.

"Don't be such a prude," Don told her, pointing downward with one finger.

"Why don't you spank her like you did me?" Betty suggested from her vantage point on the bed.

Knowing only too well that Don might be quick to adopt such a suggestion, Anne promptly sank to her knees between Don's outstretched thighs.

"That's more like it, my dear!" he complimented her. "Now, give me a complete tongue job to start off with!"

Her face a blushing crimson, Anne extended her hands to cup Don's heavy, swinging scrotum. Keenly aware that Betty was watching from the bed, she began licking at the two bloated, swollen testicles through their thin coating of sensitive flesh with her small pink tongue. Looking delightfully shamefaced, she licked them all his ball-sac until it was glistening from the effects of her saliva.

"Are you watching this, Betty?" Don asked to deliberately torment the blushing fellatrice in front of him.

"Sure am!" Betty replied in a bright voice, grinning at him from the bed.

Despite the embarrassment of having to perform such a debased act in front of an onlooker, Anne began to display rising signs of sexual arousal. Her full breasts rising and falling with deep breaths, she sucked one sperm-swollen ball part way into her mouth in a loving fashion and held it there for a few moments, sucking and tonguing on it simultaneously. She then gave the second ball a similar treat, working it between her full, ripe lips and then sucking on it while flicking it with her small tongue.

"Looks like you needed feeding!" Don remarked.

"Mmmm!" Anne admitted, darting a quick glance over at the bed to see if Betty was watching.

"Put it in your mouth!" Don told her quietly.

Holding his limp penis upward in one small hand, Anne meekly slipped the bulbous head into her warm, wet mouth. With Betty eagerly watching the performance from the bed, the attractive agent began assaulting the masculine organ with a dual combination of manual strokes and oral caresses. Sucking and tonguing the sleek head and flooding the entire area with warm saliva, she continually pulled and stroked with her smooth hand. Her efforts quickly began to pay dividends as the flaccid cock quickly began to expand and harden.

"That's the way, girl!" Don told her. "Let's see you get it all the way into your throat!"

Blushing deeply and obviously very much aware that a highly interested witness was observing her efforts, Anne soon found herself with a mouthful of rock-hard, pounding prick. The thick, virile lance made her wriggle with girlish excitement, and the salivary secretions in her mouth were matched and indeed outdone by the warm vaginal juices that leaked from her tingling pussy and trickled down her inner thighs.

"Gee!" Betty remarked from her observation post as she watched her pretty roommate working more and more of Don's husky, purplish-veined shaft into her oval-shaped mouth.

"See if you can make it disappear!" Don told her, his bare legs positioned comfortably around her kneeling body.

Anne's moan told him that that was impossible. Of course Don knew differently. Occasionally gulping on her rapidly flowing saliva, the attractive brunette began working more and more of the solid, pounding meat into her deliciously wet oral cavity. Both Don and Betty watched intently as the thick slab of bulky meat gradually began disappearing further and further between Anne's pink outstretched lips. Don felt the mushroom-shaped crown touching the roof of her mouth, scraping past it as it probed into her throat. Anne's half-strangled gulp indicated that she couldn't handle any more of it – for the moment.

"Wow!" Betty exclaimed, her voice mixing admiration with envy as she observed her kneeling roommate with what must have been at least five inches of rock hard, pounding cock in her mouth. "I can't believe she can get it that far into her mouth!" she added, wriggling prettily on the bed as she spoke.

"Now let's *really* show her what a great cocksucker you are!" Don suggested, patting Anne's head gently as he spoke.

Her crimson face straining with the effort to handle so much hard cock, Anne began moving her head up and down with long, deliciously sweet sucking movements. Both Don and Betty watched with fascination as her pretty brunette head bobbed up and down in his lap. From time to time, she twisted her head to one side or the other, allowing his bulging penis to press outward against her succulently soft inner cheeks. At the same time, her fingers played softly and teasingly over the throbbing base of his upright spear.

"*That's* the way!" Don told her, watching the sensuous movements of her full, pink lips as they moved up and down his hotly throbbing flesh.

Pausing occasionally to swallow her saliva with an audible gulp, Anne kept moving her hot, eager mouth up and down on the hotly pulsating masculine organ with rhythmic movements of her pretty head. Her cheeks drawing inwards as she sucked, she continually flicked and stabbed with her warm tongue. At times she darted a quick look over at the bed to see if Betty were watching her servile performance, and it was readily apparent to Don that his kneeling fellatrix was enjoying a masochistic thrill at having a witness to her sexual subjugation.

"All right," Don told her, "you've played with that enough for the time being. Now I want you to go kneel between Betty's legs and suck her juicy little pussy for her!!"

"Oh, *my!*" Betty gasped with sheer, delighted shock at the suggestion.

Anne drew back and looked up at Don in an appealing manner. "Please, Don, don't make me do that!" she pleaded, her hands clasped prayerfully in front of her. "Please! It's too embarrassing!"

"Go on!" he told her with an amused laugh. "You know you secretly want to, anyway!"

Their eyes met and both of them knew that he was telling the truth. Her face a blushing crimson, Anne slowly got to her feet and walked over to the bed.

"Gee, I've never been... sucked by a girl before!" Betty exclaimed, wriggling with anticipation. The shapely, raven-haired young secretary was holding her stockinged legs wantonly open, fully displaying her dripping pink gash and the damp, matted black hair surrounding it. A sluggish, pearly stream of Don's sperm dribbled out of her slightly distended vaginal tunnel and trickled over the twitching little star of her dark, crinkled anus. The rippling muscles in her young loins repeatedly tensed and flexed in anticipation of the treat to come, causing more of Don's semen to leak from her pussy.

"Well, it'll be a new experience for you," Don remarked, standing beside the bed with his blood-engorged cock feeling as hard and long as a torpedo.

Her eyes glued upon her roommate's lewdly exposed pink gash, Anne crawled on the bed between Betty's outspread legs. Looking shamefaced but excited, she leaned forward and skimmed her warm pink tongue over her lips as the delicious aromas from Betty's overheated little box assailed her nostrils. Don watched the Sapphic ceremony with great interest.

"Here, Betty," he said, grabbing a pillow. "Let me slide this under your arse."

Hotly flushed and wiggling excitedly, Betty arched her back to enable Don to slide the pillow under her. Her cute bottom, still bright pink from the spanking that Don had administered earlier, glowed prettily as the pillow slid under it. Elevated by the pillow, Betty's rosy groove gleamed with a mixture of feminine dew and male sperm as the pretty young secretary awaited the lesbian treat.

Anne, drinking in Betty's feminine charms with all of her senses, impulsively leaned forward and planted an open-mouthed kiss squarely upon the guava-pink flesh of her vulva.

"Ooooohhhh!" Betty gasped, her mouth forming into a pleased oval. "Hey... that feels *good!*"

Brushing her own hair back out of her

face, Anne extended her firm, pink tongue and began working it wetly up and down the soft, oozing groove. His brick-hard penis pounding with arousal, Don watched the lesbian performance with quiet intensity. Attired in their garter belts and stockings, these two lovely young girls were a vision of Sapphic depravity as feminine tongue met and loved feminine genitalia.

"It may be naughty but it's damn nice!" Betty remarked with a giggle, squirming her cute bottom happily as Anne's warm tongue tormented her pink vaginal slit.

Although she was blushing and obviously embarrassed to the very depths of her soul, Anne was also thoroughly enjoying the submissive lesbian role that she had been assigned. Her entire body trembled and quivered as she sliced her probing tongue between the two saucy outer lips, giving herself a sample of the deliciously juicy treats awaiting her. Using her fingers to pry open the glittering treasure trove, she formed her lips into a perfect oval and sealed them to the slippery wet gash, drinking down the delicious blend of Don's ejaculate and Betty's exudate. The highly audible sucking movements that followed quickly caught Betty's quivering little clitoris in their draft, and the pretty young secretary could feel her tiny pink bud being sucked into Anne's mouth.

"Oh! Oh! That's the way to suck my pussy!" Betty exclaimed. "Wow! I can feel my clit being pulled into your mouth! I can really feel it! Golly!"

Wriggling and squirming with provocative movements, Betty bit her lip and kept taking in deep breaths as Anne taught her the joys of girl love. Anne's mouth was like a vacuum cleaner as it sucked out the contents of her roommate's cunt and tormented her little clitoris into a rigid, lust-swollen state of sexual torment. Driven almost frantic by the debased lesbian assault, Betty pumped and thrust her hips in a wild bucking fashion. Her stockinged legs were wrapped around Anne's neck in a tight coil, giving her no chance to stop to catch her breath.

"Eat me! Suck me! Suck pussy!" Betty cried out. "Oh, my poor clit is going crazy! Eat me! Only a girl could know how to do it like that! Oh, yes, suck! *Suck!*"

Don could feel his rigid cock aching with lust as he watched the obscenely beautiful performance in front of him. Anne's lips were completely covered by Betty's plump outer folds and her nose was also partly buried in the juicy pink furrow. The liquid sucking sounds were all too audible as Anne drank in the cascading waterfall of male and female juices. Betty's pelvis was jerking back and forth with quick, jerky movements that lifted her hips right up off the bed.

"It's about time I joined this party!" Don suddenly announced, unable to endure his spectator role any longer.

His erect, blood-swollen prick so stiff that it bobbed vertically against his hard, muscled stomach, he climbed on the bed behind Anne's kneeling form and grabbed her waist.

"*Mmmmmm!*" Anne moaned. Not quite sure of which opening he would avail himself, the attractive brunette found herself in a torment of fear and anticipation. Their lithe muscles flexing wildly, her beautiful buttocks cringed at the expected assault.

"I ought to put it in your arse!" Don told her, observing her anxiety and amusing himself at her expense.

"*Nnnnnggg!*" Anne tried to protest without for a moment denying herself the tasty pleasures of Betty's steaming little box, and as a result her moans conveyed no real intelligible message.

Teasing her for a moment by letting his cockhead brush against the pucker of her anal star, Don finally guided his madly throbbing manhood toward her gaping vaginal orifice. He could feel the surging sense of relief that poured through her body when she realised he had selected the more usual target. Holding her by the waist to keep her in position, Don rammed his rigid, almost painfully aching

prick into the pink tunnel.

"Mmmmmm!" Anne moaned ecstatically as the rock-hard cock suddenly dilated her hot, eager vagina to its full capacity. Her feminine juices were flowing in copious quantities, soaking his pounding ramrod in their hot oils, and her buxom, satiny hips began churning with coital thrusts.

"Suck me! Oh, suck me!" Betty gasped, completely caught up in the throes of her first lesbian experience. "Oh, eat me! I love it! Can you taste my clit in your mouth? Can you taste it? Oh, it feels so good!"

With his madly pulsating masculine shaft buried deep in Anne's clinging, slippery vagina, Don leaned forward over her back and firmly cupped her breasts that dangled like two lush, ripened fruits. The heavy mounds quickly became stiffly suffused with erotic tension as his fingers massaged and caressed them. As he began pumping dog-fashion, he dropped one hand down to tease her quivering, lust-charged little bean of a clitoris.

"How do you like this?" he asked, although he did not expect an answer.

"Mmmmmm! *Mmmmmm!*" Anne moaned. Caught in the middle of the sexual threesome, the voluptuous young brunette found herself assaulted with an almost bewildering variety of sexual pleasures.

Betty's glorious little pussy filled her mouth with delicious feminine nectar, and Anne strove valiantly to get that throbbing little button into her mouth. At the same time, Don's pile-driving prick was driving her overheated vagina into a frenzy, while his strong, masculine hands tormented her throbbing, rigid breasts or her own, wildly sensitive, clitoral nub. The variety of sexual sensations had a cumulative effect, raising her levels of erotic awareness to heights that she had never scaled before.

"Oh, it's beautiful!" Betty exclaimed rapturously. "My pussy's died and gone to heaven. I can't believe it! I'm going to cum! *I'm going to cum!*"

Realising that his two feminine partners were reaching their sexual peaks, Don bucked and plunged his wildly aching prong into Anne's juicy vagina like a jackhammer. Draped down over her back, his hands continually clawed and twisted at her tormented breasts to tantalise her all the more. Her oven-hot cunt grasping and sucking at its masculine intruder, the sexually abandoned young woman threw her hips around in a wild, grinding motion much like a burlesque dancer's gyrations.

"I'm cumming! Oh, I'm *cummmmmmiiiinnnnggg!*" Betty's delirious scream was almost bloodcurdling. Totally beside herself, the distraught young woman flipped her hips up like a fish out of water, inundating Anne's face with a spray of her heady female ejaculate.

Caught in the vice of Betty's clinging thighs, Anne drank down the exotically flavoured juices with loud slurps.

"Mmmmmm! Ooooohhhh! Ohh! Mmmmmm! *Ooohhh!*" The ecstatic sounds of feminine sexual pleasure came from both young women, and Don could not distinguish between them.

Holding himself back as long as he could, Don finally drove his pounding cock deep into Anne's inner recesses and went off like a cannon. As the thick hot cum blasted into her, Anne arched her back sharply and Don could feel her vaginal muscles coiling tightly around his exploding prick. With the effect of a vacuum she began sucking him all the way into her, squeezing his discharging penis as though it had been caught in a powerful milking machine.

"*Aieeeeeee!*" Caught in the crossfire of the masculine and feminine climaxes, Anne experienced the most intense orgasm of the threesome. Ignited by the sparks from her hotly burning clitoris, a powerful sexual explosion racked her entire body and sent waves of electric pleasure coursing through her entire being. Collapsing breathlessly on the bed, the shapely young brunette fought to recover her sanity. "Wow, I can't believe it! I can't believe it!" she kept repeating over and over again.

"Golly, that was really something!" Betty exclaimed when at last Don untied her wrists. "Boy, when I got spanked this afternoon, I sure didn't think it would lead to this! But I still don't understand the connection between you two, and why Annie came charging in here with a gun." The pretty young secretary looked understandably puzzled.

"Well, I can't explain it to you just now," Don told her. "The two of us will just have to bribe you to keep your mouth shut about the whole thing."

"Bribe?" Betty asked. "What are you talking about?"

"If you'll just keep your mouth shut," Don said. "Anne and I, or both of us, will suck your pussy or do anything you say for the duration, and I mean anything. Okay?"

A smile spread across Betty's face. "Well, a girl couldn't beat a deal like that, could she?" she replied with a teasing glance, first at one and then at the other.

"It's a deal then?" Don asked.

"Sure!" she laughed easily. Leaning back on her elbows with her stockinged legs lasciviously spread, she grinned at them. "Now which one of you wants to go first?" she asked, indicating the spot by drawing her index finger up the sopping groove of her cunt.

Chapter 8

The disciplinary system inaugurated with Betty's spanking quickly swung into full effect. Just two nights later another roommate Linda, a pretty, bespectacled brunette in her mid-twenties, became the second victim. Crying almost hysterically and in a state of near collapse, Linda went to her fate over Don's capable lap. Once again everyone was treated to the sight of a comely young curly-haired secretary being totally bared and put over Don's knees to be given a good, crisp spanking that left her buttocks a blazing scarlet and reduced her to distraught sobs. At the conclusion of this bottom warming, her fragile knickers were declared forfeit and Don undertook the not unpleasant responsibility of removing them from around her ankles.

As he suspected, the freshly spanked young secretary eagerly followed him to his apartment afterward, like a puppy who had found its master. Linda proved to be so sex-starved, so man-hungry, so horny that neither took time to disrobe. Holding her black punishment dress up over the top of her garter belt, Linda backed against a wall and Don fucked her in a standing, 'knee-trembler' position with her stockinged legs coiled tightly about him.

The following afternoon Don met with Anne to discuss strategy.

"Since you've eliminated Betty as a suspect, that leaves only Jean, right?" Anne asked.

"Apparently so," Don replied.

"Well, she won't be so easy to trap in your little spanking game," Anne told him.

"Oh, why's that?" Don asked. "It seems to me that all you girls are getting turned on by the idea."

"Well, most of them think it's kind of wild and sexy," Anne admitted. "But not Jean. She's the one girl who makes sure she never violates a single rule."

Don was thoughtful for a moment. "Well, in that case we might arrange to have the two of you caught in a lesbian embrace. That ought to serve as sufficient justification for the two of you to be spanked."

"*What!?*" Anne flared. "Do you think I'm going to let those girls catch me..." She was too indignant to finish the sentence.

"It's part of your job," he reminded. "Besides," he added with a touch of malice, "you've been showing some distinctly bisexual trends lately."

Anne glared at him. "That's not the point," she told him. "The point is that it would be just too embarrassing for all those girls to catch me doing something like... like that."

"After this little venture, you'll never see these girls again," Don told her. "Now let's do it like this. You tell the other girls that you're planning a surprise party for Jean. That'll give you a chance to be alone with Jean, and the others can walk right in on you. I'll be with them and I'll have Jean's bare ass on view before she knows what's happening."

"All right," Anne accepted the plan quietly. "It'll take several days to set it up and I suppose in the meantime you can continue your disciplinary activities." There was a slight trace of sarcasm in her voice.

"I told you the girls would all go for the idea," Don reminded her.

Go for it they did. As plans for the surprise party began to develop, the third and fourth culprits met their fate on successive evenings. The third was a cute redheaded secretary in her late-twenties, whose name was Monica. She had been convicted of neglecting her share of the apartment chores. The fourth victim was Cheryl, a blonde, sweater-girl type in her early-twenties. She had been convicted of borrowing stockings, knickers and other items of personal apparel from her roommates without permission.

The two spankings followed the procedure that had now become well established. When Don arrived on the scene, each girl was standing in the corner attired in the standard punishment uniform of white blouse, short black gymslip, black stockings and high-heeled black sandals. Surrounded by her grinning, smirking roommates each girl was turned over Don's knee in the traditional but juvenile position.

The girls' gymslips were turned back to reveal shapely legs outlined in black stockings, bare white thighs crossed by their tautly pulled black garter belt suspenders, and clinging black knickers that fit their rotund posteriors to perfection. In each case the knickers were slowly and almost reverently lowered to reveal quivering feminine buttocks flexing in anxious expectation of the spanking to come.

The spankings were classics. In writing to her best friend back home, Monica described her ordeal.

"Of course, as you would know, all seven roomies were there to savour my humiliation. Although I tried to put up a brave front, I was simply quaking when Mr. Blake swung me face down over his lap as if I was a naughty schoolgirl instead of a twenty-eight-year-old woman. As my short gymslip was drawn back to reveal my precious nylons, bare white thighs, and black knickers and garter belt, I closed my eyes and tried to pretend that it really wasn't happening to me. But there was just no way I could blot out all those snickers, giggles, titters, smirks and so on from my assembled roommates. I'll have to admit that I had been one of the most enthusiastic advocates for spanking the other girls, and they were all just dying to see me take my medicine.

Then came the total indignity of having my knickers slowly stripped down inside out by capable masculine hands!!! Believe me, there's just no way to adequately describe the total humiliation of being completely bared before an audience like that, and by a *man!* I just wanted to shrivel up and sink through the floor. And, oh! how my roomies all smirked and giggled and acted ever so smug us they observed me lying there in total disgrace with my girlishly plump buttocks sticking up obscenely bare! Although I ever so desperately wanted to hold still, I just couldn't refrain from quivering shamefully in anticipation of the red-hot punishment my poor bottom was going to have to take.

And then it happened! My precious, tender, bare bottom that no man had ever dared punish before suddenly and abruptly received its baptism by fire from a sturdy masculine hand!! *Ohhhh!!!* Mr. Blake' palm felt as if it were travelling ninety miles an hour each time it crashed against my sensitive posterior, completely flattening my cheeks with a deafening splat! Believe me, I was no heroine about it. I simply screamed and kicked my nylon-clad legs back and forth as if I had invented some new kind of dance. And I simply had to yank and jerk my burning hips around frantically on his lap, although I knew from watching the other girls how much I was exposing myself.

Oh, what an experience!! My full, womanly backside burned and prickled and itched with a hot burning heat that made each fresh smack absolute anguish. I cried hot salty tears that blinded my vision and ran down my cheeks. My pride totally destroyed, I begged like a little baby to have my bottom spared from that burning anguish. And through it all, my seven roomies just smirked and giggled and enjoyed themselves as only a bunch of girls can do.

When it was over, my poor bottom was simply a sheet of flame and I was sobbing hard between gasps of air. As usual, Mr. Blake proceeded to collect my knickers as a souvenir. Then I was sent to the corner where I stood bare-bottomed, burning and disgraced! Can you imagine such a thing, at my age?"

In characteristic feminine fashion, Monica omitted a few details that might have given her friend a truer picture of her experiences. For example, how she had gone to Don's apartment afterwards with her bottom burning furiously and had simply begged for the privilege of putting his big, beautiful cock in her mouth. How she had gotten down on her knees and had taken that rock-hard banana out of his pants herself. How she had eagerly and joyously taken his climax in her mouth, and without even pausing to catch her breath had then sucked furiously to produce another pounding erection. How he had thereupon administered an almost-brutal dog-style fucking until she had cum several times and nearly swooned with ecstasy. And how she had begged for yet more after that.

Cheryl's post-spanking behaviour involved similar patterns of sexual hysteria, although the details were somewhat different. In the privacy of Don's apartment, the cute young blonde, still sniffling from the effects of the spanking, had brazenly turned up her deeply scarlet, furiously burning bottom and just begged to be sodomized! Although surprised by the request, Don was more than willing to oblige and the walls of the apartment shook with the comely young woman's masochistic screams as his thick, pulsating shaft violated her incredibly tight anal ring. The pounding buggery that followed would have brought an admiring gleam to the eye of the Marquis de Sade. Grinding and twisting her bright red buttocks in a savage dance of pain and ecstasy, the distraught young secretary enjoyed an intensely submissive climax as Don's hot, virile semen spurted deep into her clinging rectal passage.

* * *

Two nights later Don received his next spanking assignment. This time there were two victims who were to be punished simultaneously. The first was platinum-haired, buxom Belinda, whose ex-officio position as ringleader had not spared her from conviction for the heinous offence of stealing another girl's date. The second was a long-legged brunette secretary whose name was Lois. She had been convicted of various offences, including monopolising the telephone and stealing cigarettes.

"Well, we've got a pair of them for you tonight!" Anne told him with a grin of complicity when he arrived on the scene. As she spoke, she pointed to the wall where the two miscreants were standing with their backs to the others.

The two of them were dressed in the standard punishment outfit. Lois, the taller and leggier of the two, looked the more juvenile in her short pleated gymslip, but both of them looked highly appealing as they stood with their blushing faces to the wall. Neither of them could quite hold still and the sight of the two fully grown young women wriggling their anxious bottoms in anticipation of their spankings required Don to exercise a conscious effort to refrain from achieving an erection.

"Which one are you going to spank first?" Betty asked. She and her other five roommates were all awaiting the session with expectant smiles on their faces.

"Let's do things a little differently tonight," he suggested.

As he spoke, he took two plain wooden chairs and placed them side-by-side in the middle of the room.

"Are you going to spank them both at the same time?" Linda asked, giggling at the prospect.

"Okay, girls," Don addressed the victims. "Let's bend over the backs of these chairs.

"Come on. No stalling!" one of the girls warned.

Blushing and wriggling with a girlish naughtiness that made them look and feel all the more juvenile, the two blushing victims moved over to the chairs. Both of them kept their eyes lowered and Don noticed that their pretty, nylon-clad knees were on the verge of buckling. As he motioned for them to bend over, the two of them bent over the backs of the chairs and grabbed the seats with their hands. Standing slightly to their rear, Don watched appreciatively as their black gymslips rode up to reveal an additional expanse of black nylon.

"Mmmm, this is going to be interesting!" a feminine voice remarked behind him as the six innocent roommates lined up to watch and enjoy the proceedings. As usual, the onlookers were in a gleeful mood, the type that can only occur when females are privileged to see a fellow member of their sex punished.

"Oh, why can't you get it over with?" Lois burst out with nervous irritation, looking back uneasily over her shoulder.

Her anxiety produced mocking laughter from her roommates.

"Oh Lois, you're *really* going to need a pillow to sit on after this," one of them taunted her.

Stepping behind her, Don grasped the hem of her gymslip and began pulling it up quite slowly. There were giggles and wolf-whistles of mock admiration from the on-looking girls as the pleated garment came up to reveal long, shapely legs in clinging, full fashioned black nylons, black garter belt suspenders standing out vividly against carnation-white thighs and generously proportioned, girlishly plump buttocks encased in snug-fitting black knickers. Don carefully pulled the gymslip up until bare flesh was visible above the tops of her knickers, and then stopped for an admiring glance before moving over to his second victim.

Blushing furiously and trembling with embarrassment, Belinda said nothing as Don grasped the hem of her gymslip and began the task of unveiling the area to be spanked. Again there were titters and whistles as shapely legs attired in black stockings came into view, followed by quivering white thighs and rotund feminine buttocks encased in sheer black knickers. Involuntarily, Don licked his lips as he gazed at the twin pairs of panty-clad bottoms quivering anxiously as their owners awaited correction.

"Why don't you just get on with it?" Belinda snapped, her face a bright scarlet as she glanced back over her shoulder.

This terse request only served to draw more amused giggles from the onlookers. As usual when a spanking was imminent, the girls were talking among themselves in hushed tones of intense anticipation. The anxious victims would overhear occasional words such as 'huge' and 'hot'.

As might be expected, Don conducted the

panty-lowering ceremonies with deliberate slowness, grasping the elasticated waistbands with both hands and pulling them down inside out until they formed a ring around the wearer's thighs just above her stocking tops. Lois' knickers came down first and the long-legged brunette, blushing as red as a beet and blinking back tears of shame, trembled haplessly as her fully rounded, pink-white feminine buttocks came into view for all to see. Belinda's turn came next and the attractive platinum blonde could not conceal her deep humiliation as her curvaceously rounded, buxom hips were exposed before everyone.

"Wow, look at that!" one of the girls remarked at sight of the two upturned pairs of plump, rounded bare bottoms awaiting correction. There were similar comments from the other girls, all of who were obviously intrigued by the two quivering targets. Once again words like "big" stood out in the undertone of excited conversation.

Their stockinged knees almost buckling under them at times, the two pretty secretaries had no choice but to endure the full humiliation of having everyone's eyes fastened on their upturned and completely vulnerable derrières. Both of them remembered to hold their legs together to minimize their exposure as much as possible, but a glimpse of downy labia was still quite visible at the fork of their legs.

"Hurry up! For heaven's sakes, just *do* it!" Lois burst out, obviously unable to stand the tension any longer.

Watched by the grinning girls behind him, Don stood behind Lois and drew his right hand back.

Whack!

Don's hand smacked lustily against her exposed bottom.

"*Oww!*" Lois yelped, her head snapping back, her brunette tresses flying and long legs buckling at the knee.

The watching girls snickered and some of them clapped their hands with delight.

Whack!

The second smack landed on the opposite cheek.

"*Oww! Oh!*" Lois squealed, one hand reaching back to protect herself.

"Take your hand away!" Don warned sharply as he moved on to the next victim.

Her pretty bottom flexing obscenely, Belinda miserably awaited her fate. Don paused and slowly brought his hand back.

Splat!

Don's masculine hand landed on tender feminine flesh with a loud report.

"*Aiieee!*" Belinda squealed, her blonde curls flying as her head snapped back.

Her reaction produced gales of laughter from her assembled roommates.

Splat!

Don's capable palm smacked lustily against her other quivering mound.

"*Ow!* Not so *hard!*" Belinda cried out, squirming prettily and looking back with a worried look on her blushing face.

Both pairs of buttocks were displaying a light flush from the introductory smacks.

Smack! Splat!

Don began applying the second round of spanks to the upturned targets. The feminine squeals and wriggles that invariably followed each noisy smack produced the expected reaction from the on-looking girls, all of whom were enjoying the spectacle of their roommates' punishment enormously.

Smack! Splat! Smack!

Don applied the third round of spanks, giving each of the four cheeks a crisp whack that momentarily flattened it. By this time both victims were crying and wriggling furiously as the temperature in their bottoms began to soar. Don took his time about it, fully enjoying the aesthetic advantages of watching two lush feminine rear ends, framed by black garter belts and stockings, turning rosy pink and then an incandescent scarlet, the imprint of some of his smacks still clearly visible.

"*Wow!* Look how red their tushies are

getting!" one of the girls remarked in an awed voice the victims could clearly hear. Others joined in with similar remarks.

Smack! Splat! Whack!

Don moved up and down behind the two suffering girls, giving each plump globe individual treatment. As the building bonfires in their backsides made each fresh spank that much more painful, the two young women sang an impromptu soprano duet of pain and shame. Reddening feminine buttocks twisted furiously and sandaled feet stamped helplessly against the floor. Hot tears spilled and made their mascara run, and the two of them occasionally looked back piteously over their shoulder to appeal for mercy.

"Ouch, oh, no, not so hard!" Belinda pleaded in an anguished voice. "Please! Ow!"

"Ouch! Oh, no! Oh, oh, hoo, hoo, hoo!" Lois sang the cabaletta to the duet that Belinda had begun. "Oh, no! Please, *please!*"

The two miserable girls received no sympathy from their assembled roommates. Indeed, as their quivering buttocks turned a flaming crimson, they were only too well aware of their roommates' amused titters, giggles and cutting remarks. Some of the comments were quite devastating.

Whack! Smack!

Don began moving at a faster pace, his

hand smacking like a paper bag popping each time it came into contact with tender feminine flesh. His hand ranged from stocking tops to garter belts, and he made some effort to achieve an equally scarlet tone to all the affected areas. At times the suffering girls had to be forcibly restrained from reaching back to protect their blazing derrièrres, and the two of them constantly yanked and jerked their scarlet bottoms in anguish. It was readily apparent that neither of them would be able to sit comfortably for several days.

"Pleeeese! Pleeeese!" Lois begged, her long legs sagging weakly under her.

"Eeek! Ouch! Pleeeese!" Belinda joined her. "Please! I'm on fire!"

Slowly and methodically, Don applied the final four swats to the girls' upturned posteriors. Each new application produced a pained shriek and furious wriggles, and the two comely secretaries sobbed and pleaded throughout.

"Ouch! Oh, please! Ow! My ass just can't take any more! Ouch! Oh! Oh, God, please stop! Oooh!" Belinda shrieked hoarsely as the final smacks descended against her burning bottom.

"Ooohhh! Ouch! Oh! Pleeeese! Pleeeese! Ow! Owwww! Ouch! Stop!" Lois howled in anguish as Don applied the final smacks with crisp, wrist-snapping strokes.

At last the ordeal came to an end. Sobbing and nearly in hysterics, Belinda and Lois sagged weakly over the backs of the chairs as Don bent down to remove their knickers. As he straightened up afterward, he paused to enjoy one final glimpse at the sight of the two sobbing young women with their flaming buttocks thrust up higher than the rest of their bodies. Winking raffishly at the amused bystanders, he stuffed the two pairs of knickers into his pockets.

"Wow, you two are going to be sitting on *icepacks* for the next few days" he heard one of the girls titter as he departed.

As he retreated to his apartment, Don wondered which one of the two girls would show up first. The answer was not long in forthcoming. In about ten minutes, he heard something of a commotion outside his door.

"I was here first!" he heard Belinda say angrily.

"No, you weren't, you hussy!" Lois' voice replied.

When he opened the door, Don found himself facing an imminent catfight. Their tear-stained, hotly flushed faces strained with anger, the two of them appeared to be on the verge of an all-out hair-pulling match.

"Here, here, girls," Don told them. "Come in before you get us all arrested for disturbing the peace."

Darting angry glares at one another, the two young women entered the apartment.

"I was here first!" Belinda told him with some vehemence.

"No, she wasn't either!" Lois asserted.

"Girls, there's plenty for both of you!" Don told them with a laugh.

"*Both* of us?" they spoke almost in unison.

"Right," Don told them, seating himself comfortably in his easy chair. "Now, just follow instructions. Belinda, you kneel between my legs and see what you find there! And Lois, you stand in the middle of the room and do a striptease for me!"

The two young women looked at each other and then smiled. "Okay!" they both agreed.

A moment later platinum-haired Belinda was on her knees in front of him, her pretty face flushed with excitement as she began opening Don's fly for him. His penis was already beginning to swell in anticipation of the pleasures to come. As Lois watched eagerly from over her shoulder, Belinda hauled the masculine organ out into the open. Surrounded by her soft hand, the supple pleasure tool quickly filled with blood and expanded to reveal its true dimensions. The rock-hard, nine-inch shaft produced almost drooling gasps of admiration from the two apparently sex-starved secretaries, and Belinda's hot, wet mouth quickly encircled the broad, flaring glans with an almost desperate eagerness.

"All right, Lois, on with the show!" Don told her.

Leaning back to thoroughly enjoy Belinda's oral caresses, Don watched as Lois began her striptease. Sitting very gingerly on her freshly spanked bottom, the pretty brunette crossed first one long leg and then the other as she removed her high-heeled sandals. Standing up, she slipped out of her black gymslip. She had not replaced the knickers she had forfeited earlier and Don found himself confronted by the unusual combination of white blouse, black stockings and garter belt. The thatch of dark brown, curly hair at the apex of her thighs was glistening with a dewy wetness that was full of promise.

As Belinda's busy tongue and mouth tantalised his throbbing cock, Don watched Lois peel off her white blouse to reveal a pink half-bra that was densely packed with feminine pulchritude. Blushing prettily, she unsnapped the bra and quickly tossed it aside, allowing her melon-like, rose-tipped breasts to tumble out in a saucy, provocative manner. Moving over to watch Belinda displaying her talents as a fellatrix, Lois did not bother to remove her black garter belt and sheer black stockings. The dark garments made a vivid contrast with her milk-white body.

"Come on, Belinda, don't be such a pig!" Lois exclaimed in a petulant tone of voice. "I want to suck that jumbo salami, too!"

"Now girls! Share and share alike!" Don admonished them.

"Well, okay," Belinda agreed. Looking prettily flushed, the attractive blonde got to her feet.

Lois quickly replaced her roommate between Don's legs. Forming her pretty mouth into a wide oval, she promptly thrust it over the bulbous, purplish crown of Don's upthrust and wildly pounding prick. As her mouth and tongue went to work on his velvet helmet with almost frantic urgency, it was readily apparent that she possessed considerable talents as a fellatrix. Leaning back comfortably in his seat, Don watched appreciatively as her brunette head began bobbing up and down in his lap.

Standing directly in front of him, Belinda began her own striptease. Obviously quite stimulated by the tangy taste of hard cock in her mouth, the bosomy blonde was in no mood to waste time in disrobing. Shoes, black punishment gymslip, white blouse, brassiere, black stockings and garter belt quickly came off in that order, and Don found himself gazing at her lush young body as Lois' mouth and tongue continued to work their magic on him.

"Let's go into the bedroom," Don suggested. "The three of us ought to be able to work out some interesting combinations together!"

"Okay!" both agreed. With their cute bottoms still a bright scarlet from the spankings that he had administered, the two curvaceous young women eagerly accompanied him into the bedroom. Don quickly stretched out supine on the bed, and his two feminine companions piled on the bed along with him.

"Here, Don, I want you to kiss my bottom better for me!" Lois told him.

Don watched as the long-legged brunette turned her back to the head of the bed, and then knelt astride his supine body with her stockinged knees next to his shoulders. Suddenly, he found himself gazing up between her long, satiny smooth thighs into the enticing pink slit, partially obscured by the forest of her thick, dark brown bush. From this extreme proximity, he was clearly aware of the heat still emanating from the delectable buttocks that he had just spanked so soundly and he could glimpse the little brown rosette of her anus that nestled cosily between them.

"Okay, watch out!" Lois told him with

a laugh, slowly spreading her long legs apart and lowering her feminine charms against his face.

As the somewhat-ticklish hairs brushed against his chin and his nose fitted easily into the crevice of her widespread bottom, Don found his lips pressing against the moist outer folds of her lush vulva. Slowly but firmly, Lois dropped her weight down on his face, blocking off his vision and giving him no choice but to breathe in a delicious cocktail of her pungent, musky aromas. Trapped beneath her wriggling buttocks, Don began working his tongue up and down the pink slippery crease, working it between the plump lips, spearing up into the juicy hole of her vagina as far as he could.

As he orally caressed Lois' dripping pussy in the difficult but intriguing manner, Don soon felt Belinda's warm mouth and friendly tongue going to work on his wildly throbbing and stiffly erect penis. The luscious platinum blonde gave it a thorough tongue washing, and then eagerly slipped it into her mouth. Working the blood-distended and pounding muscle into her wet oral cavity to an almost breath-taking depth, she began sucking on it in a loving manner.

"Wow, this is *great!*" exclaimed Lois, who was the only member of the threesome who was in position to speak at the moment.

Teased by Don's probing tongue, the long-legged brunette began grinding her well-formed, spank-reddened asscheeks around on his face in a semi-circular fashion. The evidence of Lois' sexual rapture dripped down over his face and seeped into his mouth. Don worked his tongue rapidly back and forth inside the deliciously slick groove, occasionally having to pause and gulp down her delicious female exudate. His nose tightly pressed into the anal valley between her buttocks, he could only breathe by taking a gulp of air through his open mouth.

At the same time, blonde Belinda excitedly sucked and nibbled on his throbbing and aching masculine joystick. Her busy little mouth moved back and forth on the thick, desire-bloated muscle with expert movements, while her capable fingers toyed with his heavily dangling balls and the lower portions of his madly throbbing penis.

Don raised the stakes by shifting his head and stabbing his tongue directly into Lois' anal pucker, causing the girl to quiver and gasp with shocked delight.

"Oh, I'm going to *cum!* I just *know* I'm going to cum!" she cried out in a voice thick with thrilling lust. Letting her weight rest entirely on Don's face, the shapely, stocking-clad brunette wriggled her curvy hips around with rapidly jerking movements.

Feminine fluids poured over Don's mouth and into his guzzling maw, and he could feel her lust-swollen clitoris twitching violently. "I'm *cummmmmiinnngg!*" Lois cried out exultantly, bouncing her bottom happily up and down on Don's face.

Tormented beyond further endurance by the two young women, Don thrust his hips with a forceful shove and began squirting his thick, almost gelatinous semen into Belinda's anxiously waiting mouth in strong little spurts. Belinda eagerly smacked her lips as the warm milky fluid splashed against her tongue and the back of her throat. Drawing back she held the mouthful of masculine cream in her mouth as long as she could, swallowing it very slowly and savouring every drop.

"Here, let me have a taste of it!" Lois pleaded, dismounting from her position on Don's face.

Don watched as the two kneeling women, their bright pink tongues touching, transferred pearly strands of semen and saliva from one mouth to the other.

"Mmmm, that *does* taste good!" Lois remarked.

"Let's trade places!" Belinda suggested, smiling at Don as she spoke.

Allowing their masculine companion only a moment to catch his breath, the two attractive young women quickly exchanged places. Almost before he realised what was happening, Don found Belinda kneeling astride his face with her wet little muff pressed down tightly against him. At the same time, long-legged Lois stretched out at right angles to his body and quickly produced another pounding erection with her wet, hot mouth. As Belinda ground her pussy into his face, Don employed his tongue on her quivering clitoris to bring her to a climax, while at the same time Lois' pretty mouth produced a similar result on his throbbing prick.

"Wow, I never thought a spanking would get me that aroused!" Belinda remarked breathlessly as the three of them stretched out on the bed afterwards.

"Me, neither," Lois added. "What do we do next?"

"Well, I think you'll have to count me out," Don told them.

"Oh, no, you can still suck!" Belinda told him with a knowing smile.

"And kiss better the bottoms you spanked so hard!" Lois added.

The two young women playfully rolled over to show him their soft, bright red buttocks.

Chapter 9

By this time six of the eight roommates had been on the receiving end of Don's bare-hand-on-bare-bottom discipline. As a result, there were six very attractive young women who had learned at first hand, so to speak, of the erotic implications of a good old-fashioned spanking. This, coupled with the acute wartime manpower shortage, resulted in considerable competition for Don's unique services, and he found himself enjoying one heated bedroom adventure after another.

He was so occupied, in fact, that there were times when he almost lost sight of his basic mission. The party that he and Anne Carfax were trying to arrange for Jean was proving difficult to organise. Jean, whom they were now sure was Claudia in disguise, was becoming more wary with each passing day, and the quasi-lesbian relationship Anne had developed with her was beginning to taper off. Moreover, Jean was spending days at a time away from the apartment, sometimes weeks, and efforts to trail her always seemed to meet with frustration.

However, he was not too concerned about the matter. He had notified the appropriate authorities of his suspicions about Jean, and was sure that she was being fed only harmless or inaccurate information. When the invasion of Normandy went off without a hitch in June of 1944, he relaxed on the assumption that no Nazi spy would be able to accomplish a great deal after that. Yet he found himself with a lingering curiosity to find out if Jean was really the von Reichsapfel girl, the young *Fraulein* with whom he had had an affair in what now seemed the distant past. Eventually, he had his answer.

* * * *

One afternoon following a pleasant spanking and sex session with one of the girls, he decided to take a brief nap. It was quite warm and he was still naked as he stretched out on the bed and drifted off to sleep. After what seemed like several hours a slight noise awakened him. As he drowsily came to his senses, he suddenly realised that he was tied to the bed!!

"What the..." he cried out, instantly becoming fully awake. He was tied face down by the wrists and elbows in a spread-eagle position, naked and vulnerable. As he yanked futilely at the ropes that held him prisoner, he became aware that a familiar form was standing at the foot of the bed. Claudia! She had changed back to being a blonde, though she had obviously had to bleach her hair to achieve an approximation of her natural colour.

"*So... wir treffen uns noch einmal*. We meet once more!" she spat at him.

"I don't understand, Jean," Don spoke quickly, pretending not to recognize her. "What is this? Why have you bleached your hair? What are you speaking in German for? Some kind of game?"

"Some kind of game, *ja?*" she taunted, stepping around to the side of the bed where he could see her easier.

Don's heart skipped a beat when he saw the gun in her hand, and his wrists pulled futilely at the ropes that held him to the bed.

"Some kind of a game, ja?" she repeated, once again deliberately, mockingly speaking in an almost theatrical German accent.

"I still don't understand," Don continued to feign ignorance.

"Oh come *on*. You know who I am!" Claudia told him. "When you first came here, I didn't think you were after me. But then the other day I found out that someone had tipped them off about me, and they've been giving me useless information for months. And that could only have been you!" She brandished the gun in a threatening manner as she spoke.

"I don't know what you're talking about,"

Don persisted. Trying not to be obvious about it, he kept working to loosen the ropes at his wrists. However, they had been tied quite efficiently and the task seemed hopeless. Knowing that Claudia probably had no intention of letting him escape alive, Don felt his hopes sinking.

"But it was really your girlfriend who gave you away," Claudia went on.

"Girlfriend? What girlfriend?" Don replied, trying to conceal his rising sense of terror.

"You know who," Claudia replied contemptuously. "Anne! That fake lesbian you've had sniffing after me for months! She got a little careless talking to some of the other girls, and I put two and two together!"

Becoming more desperate, Don jerked against the bonds that held him helpless. "Look, Claudia," he protested, instantly realising his mistake.

"Ah, so you *do* know who I am!" she flashed a knowing smile at him.

"Okay, Claudia," he spoke breathlessly and quickly. "Don't get yourself involved in a murder. The war's almost over. If you turned yourself in now, I'll see to it that the worst you'll get will be a few months in prison."

"That's what you say!" she spoke derisively, once again brandishing the gun in a manner that made Don flinch. "No, my friend, I'm afraid I can't let you out of here alive. Others only suspect who I am, but you *know*. Besides, there are plenty of better suspects for your murder than me – *I* wasn't one of your little playmates and *this*," she nodded at the automatic in her hand, "is Miss Carfax's gun!"

Don gulped and tried to think quickly, but fear was beginning to paralyze his mind. His entire body felt cold and numb.

"But first there's something else I'm going to do," she spoke slowly with an undertone of pleased expectation in her voice.

What? Don wondered but could not bring himself to ask. He relaxed slightly when he saw Claudia put the gun on the nightstand. She was looking at him steadily and with amused pleasure, like a cat that had cornered a mouse.

"First, I'm going to punish you!" she told him.

Don tensed as he saw her unbuckling the wide leather belt at her waist. "Don't!" he burst out impulsively.

"How the tables have turned!" she taunted, removing the belt and caressing it through her hands in a manner designed to increase his anticipation. "The disciplinarian gets disciplined!"

A cruel look in her eye, she raised the leather belt high over her head. Cringing in expectation of the blow, Don lay frozen on the bed with his teeth clenched, determined not to show any reaction to the pain that he was about to endure.

Thwack!

The wide belt whistled through the air and cut savagely across his back.

"Uhh!" Don gasped. The air seemed to go right out of his chest, and he felt the fiery pain of the belt starting to penetrate. His arms and legs both jerked reflexively and were abruptly stopped by the bonds at his wrists and ankles.

"How do you like that?" Claudia asked, laughing.

Don deliberately refrained from answering.

"Oh, I'll have you begging by the time I'm through," Claudia assured him.

Once again the belt sliced across his back, and Don's entire body jerked with the sudden jolt of pain.

"Take *that!*" Claudia spat. "And *that!*"

Once again the belt cut unmercifully across his back, sending waves of pain racing through his body. But with the anguish there came a slight ray of hope. As his body jerked against the ropes, he felt the rope at his right wrist loosen slightly. I must work it loose, he told himself, while Claudia is distracted with her whipping activities.

Whack!

Once again the belt flicked across his bare back with an agonizing lick of fire.

"Ungggh!" Don gasped involuntarily, his entire body twitching with an involuntary reflex to the sharp stab of pain.

"How does *that* feel?" Claudia asked. A little breathless, she was obviously enjoying the chance to get even with him. Without waiting for a reply, she drew the belt back and lashed it downward against his exposed buttocks.

Whack!

The sleek leather landed painfully across his bare flesh and cut a deep weal into the tender skin.

"*Arrrghh!*" Don croaked, instinctively twisting in an effort to avoid the full effect of the blow. At the same time he kept yanking at the rope at his right wrist, and could feel it starting to give.

"Take *that!* And *that!*" Claudia screamed at him, a vengeful look on her face. "It's about time you found out what it feels like!"

His vengeful former pupil began frenziedly lashing at his bare hips and upper thighs with the belt. The smooth, supple leather coiled about the curves of his body with burning strokes that were starting to lacerate his back and buttocks. The pain quickly became quite intense and Don felt himself desperately clenching his teeth and fighting back the mist of tears that threatened to blind his vision. But at the same time he could feel the rope at his right wrist becoming loose.

"Go ahead! Whip me, you little bitch!" Don spat at her through gritted teeth while he worked his wrist free.

Whack! Whack!

Claudia continued applying the belt at various angles, and the pain was becoming almost unbearable. From shoulder to thigh, Don's body was an agonizing mass of bloody weals from the effects of the vindictive whipping. But at last his wrist was free and he was waiting for Claudia to get close enough for him to grab. In the meantime there was nothing he could do but absorb the punishment she was administering.

"You will die in agony!" she told him with a tone of obvious satisfaction in her voice.

"There!" Don cried out as he suddenly grabbed her wrist in a tight vice and desperately held on.

"*Aieee!*" Claudia screamed in surprise. "Bastard! *Schweinhund!*" With that she lapsed into a torrent of her native German.

As the angry young woman flailed at him with the belt, Don pulled her toward him so that he could get her under control. Despite her resistance Claudia came down on the bed on top of him in a wild tangle of arms and legs. Abandoning the belt she clawed furiously at him with her long fingernails and kicked at him with her high-heeled shoes.

"You little bitch!" Don exclaimed as he fought to control the wildly struggling young woman.

"*You bastard! Schweinhund!*" Claudia kept yelling at him in an abusive fashion, but most of what she said was in German.

The two of them struggled wildly on the bed, and Don's greater strength gradually began to prevail despite his handicap. He slowly twisted Claudia's wrist behind her back and began pulling it up short. Developing his strategy as he went along, he decided to try to pin her body under his while he tried to untie his other wrist.

"Stop! You're breaking my arm!" Claudia pleaded, the resistance suddenly going out of her.

"Okay, but only if you untie my wrist with your other hand!" he told her, keeping an iron grip on her wrist.

Crying with frustration and discomfort, the young woman haplessly untied his other wrist.

"Now my ankles!" Don told her.

He retained a firm grip on her wrist as she twisted around to untie his ankles. As she did so, her dark skirt rode up over the tops of her black stockings, providing an intriguing glimpse of bare white thigh and black garter belt suspenders. In a few moments Don's wrists were free, and he twisted into a sitting position with Claudia across his lap, her stockinged legs swinging back and forth.

"*Nein! Nein!*" she protested, struggling half heartedly, the fight seeming to go out of her.

"*Ja! Ja!*" Don mocked her, holding her firmly in position with one hand and he worked her skirt up with the other.

In a moment Claudia's stocking-clad legs, ivory white thighs, black garter belt and knickers were on full view. The knickers came down slowly to reveal her beautiful, shimmering buttocks. The two lush, pale pink globes quivered like bowls of firm jelly as Don worked the knickers all the way down her legs and off her feet.

"Please!" Claudia protested. "You have no right to do this! Please!"

After what he had just endured from her belt, Don was in no mood to be lenient. "Oh but I have every right. You're going to get what's coming to you, you little Nazi trollop!" he told her in an angry voice. As he spoke he raised his right hand high in the air.

Splat!

Don's hand crashed noisily against Claudia's bare bottom, landing squarely across the crevice and flattening both cheeks.

"Oww!" Claudia screamed, her stockinged

legs flailing upward and her body bucking up wildly on his lap. “Don’t! Stop! You can’t…!”

Whack!

Don brought his right hand down just as hard as he could on her right buttock.

“Yeow!” Claudia shrieked, twisting frantically in an effort to avoid the punishing blows. “Stop it! You cannot do this…”

Smack! Don’s hand crashed against her left bottom-cheek with a loud report.

“Owwww!” Claudia wailed, her shapely, nylon-clad legs waving back and forth and her entire body twisting in worm-like fashion. “Stop! Please! It hurts! Please, you have no right to do this!”

“After trying to kill me, now you’re talking about your rights?” Don chuckled derisively.

Smack! Whack! Splat!

Don began spreading crisp and noisy spanks around over the inviting target. As the soft, tender flesh quickly turned a bright pink, Claudia squealed and wriggled delightfully with her nyloned legs prettily kicking back and forth. Crying with humiliation and pain, she continually looked back over her shoulder with an apprehensive look on her face.

“Ouch! Stop! It hurts!” she protested in a distraught voice. “Please! I’ll do anything you say!”

“I’ve hardly started with you, you

vicious little bitch!" Don told her, easily controlling her wildly struggling young body with his superior strength. By this time he had developed a pounding, thoroughly exhilarating erection and was prepared to enjoy himself thoroughly.

Smack! Whack!

Claudia haplessly wriggled her saucy bottom as Don's husky palm continued to torment her with energetic smacks. With her pretty posterior prickling and itching and burning brightly, the comely young woman simply had no choice but to jerk her shapely, stockinged legs back and forth in a thoroughly provocative manner. From time to time, the fat outer lips of her cunt flashed into view along with the fleecy crop of blonde hair between her legs.

"Please! *Ouch!* Oh, no! *Please!*" she implored him between exclamations of pain. "Oh, stop! You brute! My God – it hurts so much!" Tears were streaming down her eyes, and she was breathlessly wriggling around on his lap in a futile effort to avoid the full force of the blows as much as possible.

Whack! Crack!

Don continued applying his hand to the lush feminine target, spreading the spanks around to even up the colour scheme. As her rotund bottom turned a charming shade of red, Claudia sobbed like a girl and kicked her shapely legs back and forth with uneven jerks that provided tantalizing glimpses of pink girl-meat.

"Ow! Oh, no more! Please! I beg you!" the attractive young woman begged hoarsely. "Arghhh! Please! It hurts! Please stop, I'll do anything! *Anything!*"

Applying his capable palm with even strokes, Don appreciatively watched the undignified but appealing performance that she was putting on for him. Once again she was reinforcing his opinion that there was really nothing more attractive and erotically appealing than a tearful and obviously distressed young woman wriggling her scarlet bottom and kicking stockinged legs back and forth with increasing desperation.

"Stop! Oh, no, please! *Pleeeeeeeeeeese!*" Claudia pleaded between sobs. "Please, I can't take it anymore! I just can't!"

Despite her tears and protests about the mistreatment that her pretty hindquarters were receiving, it was quite apparent that Claudia was finding considerable masochistic pleasure in her torment. Don was quite aware of the moisture seeping from her pussy over his bare thigh, and could see that her hips were jerking with coital-like movements each time that his hand descended against them. Her buttocks were a bright scarlet and it was obvious to him that they were simply burning up.

"Now I think it's about time for this!" Don said, reaching back for the belt she had used on him earlier.

"Oh, no! Not that!" Claudia screamed when she realised what he planned to do. The miserable young woman turned her tear-stained face back over her shoulder to plead with him with her eyes. "Please! I couldn't stand..."

Don watched the pretty muscles in her red bottom tightening in fearful anticipation as he doubled up the belt.

Whack!

The belt coiled around her scarlet, cringing buttocks.

"Owwww!" Claudia shrieked in a pain-stricken voice, her feet flying upward and her entire body giving a convulsive jerk. "Please, I can't stand it!"

Whack!

Once again the belt descended against her defenceless posterior with a loud smack.

"*Aiieee!*" Claudia emitted a soprano shriek, her scarlet buttocks wriggling furiously and her stockinged legs flailing back and forth in a revealing manner.

Despite Claudia's shrieks and sobs of anguish, Don proceeded to give her a thorough working over with the belt, though with enough restraint not to break the skin in the way that she had done to him. Squirming and wriggling frantically, Claudia was in hysterics when he finally stopped. Pausing to catch his breath for a moment, Don admired the intriguing combination of a reddened, weal-striped, female bottom and shapely legs attired in black, full-fashioned nylons.

"Now, Claudia, get into a kneeling position on the bed with your skirt up!" he told the sobbing young woman.

Claudia haplessly complied. "Please! Please, you're not going to spank me anymore, are you?" she tearfully pleaded in a distraught tone of voice. "Please, please, I couldn't stand it! I'm just blistered all over!"

"No, I'm not going to spank you!" the former headmaster told her, standing up with his jutting erection pounding for release. "Spread your legs apart!"

"What are you going to do?" Claudia asked in a very small voice as she reluctantly spread her stockinged knees apart. "Oh, no, you wouldn't!!" she gasped with horror when she began to realise what he had in mind.

Without replying, Don moved into a kneeling position behind the cringing, miserable young woman.

"Oh, *NO!*" Claudia shrieked. "You wouldn't!!! Please, not *that!* It's too humiliating! Please!" She twisted wretchedly in front of him, looking back haplessly over her shoulder to plead with him. "No, don't bugger me! Please – I can't take your..."

"Stay in position!" Don demanded, ignoring her fervent entreaties.

Sobbing and shaking with fear and humiliation, Claudia miserably remained in position on her knees and elbows with her scarlet, blistered bottom sticking up all too vulnerably. Don caught her by the waist and began manoeuvring to start the anal insertion.

"Please! Please! Don, please!" Claudia wept. "It'll hurt too much! Please, it'll never fit! You're too big! Please put it in my mouth... or anything!"

Don employed his thumbs to open her scarlet bottom cheeks as much as possible and reveal the brownish pucker of her rear entrance. Claudia winced with pain as his masculine fingers brushed against her blistered bottom, and between sobs begged and pleaded to be spared the final indignity.

"Hold still!" Don ordered.

"Oh, no, please! Please! *Please!*" Claudia buried her face in her hands and sobbed as she made her final appeals. "Oh, please! You musn't... please!"

Her young body limp with fear, Claudia shuddered as she awaited the insertion of his long, thick phallus. He moved closer to her, allowing his rigid penis to slide into the crevice of her rotund buttocks. The contact produced violent quakes from Claudia, who collapsed into blubbering tears and unintelligible pleas. Slowly, Don allowed the bulbous head of his prick to rub against her wrinkled little anal sphincter.

"Oh, no!" Claudia sobbed. "Please, it won't fit! It won't fit! It's too big!"

Holding the squirming, sobbing young woman at the waist, Don began inserting his thick, hot penis into the small opening.

"*OWWWW!*" Claudia screamed at the top of her lungs as the huge crown began penetrating her short anal canal, dilating the small opening in a highly painful manner. "Oh, for heavens sakes, no! Take it out! Take it out! It's much too *big!*"

As the head of his massive cock disappeared into the tiny pinkish brown aperture, Don paused for a moment and then began thrusting forward to complete the Nazi spy's shameful buggery. Claudia wept bitterly as she became impaled on the huge masculine weapon, and her sphincter muscles flexed desperately in an vain effort to expel the foreign intruder. Her kneeling body was convulsed with sobs, and her spasms provided added thrills for his madly pounding shaft.

"Please, I can't stand it!" Claudia begged. "Please, take it out! You're killing me!"

"Now you're really going to get arse-fucked, you little Nazi!" Don told her.

Don began thrusting his rock hard, thick penis back and forth past the warm, incredibly tight anal canal and deep into the girl's rectum. Each forward thrust produced a convulsive sob from the distraught young woman. Pumping with firm thrusts, he slipped his hands down between her legs and began to fondle her dripping-wet cunt. Claudia's fountain began to gush its warm liquids over his fingers, and her bright red bottom wriggled girlishly as he worked his fingers between her slippery cuntal lips. Probing her hot, sticky pussy with his fingers, he continued thrusting his wildly throbbing penis back and forth inside her tight little bottom.

"Ooooooohhhhh! Ouch! Oh! Ouch!" Claudia began to reveal in the mixture of pain and pleasure. "Oh! It hurts but it's... Oh! Ouch! Oooh! Oh! *Ooooohhhh!*"

As Don's probing fingers aroused her more and more, Claudia began moving heir spank-reddened bottom around with progressively more frantic gyrations. As his pulsating shaft slid back and forth in the tight confines of her rear, Don could feel her anal muscles clutching frantically at his sex as it ploughed far beyond her anus and deep into her rectum. His blood-dilated cock was aching for release and he made no attempt to hold himself back. Sliding his fingers past her lust-crazed clitoris and into her vagina, he began thrusting with almost brutal strokes that sent his rock-hard prick deep into her constricting anal tunnel. Finally, he simply let himself go and blasted his hot semen into the furthest recesses of her rectal channel with voluminous spurts.

"Oh! Ooooohhhh! *Oooooohhhhh!*" Claudia wriggled and squirmed frantically and Don could see that she was deep in the throes of an intensely masochistic orgasm.

Afterwards, Don quickly picked up Anne's gun that Claudia had placed on the nightstand earlier. "Okay, Claudia, I'm afraid the party's over for you for the duration!" he told her.

As he expected, Claudia lost no time kneeling before him with her hands folded prayerfully in front of her. "Please! Please!" she begged. "Don't turn me in! I'll do anything you say! I'll suck your dirty penis. I'll be your slave! Please! Oh *please!*"

"I'm afraid not, Claudia!" Don told her. "You're a real temptation, but this time I'm afraid we'll have to put duty ahead of pleasure." As he spoke, he reached for the telephone and Claudia collapsed in sobs on the floor.

* * * *

"What will they do with her? I thought spies were usually shot." Anne Carfax asked

when the two of them met at Don's apartment later that evening.

"The war's virtually over. I don't think we'll shoot her," he replied. "She'll probably get a thorough grilling and then be sent back to Germany."

"Well, I suppose that concludes our assignment together," Anne remarked with a trace of regret in her voice.

"Not entirely," Don replied.

"What do you mean?" she asked, obviously puzzled.

"Claudia caught on to us because of your carelessness; and you let her steal your gun," Don told her in a matter-of-fact voice.

Anne quickly understood the implication. "And I suppose you intend to discipline me for that," she remarked, a tremulous thrill in her voice.

"Don't you think you deserve it?" Don asked quietly.

Without answering him and blushing deeply, Anne submissively hitched up her skirt, lowered her knickers and proceeded to drape herself across Don Blake's knee, her pale, rounded bottom cheeks presented to his implacable gaze.

His arm rose above shoulder height, and then descended with full force.

The End